LISTEN

FOR THE

LIE

LISTEN

FOR THE

LIE

AMY TINTERA

CELADON
BOOKS
NEW YORK

LISTEN FOR THE LIE. Copyright © 2024 by Amy Tintera. All rights reserved. Printed in the United States of America. For information, address Celadon Books, a division of Macmillan Publishers, 120 Broadway, New York, NY 10271.

www.celadonbooks.com

Designed by Meryl Sussman Levavi

The Library of Congress Cataloging-in-Publication Data is available upon request.

ISBN 978-1-250-88031-4 (hardcover)
ISBN 978-1-250-35161-6 (international, sold outside the U.S.,
subject to rights availability)
ISBN 978-1-250-88032-1 (ebook)

Our books may be purchased in bulk for promotional, educational, or business use. Please contact your local bookseller or the Macmillan Corporate and Premium Sales Department at 1-800-221-7945, extension 5442, or by email at MacmillanSpecialMarkets@macmillan.com.

First U.S. Edition: 2024

First International Edition: 2024

3   5   7   9   10   8   6   4   2

For Laura, Emma, and Daniel.
Thank you for having so many ideas.

LISTEN
FOR THE
LIE

LUCY

A podcaster has decided to ruin my life, so I'm buying a chicken.

I make plans for this chicken as I sit in my cubicle at Walter J. Brown Investment Services, waiting to be fired. I stopped pretending to work two hours ago. Now I'm just staring at recipes on my phone, dreaming about sticking lemons up a chicken's butt.

It's an apology chicken, for my boyfriend.

It's like that engagement chicken. The one women make to persuade their boyfriends to propose? Except this is a "sorry I didn't tell you I'm the prime suspect in my friend's murder" chicken.

Apology chicken, for short.

"Lucy?"

I look up from my phone to see my boss standing at the door of his office. He adjusts his tie and clears his throat.

"Could you come in for a minute?" he asks.

Finally. They clearly decided to fire me this morning. Glass office walls are a strange choice always, but especially when you have a meeting with three other managers, and none of them can stop glancing over at your assistant, whom they are clearly discussing, for the entire conversation.

"Sure." I slide my phone into my pocket and follow him into his immaculate office.

I'm struck by how pristine it is, even after nearly a year of working for him. There's nothing on the beige walls. No boxes piled in a corner. The desk is completely bare except for the monitor and the keyboard.

Every evening, when Jerry Howell walks out of his office, he leaves absolutely no evidence that he was ever there. He probably missed his calling as a serial killer.

Of course, he's only in his midforties. Plenty of time to take up a new hobby.

I sit down in the chair on the other side of his desk and try to put a pleasant expression on my face. One that doesn't betray the fact that I was calmly thinking about him murdering people.

(A side effect of being accused of murder is that you spend a lot of time thinking about it. You get used to it.)

Jerry reaches up to touch his hair, and then quickly folds his hands on top of his desk. He does that a lot. I think he used to play with his hair, but he's balding now, and it's cut very close to his scalp.

"I'm sorry, Lucy, but we have to let you go," he says, to the surprise of no one.

I nod.

"We're downsizing, unfortunately." He looks at a spot just past my shoulder instead of at my face. "Having assistants double up. Chelsea is going to assist both me and Raymond. I'm sorry."

Chelsea's really getting the short end of the stick here. Double the work, all because of a true crime podcast.

"I understand." I get to my feet. Jerry looks relieved that I'm not going to make a scene.

Through the ill-advised glass wall of the office, I can see a security guard already standing at my desk. It's standard procedure when someone is fired, but I can't help but notice that all three of the assistants who sit in my cubicle pod have fled.

I guess we're not getting "sorry you were fired for being a suspected murderer" drinks.

My desk is not as clean as Jerry's, and I have to take a minute to gather up my mug, water bottle, purse, and several tubes of lip balm. The security guard hovers the entire time.

He marches me through the now-silent office to the elevator while everyone either watches or pretends not to see. Chelsea looks pissed.

I step into the elevator. The door slides shut.

The security guard leans closer to me with a grin. One of his front teeth overlaps the other.

"So, did you do it? Did you kill her?"

I sigh. "I don't know."

"Seriously? That's the truth?"

The elevator door opens again with a *ding*. I step out and look at him over my shoulder.

"The truth doesn't matter."

CHAPTER TWO

LUCY

It's probably unfair to say that a podcast ruined my life.

Technically, my life was destroyed the night Savvy was murdered.

And then it was destroyed again, the next day, when I decided to take an early-morning stroll with her blood drying on my dress.

And for a third time, when everyone in my hometown decided that *I* was the one who killed her.

But a podcaster dragging the case into the public eye, five years later, doesn't exactly *improve* my life.

I'm making the apology chicken, because my former coworkers aren't the only ones listening to Ben Owens's newest season of his true crime podcast. My boyfriend, Nathan, was weird when he came home from work last night. He was late, and smelled like beer, and he wouldn't look at me. Clearly, someone clued him in.

To be honest, I never had any intention of telling him. Nathan has almost no interest in anything besides himself. I didn't think it would come up.

I've known plenty of self-absorbed men, but Nathan takes the cake. It's my favorite thing about him. I can't even remember the last time he asked me a personal question. When I told him that I'd been married for two years, in my early twenties, he said, "No worries, want to go to a movie?"

I'm sure he must have googled me at some point early in our relationship, but the case didn't generate national media attention, and I was never actually arrested for the crime, so you have to do a tiny bit of digging to find me. That is way too much effort for Nathan.

But now, thanks to my least favorite podcaster, murder is the very first thing that pops up when you google "Lucy Chase." So I'm making apology chicken and preparing to get dumped. Immediately after getting fired.

To be fair to Ben Dipshit Owens, Nathan and I probably wouldn't have made it more than another month or two, even without a surprise murder thrown into the relationship. We'd only been dating for three months when he offered to let me move in with him. My lease was up, and we were still in the sex-all-the-time phase of our relationship, so it seemed logical. I was there every night anyway.

Unfortunately, that phase ended about two weeks after I moved in. I'm pretty sure Nathan regretted his decision, but he's the kind of guy who avoids conflict at all costs. So, we've been awkwardly living together for two months now, even though I'm pretty sure neither of us is all that thrilled about it.

Let this be a lesson to all the men out there who can't handle conflict—man up and dump your girlfriend, or you might end up living with a suspected murderer indefinitely.

The front door opens, and Brewster runs over to greet Nathan, tail wagging.

I'd be lying if I said that Brewster's little furry yellow Lab face didn't factor into my decision to keep living with this man. He may be a deeply average dude, but he has great taste in dogs.

Also, decent taste in apartments. The recently renovated nine-hundred-square-foot one-bedroom with a dishwasher *and* an in-unit washer/dryer is more than I've ever been able to afford in Los Angeles. It has these gray hardwood floors and bright white marble countertops that aren't all that trendy anymore, but still clearly signal that you pay a monthly rent that would horrify people in most other parts of the country.

"Hi, boy." Nathan spends a long time petting his dog, trying to avoid looking at me. "Something smells good."

"I made chicken."

He stands, finally glancing my way. His attention turns to the chicken, cooling on the stove.

"Great." He loosens his tie and pulls it off, unbuttoning his collar.

I used to love watching him do that. He always stretches his neck to one side as he pulls free his top button, and there's something really sexy about it. Every time he'd come home, I'd stop what I was doing and hop over to give him a kiss. I'd run my hands into his dark hair, perfectly combed to one side for work, and muss it up a bit, because I think it looks better that way.

He notices me staring at him and suddenly looks alarmed. "I, uh, I'm going to change." He rockets into the bedroom like I might chase him down for a kiss.

I pull out a carving fork and knife. The chicken now seems like a bad idea. Maybe I don't care enough to apologize.

Then again, I'm going to have to find a new place to live if Nathan kicks me out, and landlords tend to require pesky things, like proving you have an income.

I pierce the chicken just as Nathan walks back into the room. He swallows, his Adam's apple bobbing, and I briefly imagine stabbing the fork straight into his neck. It's two-pronged, so it would leave twin bloody little holes, like a vampire bite.

My other hand is holding the knife, and I stare at him as I double-fist my weapons, waiting. I want him to say it first. He's the one who clearly thinks I'm a murderer; he should have to say it first. I'm pretty sure those are the rules.

I stare. He stares.

Finally, he says, "How was work?"

"I was fired."

He edges around me and reaches into the counter next to the fridge. "Cool. You want some wine? I'm going to have some wine."

I wait for my words to sink in, but he just reaches for the bottle of wine, oblivious.

I stab the knife into the chicken, right between the breast and thigh. I may have used a bit more force than necessary.

Nathan jumps. I smile.

At this rate, he's going to end up married to a murderer.

Listen for the Lie Podcast with Ben Owens

EPISODE ONE—"THE SWEETEST GIRL YOU EVER MET"

Maya Harper: She got away with murder, and everyone knows it. Every single person in Plumpton knows that Lucy Chase killed my sister. It's just that no one can prove it.

Maya Harper was eighteen years old when her older sister, Savannah, was murdered. She describes Savannah as fun and sweet, the kind of woman who could organize a party in less than an hour and make it look like she'd worked on it all month.

Maya: She was just so nice and welcoming to everyone. And she was the best sister. When she was in high school, she'd let me hang out with her and her friends sometimes. And we weren't even close in age. She was six years older than me. I didn't know anyone else who had a big sister who let a little ten-year-old tag along to football games.

Maya was happy to talk to me, but she was skeptical that I'd find anything new.

Maya: You know that my family has hired three different private investigators, right? Like, my parents did not give up. I don't know if there's anything left to find.

Ben: I'm aware, yeah.

Maya: I guess it couldn't hurt, though. I mean, it's been five years and it's like no one even cares anymore that Savvy is dead. They've all given up.

A quick note here—you'll often hear people who knew Savannah refer to her as "Savvy." It was what most people called her.

Ben: So you haven't heard any updates from the police or the DA or anyone?

Maya: Not in years. They all knew Lucy did it, they just couldn't prove it, I guess.

Ben: There have never been any other suspects?

Maya: No. I mean, Lucy was covered in Savvy's blood when they found her. She had Savvy's skin underneath her fingernails, there were scratches on Savvy's arm and bruises shaped like Lucy's fingers. People saw them fighting at the wedding. Lucy killed her. She killed my sister and got away with it because the useless police department said there wasn't enough evidence for an arrest.

Ben: Have you had any contact with Lucy recently?

Maya: No, not since she left Plumpton. She's never come back, even though her parents still live here.

Ben: As far as you know, is she still claiming to have no memory of the night Savannah died?

Maya: Yeah, that was her story.

Ben: Do you believe her?

Maya: Of course I don't believe her. No one believes her.

Is it true that no one believes Lucy Chase? Is she hiding something, or have the people of Plumpton accused an innocent woman of murder for five years?

Let's find out.

I'm Ben Owens, and this is the *Listen for the Lie* podcast, where we uncover all the lies people tell, and find the truth.

CHAPTER THREE

LUCY

Nathan, as it turns out, has no balls.

We ate chicken. We drank wine. I played with the giant carving knife just to watch him sweat. He rambled on about work.

He did not ask whether I'm a murderer.

At this point, I'm curious how long this can go on for. He's clearly wanted to break up for a while, and now he's worried I'm going to murder him. Surely he will locate his balls and actually say the words "Please move out of my apartment and never contact me again" soon?

On the plus side, I have more time to look for a new place while I wait for the inevitable. Just this morning I found a very promising one-bedroom with no income requirements. It looks like a dump in the pictures, and the landlord asked to see a picture of my feet when I emailed, but, hey. It's cheap.

Sometimes I think about the fact that the twenty-two-year-old version of me would be absolutely horrified by almost-thirty me. That shiny, smug newlywed with a four-bedroom house was so certain that she had life figured out and it was all going her way.

Guess what, asshole?

I also halfheartedly applied for a couple of new jobs over the weekend, and already got a rejection from one. I'm really killing it lately (pun intended).

But I don't actually want a new job, if I'm being honest. I've published three romance novels under a pen name, and the third one is actually selling some copies. It's an unexpected turn of events, considering how few people bought my first two books, but it means I've had to work overtime on the next one, so I don't lose momentum.

And maybe, with a little luck, they'll start selling enough copies so that I don't have to worry about finding another mind-numbingly boring day job.

Of course, now I have to worry about a podcaster shining a very bright light on my past, and possibly someone finding out that it's actually a suspected murderer writing their new favorite rom-com. No one except my agent, my publisher, and my grandma knows about my career as a romance author, but I'm a favorite subject for the amateur internet sleuth.

The thought nags at me all weekend. Monday morning, I run extra miles on the treadmill in the gym at Nathan's complex, and then head to the grocery store because I need to tell my feelings to chocolate. Lots of chocolate.

The grocery stores are never empty in L.A., even on a weekday, because no one here has a real job. I maneuver around a woman at the entrance who is talking on her phone and wearing leggings that probably cost more than my entire outfit. They make her butt look great, though.

I turn my cart into the produce section. Maybe I'll get something to chop into tiny pieces in front of Nathan.

(A nicer person would just say, "Hey, you heard about the podcast, didn't you?" and put him out of his misery. I should try to be less of an asshole. Tomorrow, maybe.)

A slim blond woman is tapping a butternut squash with one finger, and I try very hard not to imagine smashing the squash against her head.

I fail. Squash, as it turns out, is a weakness of mine.

I wonder whether it would even hold up after being smashed against a human head. It would probably explode and you'd just end up with a headache and squash all over your face.

The woman looks up and notices me staring at her. I smile like I wasn't just imagining bludgeoning her to death. She walks away, casting an alarmed glance over her shoulder at me.

I really should try to be less of an asshole.

I don't *want* to think about murder, but I can't seem to stop it. I don't do it with everyone, but I've imagined killing a whole lot of people.

It started not long after Savvy died. Everyone said I was a murderer, and I couldn't say for sure that I wasn't, so I started thinking of all the different ways I *could* have killed her. I thought that if I went through enough options, I might actually land on something that sparked a memory.

So far, no luck. But maybe one day I'll stumble on it. I'll imagine killing a waitress with my empty milkshake glass and it will all come rushing back. *Ah yes! That's right! Savvy and I fought over whether strawberry or chocolate milkshakes were best and I flew into a rage and murdered her with my glass. Take me away, Officer!*

I really wish the police had found the murder weapon. It would have spared me a lot of imaginary killings.

My phone buzzes. I glance down at the screen to see the word *Grandma*, which is unsurprising. Telemarketers and Grandma—the only people who use the phone in the way it was originally intended.

I accept the call and press the phone to my ear. "Hey, Grandma."

The guy next to me gives me a small smile, like he approves of me talking to my grandma. I push my cart to the corner, in front of the cabbage.

"Lucy, honey! Hi. Are you busy? Am I interrupting?"

She always asks whether she's interrupting, like she thinks I have a packed social calendar. I don't even have any close friends. Just some work acquaintances who will definitely never speak to me again.

"Nope, just grocery shopping," I say.

"How's Nathan?"

"He's . . . you know. Nathan."

"You always say that, and I don't know what you mean. I've never met the man."

"He's fine."

"I see." She clears her throat. "Listen. I have a favor to ask."

"What's that?"

"It's a small favor, really, and I'd like to remind you that I'm nearly dead."

"You've been saying you're nearly dead for twenty years."

"Well, then it stands to reason that I must really be getting close then!" She cackles.

"Are you drunk?"

"Lucy, it is two o'clock in the afternoon. Of course I'm not drunk." She pauses. "I'm merely slightly tipsy."

I bite back a laugh. "What's the favor?"

"I've decided to have a birthday party. A big one. It's the big eight-oh, you know."

"I do know."

I actually do. Grandma's birthday is the only one I can remember without the calendar reminder.

"You'll come, of course?" Her voice is hopeful.

Shit.

"I can't have it without my favorite grandchild there." She's switched to guilt.

"You do know that it's tacky to tell me I'm your favorite when you have three grandchildren?"

"We both know that Ashley and Brian are assholes."

"I think we're supposed to pretend to like them anyway."

"Well. I can't have a birthday party with only the assholes."

I would laugh if it weren't for the swiftly mounting dread.

"Do you think you could take some time off work?" she asks.

"I was fired."

"Oh, perfect! I mean, I'm sorry," she adds hurriedly.

"You know I didn't like that job anyway."

"I retract my apology. Congratulations on being fired."

"Thanks."

"Since you have so much free time, maybe a longer visit? A week? I've already talked to your mom, and she says you can stay with them as long as you want."

"A week?" I shriek the words so loudly that a passing woman looks very startled.

"Well, this is all very last-minute, and your mom has that broken leg . . . we would need some help getting everything together. I'd let you stay with me, but there's no room, of course."

The prospect of spending one day in my hometown is bad enough, but *an entire week*?

Seven days in the place where I'd once been successful, and married, and had lots of friends who were jealous of my (fake) happiness.

It would be the opposite of a triumphant return. Five years later, I stumble back in, an unemployed divorcée with no friends. I can't even tell people I've published three books. I shiver as the produce mister turns on, spraying my arm as well as the cabbage. I inch away from it.

"Unless you'd rather bring Nathan and stay in a hotel? I'm sure your mom would understand you staying in a hotel if you bring him."

I imagine, briefly, inviting Nathan to come to Plumpton, Texas, with me. I wonder whether that would be the thing that finally gets him to dump me. Visiting the scene of the crime is probably a bridge too far, even for him.

"You can say no." I hear a clinking sound on the other end, like ice cubes against glass. "I know you must be very busy . . ."

"You know I'm never busy."

"It's so weird how you always say that. People your age are usually so proud of being busy. One of the girls from church has told me at least a hundred times about how busy she is. I'm starting to wonder if it's a cry for help."

"You talked to Dad too? About me staying with them?"

"Of course not; I try to avoid having conversations with your father whenever possible. But Kathleen talked to him. We wouldn't just spring you on him."

"He never did like surprises."

"No. Does that mean you'll come?"

I stare at the butternut squash and consider smashing it against my own head.

"Lucy?"

I blink. "Sorry. Squash."

"Don't buy squash, you're coming to Texas!"

"Oh my god."

"Right?" She's hopeful again.

I sigh. I can't say no to the only family member I like. One of the only *people* I like. "Yes. I'm coming to Texas."

A soft voice, a voice I always try to ignore, whispers in my ear, "*Let's kill—*"

I grip the phone tighter and will the voice away.

"Oh, wonderful! Do you think Nathan will want to come?"

I take a shaky breath. The voice seems to be gone. "I don't think he can get off work."

"Oh, sure. Well, I'll just buy you a plane ticket then. You okay to leave this weekend?"

"You don't have to do that."

"Nonsense, I want to. I'll be dead soon anyway."

We might all be dead soon, but that seems like too much to hope for.

"Sure, this weekend." I reconsider her last statement. "Wait, are you sick?"

"Not that I know of, but my friends are dropping like flies, so really, it's only a matter of time."

"That's the spirit."

"Now, listen, I don't drive much anymore, but I can probably make it to Austin to pick you up. If my car starts. You never know these days."

"Don't worry about it. I'll rent a car. And I'm getting a hotel."

"Well, your mother won't like *that*."

I pinch the bridge of my nose with my fingers.

"And Lucy?"

"Yeah?"

"You heard about that podcast, right? The one about you?"

CHAPTER FOUR

LUCY

I have to buy a suitcase because I never travel. I had a beautiful matching luggage set once, but I left my ex-husband with clothes stuffed into garbage bags.

Brewster greets me at the door when I come in, excitedly sniffing the new purple luggage. Nathan is home, still in the black pants and white button-up he wore to work. His face lights up when he sees the suitcase. Subtle, dude.

"Going somewhere?"

I drop the bag on the floor. "No, it's for a dead body."

His lips part. He looks from me to the suitcase.

"What?" I glance down at it. "You think I should have gotten a bigger one?"

He stares at me for several seconds before letting out a long, annoyed breath. "Jesus Christ, Lucy."

I lean down to pet Brewster. He licks my hand, oblivious to the tension in the room. Dogs don't know about murder podcasts. Lucky bastards.

"You weren't even going to pretend, huh?" I ask.

"What?" The tiny dent between his eyebrows appears. He has perfect L.A. eyebrows. Sculpted by a professional. I'd liked that he was the kind of guy who didn't feel his masculinity was tied to his beauty routine (or lack thereof).

Now I'm annoyed by those two immaculately plucked eyebrows.

"A lot of people pretend to think I didn't do it," I say. "They act like they want to hear my side, like they haven't already made up their mind."

"Oh. I, uh, I do want to hear your side ..."

I roll my eyes. That was so insincere I don't bother responding to it.

Some guys actually like the suspected-murderer thing. The first couple of years after it happened, I'd get the occasional email with a flirty request for a date. Thrill seekers, I guess. Or they want to save me. I'm a real fixer-upper.

Not Nathan, apparently.

"You're ... going somewhere?" he asks, after a long silence.

"Texas. My grandma is having a birthday party."

"Oh."

"She invited you too."

He blinks. "I, um ... I don't know if I can ... you know, with work."

"Sure."

"When are you leaving?"

"Friday. I'll be gone about a week."

He nods. I wait for him to suggest that I take all my stuff with me when I go. The only sound is Brewster's loud sniffs as he thoroughly examines the ends of my jeans.

"Are you going to tell me?" he finally asks.

"What?"

"Your side."

For fuck's sake. Men are such babies. They're too scared to actually break up with you, so they just get mean or fade away until you get mad and dump them.

Risky move, making a suspected murderer angry enough to dump you.

"Would you believe me if I did?" I ask. My phone buzzes. I pull it out of my purse to see a text from my mom.

You're not staying at a hotel. I'm getting the guest room ready now.

I quickly type out a response. I'm fine at a hotel.

I look up at Nathan to see that the answer to my question is clearly *no*.

"Yes," he lies.

"I still have no memory of the night, but I never would have hurt Savvy." The words tumble easily out of my mouth. I've said them a hundred times.

Nathan stares like he expects more. They always do.

My phone rings, my mom's name on the screen. I sigh and swipe to answer it.

"You're not staying at a hotel." Her tone leaves no room for argument.

"Hi, Mom, how are you?" I ask dryly. Nathan is still staring at me as I step out onto the balcony.

"I'm fine. You're not staying at a hotel."

"Grandma said you broke your leg." I look down, watching as a woman on the street pushes a stroller down the sidewalk. A small pug pops his head out, tilting his smushed face up to the sun.

"Stop changing the subject."

"I thought you liked it when I try to make small talk. Act like a normal person and all that."

"*Lucy.*" She's already incredibly tired of me, and I haven't even arrived yet.

"Let one of my cousins have the room. They'll be in town, right?"

"Only for a night or two. You're staying with us. We have plenty of room. Besides, everyone will talk if you don't stay here."

Ah. There's the only reason that matters.

I turn around and lean against the railing. Inside, Nathan is furiously texting. "God forbid people gossip about me. I can't imagine what that would be like."

"The cheapest hotel in town is like eighty dollars a night anyway, and I doubt it's up to your standards."

"Bold of you to assume I have standards." Though, she has a point. Considering that I've just lost my job, I don't need to be spending several hundred dollars on a hotel room.

"Just stay with us, Lucy. Don't make things harder."

She left off the "like you always do" at the end of that sentence. I guess it's implied.

"Okay. Thank you."

"Oh." She sounds surprised, like she didn't actually think she'd succeed. I'm going soft, I guess. "Good."

"Seriously, how'd you break your leg?"

"I fell off the stair machine. You know the one at the gym, with the stairs that go round and round to nowhere? Well, it's quite high up, and I missed a step and . . . it was embarrassing, to say the least."

"Sounds painful."

"It was. Anyway, I'll let you go. Oh, and did your grandma tell you about that—"

"Yes, I know about the podcast."

I've actually probably known about the podcast longer than anyone. I received the first email five months ago.

From: Ben Owens
Subject: Listen for the Lie *Podcast*
Hi Lucy,

My name is Ben Owens and I'm a journalist and the host of the podcast *Listen for the Lie*. I'm doing some research into the murder of Savannah Harper, and I'd love to sit down and talk with you. I actually live in Los Angeles too, so I'd be happy to come to you. Please feel free to email me or call at 323-555-8393.

Cheers,

Ben

I didn't reply.

My research turned up the first season of his podcast, and quite a few news articles that gave him decidedly mixed reviews.

"*Questionable ethics,*" one article said, "*but you can't argue with the results!*"

Another article described Ben as having "*boyish good looks,*" which had only made me hate him more. I've never liked men who can be described as having *boyish good looks.* They're always smug.

But I never reply to emails about Savvy, and I wasn't making an exception for this smug bastard, so I archived it and moved on.

Of course, most emails about Savvy don't require a response. They're usually some version of "*How do you live with yourself, you heartless bitch?*" or "*You're going to hell,*" except almost always with the wrong *your*, which is extremely distracting. An insult doesn't have the intended impact when spelled incorrectly. I'd reply to let them know, but, in my experience, dumbasses don't appreciate having their spelling corrected.

I sit down on the bed next to my open suitcase, scrolling through the emails that Ben sent me months ago. Brewster nudges the bag of jelly beans on the nightstand with his nose, and I shoo him away from it and pop one in my mouth.

A second email had arrived a few weeks after the first, asking again for a meeting. And then a third:

From: Ben Owens
Subject: Listen for the Lie *Podcast*
Hi Lucy,

One last email! I'd really love to interview you, and get your side of the story. I'm willing to meet on your terms. The podcast is really coming together, and I think it's important to hear your side of the story.

Cheers,

Ben.

Oh, sweet, naive Ben. No one gives a shit about my side of the story.

To be fair, my side of the story is "I don't remember anything," so it's not exactly exciting. Or believable, apparently. I glance out the door at Nathan, who is drinking away his awkward feelings about his murderous girlfriend on the couch, the glow from the television flickering across his tense face.

I've tried to avoid thinking about just how popular this season of the podcast is, but now I can't stop myself. I google *Ben Owens Listen for the Lie*. A picture of him pops up. He looks very smug.

There are numerous articles about the podcast. The usual true crime websites have picked up the story, but it's splashed across national media as well. *Entertainment Weekly* and *Vanity Fair* and a dozen other places have articles with headlines like "This Small-Town Murder Will Be Your New True Crime Obsession" and "Come for the Murder, Stay for the Accents: *Listen for the Lie* Podcast Digs Up a Cold Case in Texas." Twitter is having an absolute field day with theories.

People seemed to have formed teams, given that I keep seeing "Team Savvy" pop up. Logic dictates that there must also be a "Team Lucy," though I don't see evidence of it.

Given the flurry of media attention, everyone in Plumpton is definitely listening to the stupid thing.

I look down at Brewster, wishing I'd come up with an excuse to avoid the whole trip. I should have pointed out to Grandma that my presence at her birthday will likely ruin the whole thing. I'm the relative that you tell everyone about at parties, when you're comparing fucked-up families. I make for a good story. You don't *invite* me to the party.

But my grandmother never asks me for anything, and I haven't seen her since I left Plumpton nearly five years ago. She's never been on a plane, and she's *sure as shit not starting now*, to use her words. She's also expressed concern, more than once, about being force-fed kale if she ever visits California.

Texans hate California. It's one of the reasons I made it my home.

Plus, my cousins really are assholes. Grandma is right—she can't have a party with just the assholes.

If I'm going to go, I might as well go armed with knowledge. I open my podcast app and find *Listen for the Lie*.

I put on the first episode as I pack.

Listen for the Lie Podcast with Ben Owens

EPISODE ONE—"THE SWEETEST GIRL YOU EVER MET"

I arrive in Austin on a Tuesday, and honestly, I'm disappointed by the lack of cowboy hats.

It's my first time in Texas, and I had visions of streets lined with nothing but barbecue joints and stores that sold boots and whatever else you need to ride a horse. Saddles? I don't know. I know nothing about horses. I've never even done that touristy L.A. thing up in the hills where you can ride a horse to a Mexican restaurant, load up on margaritas, and then ride back. Always seemed like a bad idea to me.

The Austin airport is extremely Austin. I can tell this immediately, even though it's my first time in the city. There are signs advertising that it's the live music capital of the world, and there's a band playing in one of the food courts, in case you doubted this. There are decorative guitars in baggage claim. There isn't a single Starbucks or McDonald's in the whole airport, because you know that saying? *Keep Austin Weird*? The second part of that saying, the part no one remembers, is *support local businesses*. There are only local businesses in the Austin airport.

I consider eating barbecue before I leave, but eating dinner at an airport after *arriving* seems sad. So, I jump in my rental car and head for Plumpton.

And this is where Texas is no longer as expected. It's very green. I guess I thought it was a desert. And just to really prove that I'm an idiot, it starts raining so hard that I have to pull over onto the shoulder for several minutes because I can't see the road. It's raining like the apocalypse is nigh, and I start to wonder whether it's a sign that this case was a poor choice.

I'm going to be honest with you guys. While I was sitting in that car, watching the apocalypse rain, I seriously considered going back to the airport and flying straight back home.

And honestly, I was still thinking about that barbecue.

When the rain finally lets up, I soldier on, hungry and nervous. About two hours later, I arrive in Plumpton, Texas.

[country music]

Plumpton is a quaint, charming town in the Texas Hill Country. It's home to about fifteen thousand people, a number that's growing every year. It's a tourist town, due to its close proximity to several Hill Country wineries, but it's also become a popular spot for young couples looking to escape the big cities. The public school system is one of the best in Texas.

The downtown area is bustling with tourists when I arrive, but when I take a stroll around the block, several locals recognize me. One man even yells that he's looking forward to the podcast. My reputation precedes me.

The town is mostly local businesses, but a few chains have made their way to Plumpton as the town has grown over the past ten years. The first Starbucks opened here a couple of years ago, which at least five people complain to me about within my first two days in town.

But Plumpton's main claim to fame is Savannah Harper, to the chagrin of nearly everyone who lives here. Most people in this town don't want any part of the big-city life—they've either lived here for generations, like Lucy Chase's family, or they moved here specifically to get away from the city, like Savannah Harper's family. They don't like being known for a grisly murder.

It's a common sentiment in Plumpton—this wasn't supposed to happen here. This sort of thing happens in bad places, not in a town where all the locals know each other and attend the same church.

Norma gives me a few Plumpton tips when I check into my hotel. She's a friendly woman in her fifties, and she works the front desk until six in the evening every weekday.

Norma: And don't go to the bar on Franklin, that's where all the tourists go to get sloppy. A bachelorette party was throwing around penis confetti last time I was there, if you can believe that. I was finding penises in my hair for hours.

Ben: That's . . . unfortunate.

Norma: Go to the bar down the road a bit, on Main. Bluebonnet Tavern.

Ben: I'll keep that in mind, thank you.

Norma: You're from California?

Ben: Yeah, Los Angeles. Well, San Francisco, originally. I live in L.A. now.

Norma: That whole state is going to break off into the ocean after a big earthquake, you know.

Ben: I've heard that.

Norma: You know Lucy Chase lives out there too? Horrible woman. Savannah was an absolute peach. Just the sweetest girl you ever met. I hope you nail Lucy's murderous ass to the wall.

This, I should note, was a common theme in my first few days in Plumpton.

CHAPTER FIVE

LUCY

The house on Clover Street is the same house I grew up in. I sit in my rental car, parked on the street in front of the house, for several minutes and just stare at it.

They've painted it a new color—a subtle shade of peach that's an odd choice for the exterior of the house—but otherwise it's the same. There are bushels of purple flowers planted along the porch. A nicely trimmed lawn. A front porch swing that you can't sit on six months out of the year because it's too damn hot.

I finally muster the strength to step out of the car. It's six o'clock in the evening, still light out, and still hot as balls. The heat's relentless this time of year. It was a real dick move on Grandma's part to be born in August.

I grab my bag and trudge across the grass to the front door.

Dad opens it before I can knock. His smile is wide, friendly. Dad's so good at that Texas thing where you act polite to people's face and then talk shit behind their back.

"Lucy!" He steps forward and embraces me briefly.

"Hi, Dad."

"I'm so glad you're home, finally. Come in!" He steps back, sweeping his arm out dramatically.

I step inside. It's cold and dark inside, as always. The house has never gotten good light downstairs.

He shuts the door behind me. His dark hair is grayer than last time I saw him. Dad's eyes are deeply set, giving him a soulful appearance that is always more pronounced when he looks at me. There's disappointment in every line of his face.

"How was your flight?" His gaze is on my suitcase.

"Fine." Lies. I ate too much chocolate, we hit turbulence, and I almost puked. I spent the last fifteen minutes of the flight clutching the vomit bag.

He nods, briefly meeting my eyes, and then quickly looks away. He still can't look at me, apparently.

I turn away and survey the living room. The furniture is mostly new. Or new to me, anyway. There's a plushy brown sofa, and an uncomfortable-looking chair with ugly pink-and-orange-striped upholstery. The frame of the chair looks old, but the upholstery brand-new, like someone recently did that to the chair on purpose. Mom has always had questionable design taste.

On the table next to this awful chair is a picture of me and Savvy, with a few other women. It was taken at a wedding, not long after I moved back to town. We look like a photo shoot for *Southern Living*, a bunch of white ladies in pastel dresses with perfectly wavy hair.

The picture seems in incredibly poor taste to me for two reasons—one, most people think I murdered Savvy, and maybe they have a point; and two, she died after going to a wedding. Not *that* wedding, but people who come over don't know that. Do they react with horror and say, "*My god, was this taken the day she died?*" And then Mom has to launch into the whole story.

Actually, I just realized exactly why she chose that picture. Most people wouldn't want to talk about their maybe-murderer daughter, but not Mom. She knows how to work a room, and there is no better way to command attention than to tell the worst fucking story in the world.

"Your mother is in her bedroom. I think she was taking a nap, but she's probably up now." Dad smiles and takes a step back so there's a wide swath of space between us. "Why don't you go on up and say hi?"

The lamp on the table next to the sofa isn't new. We've had it for as long as I can remember. It's a long cylinder, solid ceramic, and heavy. But not *too* heavy. I could lift it, and swing it, and bash it right into his head. Maybe the lamp wouldn't even break. It's quite sturdy. Mom would appreciate that. She must like that lamp, considering how long she's had it.

She would not appreciate the mess, though. Blood would spurt out of his mouth and splatter across the walls. Maybe on the sofa too, and it does *not* look like the kind of sofa that's easy to get blood out of.

Not that I know which sofas are easy to get blood out of.

Maybe it would be less messy if I hit him in the back of the head. That would also be convenient, because now he's turned away from me. He wouldn't even see it coming.

Not in the moment, anyway. I don't think anyone—least of all my father—would be surprised by my murdering someone.

"You okay?"

Dad's words startle me, because he's turned back around while I was killing him, and now he's staring at me.

"You have a weird expression," he says. "Is something wrong?"

"I'm just tired from the flight."

I start to push the murder thoughts away, but every therapist I've been to (and I've been to several) has wanted me to deal with the violent fantasies instead of just trying to make them stop.

I recently admitted to my latest therapist that trying to avoid murdering people in my head has just resulted in me murdering even *more* people in my head. She was very supportive of my idea to just let the thoughts fly and see what happens.

So, I imagine Dad's brains splattering across the couch again and head upstairs to see Mom.

Listen for the Lie Podcast with Ben Owens

EPISODE ONE—"THE SWEETEST GIRL YOU EVER MET"

Savannah's body was discovered early in the morning, only a few hours after her death. Gil Bradford was out for a run when he came across the body.

Gil: Yeah, it was a Sunday, which is when I used to do my long runs. I was really into running back then, but my knees are pretty wrecked these days. Anyway, I used to jog on this trail near the Byrd Estate, which is where they have all these fancy weddings and stuff. Savannah had been at a wedding there the night before.

So, I was out on that trail when I saw this flash of pink out there in the trees. Her dress—Savannah's dress—was a pretty bright color, so I just saw her right away.

Ben: You saw her body right away? Or just the dress?

Gil: I saw her body maybe half a second after noticing the dress. She wasn't hidden at all. This was real early—like the sun had just barely started coming up, but I could still see her there, plain as day. So I ran over, and I think I was yellin', asking if she needed help.

But when I got close, I could tell she was already dead. Her eyes were open, and she was pale and soaking wet. Huge gash on her head, like someone had hit her with something. It rained real hard that night, I'm sure you heard. It had only just let up when I left for my run.

But I seen all those cops shows, so I moved away, didn't touch her at all, and called the police. Of course, it didn't matter, turned out that the rain had washed away all the evidence anyway.

(Just a note here, for those of you who are wondering—I tried reaching out to the Plumpton PD many times to see if anyone would talk to me about the case. They were . . . less than friendly, to put it nicely. The unsolved murder of Savannah Harper is a sore spot with the police department here, and it was made very clear to me that they would not be cooperating with the podcast in any way. We are on our own here.)

Ben:	Had you ever met Savannah before that day?
Gil:	Nah, I live out on the edge of town, and I mostly keep to myself. I knew the Chases, of course, but no, I'd never met Savannah. I had no idea who she was when I called 911.
Ben:	What happened when the police came?
Gil:	They sealed off the area, asked me some questions. Found her car on the side of the road—no one had been down the road that morning yet, because it got washed out in the rain. The cops had to come down the trail like me. It was hours before they could get to the car.
Ben:	How did the other wedding guests get home?
Gil*:*	There are two roads out of the Byrd Estate. A little country road, and the main road. Savannah and Lucy left the wedding before it started raining, from what I heard later. So, they went down that little country road. But when the other guests left an hour or so later, it was already pouring, and that road was flooded. The people at the Byrd Estate roped it off. Everyone had to take the main road.
Ben:	What happened after the police came?
Gil*:*	They had me come down to the station a couple days later. I gave them a DNA sample—I guess I didn't have to, but I said, "Look, if it'll help, just swab my cheek or do whatever you wanna do, I don't care. I know I didn't kill nobody."

Lucy was found an hour later, walking barefoot down the two-lane road that led out of town, still in her baby-blue dress. A man named Billy Jack spotted her as he headed out of town to visit family.

Billy Jack:	I was just driving, and I saw this girl walking. I hadn't heard nothin' about a missing person or anything like that, but she looked like she was in trouble, you know? She was barefoot and walking all funny. Staggering around like a drunk. She was wearing this dress—like a nice dress. And it was filthy. Like she'd been rolling around in the mud or got up to somethin'.
	So I stopped, 'cause I'm not gonna just keep driving when this girl is clearly in some kind of distress. I rolled down the window and hollered, "Hon, you need some help?"

She stops, and she looks over at me. And I'll tell you what, I damn near had a heart attack. She had this huge welt on her forehead. Clothes soaking wet, and her makeup was all down her face. She had blood caked to her hair, I think, but it was hard to tell. Could have been mud. She was a mess.

You know how you can look at people sometimes and tell they're not all there? Man, when she looked at me, she didn't see shit. The lights were on but nobody was home. She looked like a ghost in a goddamn horror movie.

Anyway, she just turns away and starts walking again. Or staggering, really. So, I'm like, shit, I can't just drive away. And I'm sure as hell not going to drag this girl into my truck with me.

So I call the cops and tell them where she is and say I'm gonna slowly follow her until they get there because I'm real worried. I didn't know this at the time, but they had every cop in town out looking for Lucy because they'd already found Savannah's body and feared the worst, you know? Anyway, a cop gets there so fast. I could see him in my rearview mirror, doing like a hundred.

The cop catches up with her and I wait around for a bit because they want me to give a statement. An ambulance comes and at least seven other cop cars. I'd never seen such a ruckus in Plumpton before. One of the cops tells me about Savannah and I'm just like, shit, this girl must have gotten so lucky. And the cop was like, "Yeah, no kidding, hope she can tell us who did this to them."

I don't think that a single cop at that scene was thinking that this girl was the one who killed Savannah. Everyone was so relieved. They thought that Lucy was dead too and they were so happy to have found her.

We didn't know. We couldn't have even dreamed it.

CHAPTER SIX

LUCY

The wooden stairs creak as I walk up to them, much worse now than when I was a kid. I'd have a hell of a time sneaking out these days.

I glance back at Dad as I go. He's in the kitchen, taking a breath so big I can see his shoulders rise with the effort. My presence makes many people uncomfortable, but none more so than my own father.

I think about Nathan, standing in the corner of his bedroom yesterday, rambling about work as he watched me pack. I could feel the nerves rolling off him.

Fuck, he reminds me of my father. Wonderful. My therapist is going to love this.

The master bedroom door is cracked and I can hear the sound of a humidifier coming from inside. I press my hand to the wood, nudging it open.

Mom sits on the bed, back propped up with pillows, legs stretched out in front of her, one in a giant white cast. Her blond (fake, she's brunette like me) hair is pulled up in a ponytail, and she's wearing a full face of makeup. I've rarely seen Mom without makeup. Plumpton is the sort of town where people drop by unexpectedly.

She spots me creeping at the door and smiles. "Lucy! I thought I heard you down there. Come here, hon."

I step inside. The master bedroom used to have an elaborate

gallery wall over the bed of me growing up—at least a dozen pictures of me being cute as hell throughout the years—but there's a large blue and white quilt there now. It was probably handmade by Mom, but I'm still a little salty about being replaced by a blanket.

"Hi, Mom."

"Come here and give me a hug. I know I look dreadful, but don't worry, I'm fine."

She does not look dreadful. She does look older, though. Maybe that was what she meant by *dreadful*. My mom, like her mom, is blessed with smooth, beautiful skin that has always made her look a good ten years younger than she really is. Now, at fifty-five, she's starting to actually look like she's in her fifties.

I inherited this great skin, but I look twenty-nine. I might look well into my thirties, on a bad day. Being accused of murder has aged me prematurely.

I walk to the bed and give her a quick hug. She smells like perfume. Probably expensive, but I wouldn't know. All perfume smells like flowery garbage to me.

"I'm so glad you came," she says. "Your grandmother is being impossible about this party. The woman won't even let us take her out to dinner for most of her birthdays and now she suddenly wants a huge shindig with the entire family? And she tells me *two weeks* beforehand? I think she's trying to kill me just so she can brag about outliving her daughter."

I don't argue, because that does sound like Grandma.

I perch on the edge of her bed. "How's the leg? Did they give you some good pain meds?"

"I don't need pain medication." She waves her hand dismissively. Mom has more of a Texas accent than Dad or I do, and it makes everything she says sound friendly. She grew up here, in Plumpton, but Dad didn't move to Texas until college. I lost what little accent I had after a couple of years away. I'm not sad about it.

"How'd you even get up here?"

"I just used my crutches." She flexes her biceps. "The doctor said it would be difficult, but it was a breeze. All those sessions with the personal trainer are paying off."

"When did you become a gym rat?"

She wrinkles her nose. "I don't believe I like that term. But exercise is very important for older women. Do you still spend all those hours on the treadmill?"

"Yes." Running until I can't think is the only way I stay sane, most days.

Well, relatively sane.

"Maybe they'll let you use my pass while I'm injured. I'll remind them that I'm not suing."

"Very big of you."

She pats my hand. "Now, I want you to feel free to go wherever while you're in town. I told several people that you're coming so that no one will be surprised. I'm sure it's spread all around town by now."

"I'm sure."

"I do hope you'll go out and see folks." Her hand is still on mine, and she looks at me anxiously.

"No one wants to see me, Mom."

"Sure they do. And I think it's best if you don't hide. You don't have anything to be ashamed of, do you?"

It's a genuine question, one that requires my response. Mom asks me constantly, in a million different ways, whether I murdered Savvy. Maybe she thinks that if she asks enough, I'll eventually let it slip that I did indeed bash my friend's brains in. I have to admire her persistence.

"No, I don't have anything to be ashamed of," I lie.

"That's right, dear." That's what she always says when she thinks I'm lying.

And my mom *definitely* thinks I'm lying about not remembering the night that Savvy died. She tried for years to get me to confess.

She pestered me to come back home after I left for L.A.—"*If you're back here, you might remember something. Or you might feel compelled to share something new. Have you seen the memorial they did for Savvy?*"

She tried the god approach—"*You need to confess and atone for your sins here if you want to be forgiven in the next life.*"

She gave logic a whirl—"*You were the only one with Savvy that night, so I think that it's time to face facts.*"

She went for guilt (by far her favorite)—"*Do you know what that family is going through? They need an explanation.*"

There is nothing my mother wants more than for me to confess to killing Savvy. Not just because she thinks it's the right thing to do, but because she would excel as the mother of a murderer.

She'd be a star at church. She'd give long speeches about forgiveness. She'd write a book about overcoming the guilt she felt at raising a murderer. Sometimes I think that she's angrier about me depriving her of this than she is about me actually (maybe) murdering someone. Mom enjoys being the best at everything, and I've denied her the opportunity to be the best mother of a murderer. You can't be the best mother of a woman *suspected of* murder. That just doesn't have the same ring to it.

I stand, and her hand slips off mine. "Do you need anything?"

"No, I'm fine, hon." She smiles up at me, and I head to the door. "By the way, I don't know if anyone told you, but that podcaster is back in town. Might want to keep an eye out."

Listen for the Lie Podcast with Ben Owens

EPISODE ONE—"THE SWEETEST GIRL YOU EVER MET"

Savannah's mother, Ivy Harper, invites me to her home shortly after I arrive in Plumpton. It's the first of several conversations.

Ben: Hi, Mrs. Harper?

Ivy: Ben! It's so nice to meet you, finally. Come in, come in. And please call me Ivy.

Ivy is a small woman, just barely over five feet tall, with blond hair that is neatly braided every time I see her. Savannah took after her mom, which I mention when I see the pictures of her hanging on the wall.

Ben: Wow, how old is she here? She looks just like you.

Ivy: That's tenth grade, so about fifteen. We took these after services on Easter Sunday.

The Harper home is the same one that Savannah grew up in. It's a large, four-bedroom house that's sparsely furnished, making it seem even bigger. There are pictures of Savannah everywhere—on the walls, in picture frames on the tables, in the slideshow playing on the television.

Ivy and I sit at the round table in the breakfast nook, a bright room just off the kitchen, and she tells me about Savannah. Or Savvy, as everyone in her life called her.

Ivy: Savvy was so happy. Her whole life. Even as a teenager! She was the worst baby, just crying all the time, constantly, but about age two she just became as cheerful as could be, and that never let up. She had her days, I guess, but for the most part she was just a really joyful woman. Maybe *too* joyful.

Ben: How do you mean?

Ivy: Well, I used to tell her to calm down, to think things through. She'd just get so excited about something and want to do it immediately. She was so excited to experience new things, sometimes it was like she wanted to do everything all at once. I wanted her to slow down. I'd tell her she had her whole life. But I guess she knew that wasn't going to be long.

Ben: Can you give me an example?

Ivy: When she was ten—or maybe eleven—and we were still living in New Orleans, she decided she wanted to try out for this local production of *Romeo and Juliet*. For the role of Juliet. And I said to her, "Savvy, that role isn't for a child. Only adults can audition for that role. Maybe a teenager could, but not a ten-year-old." She was *so* mad at me. She begged me and begged me to go audition, and I said no, so she just hopped on a city bus after school one day, marched over there, and auditioned all by herself.

Ben: Did she get it?

Ivy: No, but they gave her another small role. But, of course, she didn't want that one, she wanted Juliet. So she didn't do it. She did play Juliet eventually, when Plumpton High did a production. She was fifteen then. It was a big commotion when the role went to a sophomore.

Ben: When did you move to Plumpton? You said you were in New Orleans when Savvy was ten.

Ivy: When she was twelve. Keaton—my oldest—was about to start high school, and Jerome and I had always planned to move back to Texas. I grew up in San Antonio, and we both love it here. They were building all these new homes back then for a really good price, so we jumped on it.

Ben: Did Lucy and Savannah know each other in school?

Ivy: Oh, sure, of course. It's a pretty small town. All the kids knew each other, especially if they were the same age.

Ben: But they weren't friends?

Ivy: No. They didn't have anything in common. Savvy was a cheerleader, she was on student council, she was homecoming queen. Lucy was . . . not . . . any of those things.

Ben: When did they become friends?

Ivy: After Lucy moved back to town. Savvy was already here . . . well, you know. She'd been back in Plumpton for a couple years, after college didn't work out. She came over for Sunday dinner and she said, "Mom, you remember Lucy Chase?" I didn't, actually. She'd had to remind me. That girl who once got suspended for punching a boy. That's how Lucy was known back then.

So, she says, "Yeah, she got married to a guy she met at UT"—that's the University of Texas in Austin, hon—"and they just moved back to town. We got to talking when she came by the Charles." The Charles is this fancy restaurant downtown—Savvy used to bartend there.

Ben: So they hit it off then?

Ivy: Yeah. Savvy said it was a little weird at first. Lucy immediately asks how Savvy had liked Tulane, and of course Savvy had to tell her that she left after her freshman year. She was . . . [*long sigh*]. Savvy was doing this thing then, where she was making light of it and sort of poking fun at herself. Making the joke before someone else can and all that. I didn't like it.

Ben: What would she say?

Ivy: She would tell people things like, "I majored in partying," or "I was a terrible college student, but a truly excellent sorority girl." It just made her sound dumb, and she wasn't dumb. She'd gotten a scholarship to Tulane. She was her high school salutatorian, for god's sake! She was just too young. I know plenty of eighteen-year-olds do just fine leaving home, but she didn't. She was a sweet girl who just wasn't ready to be on her own. She was finally starting to get her feet under her again when Lucy moved back to town.

Ben: And you said it was awkward at first? Because of the college thing?

Ivy: Savvy said that Lucy looked really uncomfortable at first, and Matt had to jump in and save her. Matt was always doing that. He's a real charmer. No idea what he saw in Lucy. But I guess Lucy and Savvy got to talking, and they decided to meet up for drinks the next day. I was turned off by the whole thing right away, honestly.

Ben: Why?

Ivy: It just sounded like Lucy was taking pity on Savvy. Lucy had moved back to town with her rich, handsome husband,

they'd bought this gorgeous old house, and she was helping her husband open this fancy brewery restaurant thing.
And then she comes across the former homecoming queen,
who has dropped out of college and is now a bartender?
Please. It was so obvious that Lucy liked how the tables had
turned.

Ben: Did Savvy get that impression from Lucy?

Ivy: No. Not that she said, anyway. But that girl had blinders on
when it came to Lucy. She didn't see the real woman. Not
until it was too late.

CHAPTER SEVEN

LUCY

The bedroom I lived in for the first eighteen years of my life looks nothing like it did when I was younger. Before leaving for Los Angeles, I cleared out the entire room. Took everything off the walls and boxed it all up, emptied the closet and dresser, tossed all the old notebooks and school assignments in my desk.

Mom replaced the furniture at some point—the twin bed is now a queen, and the dresser and desk are new—and so the room is completely different than when it was mine. It's a relief.

I pull my laptop out of my bag and plop down on the bed, which is hard as a rock. Mom thinks that soft beds are bad for your back, and she won't be convinced otherwise.

I have a few emails, a couple book-related, one hate-mail-related (*"Who did you sleep with to get the charges dropped, you evil bitch?"*), and one from my agent, Aubrey. Aubrey Vargas is a perpetually upbeat woman, and she has sent me an email with a lot of exclamation points about how she's not at all worried about the podcast. *"Your real name will be kept under wraps here as usual! I hope you have a great time in Texas!"*

Sure, Aubrey. The best time.

I also have a mountain of social media notifications, and I scroll through them quickly. I only have active social media accounts under the Eva Knightley name. I had Instagram, Facebook, and

Twitter accounts once upon a time, but I shut them down a long time ago. It felt too risky. I'd just barely skirted beneath the radar of social media for years before this podcast. I never wanted to tempt fate.

Eva Knightley is just a bubbly romance author with lots of (strictly online) friends. No one thinks she's murdered anyone, with the exception of the occasional fictional character.

I scroll through the comments on my Facebook reader group page, where a few people are discussing Clayton, the evil ex-boyfriend in my last book.

"*Am I the only one who thought that Clayton was going to mysteriously die at the end?*" Amber Hutton wrote.

"*Yes!*" Erica Burton replied. "*When Poppy says 'literally no one would miss you if you disappeared tomorrow, Clayton,' I was like, she is going to murder that dude! And I'm not going to be sad about it!*"

"*LOL,*" Amber replied, "*100%. For a minute I wondered if I'd picked up a really weird romance novel, because the heroine doesn't usually kill people.*"

"*Eva, maybe you should be writing serial killer books too!*"

I snort as I type out a reply. "*Not a bad idea. Watch out, world—I'm entering my murder era!*"

The comment immediately starts to get likes and laughs. I have to wonder if they'd think it was funny if they knew who I really was.

"*Lucy, dinner!*" my mom calls from downstairs, and suddenly I'm sixteen again. I wish I'd gotten the stupid hotel room.

Dad made dinner. Both my parents cook, but Dad does it most of the time. He's better at it, and he enjoys banging the pots on the stove really loudly when he's annoyed.

There's been a lot of banging tonight.

I offered to pick up Grandma so she could join us, but she claimed exhaustion and told me to come over in the morning. "Exhausted means drunk," Mom helpfully explained when I got off the phone.

Now, I sit at the table across from my parents. They're both on the other side, united against me. Or maybe they always sit there. It's weird, but perhaps they don't want to look at each other.

I take a bite of roast chicken. Dad's disappointment doesn't transfer to his cooking. People like to claim that food tastes better when it's made with love—like how their grandmother's pie didn't taste right when they made it, so it must have been the love that made it good.

This is bullshit, in my opinion. It was probably just extra butter or better-quality sugar that made it good.

Dad's cooking is proof of this. It is not made with love; it's made with resentment and disappointment. And it still tastes fucking great.

"How is work, Lucy?" Mom's using her long, peach fingernails to slowly peel the skin off her chicken breast. She banishes it to the edge of her plate, which seems a shame to me.

I look at my food instead of at her. "Fine. Same as usual." My parents don't need to know I was fired. Their opinion of me is low enough already.

"That's good. You're still working for that educational publisher, aren't you? Doing copyediting and such?"

"Yep." I did have that job for a few months, two years ago. Close enough.

"You *always* noticed misspellings and grammar mistakes. Don, you remember, don't you? She used to mark up the church program and give it to the pastor."

"I remember," Dad says. "I think that Jan has held a grudge about that forever."

"Jan should have done a better job typing up the programs," I say.

Mom laughs, because it's true. Those programs were an embarrassment. For years I amused myself during sermons by counting all the mistakes, but by about age fifteen I couldn't take it anymore and

I'd hand over my corrections to the pastor after the service. I must have looked like a little asshole to Jan, the receptionist whose job it was to type them up every week.

They replaced Jan after I pointed out that she'd used *pubic* instead of *public* in the newsletter. My youth group lost it. *Plumpton Baptist Church Pubic Events* was the funniest shit we'd ever seen.

Jan was given another job in the church, but she definitely always hated me after that. It's not my fault that Jan couldn't be bothered to proofread her work.

I wonder whether anyone (besides my parents) remembers that now. Aggressively copyediting church documents seems rather tame, considering the events of the next few years.

Listen for the Lie Podcast with Ben Owens

EPISODE 2—"SHE WOULD NOT HESITATE TO CUT A BITCH"

There's a wealth of information out there about Savannah. Most of her friends and family have been forthcoming with stories about her life. But Lucy? She's more of a mystery. A lot of people I spoke with said they wanted the focus to remain on Savannah, not on Lucy. Savannah was the one who was murdered, after all.

However, you can't talk about Savannah without also talking about Lucy. So, I pressed people for details about her, and what they remembered about her from before the murder. Here's Ross Ayers, who grew up in Plumpton and went to school with Lucy.

Ross: I mean, Lucy was . . . she was okay when we were little. Like, she was sort of nice, I guess. But later she . . . I don't know. She . . .

Ben: She what?

Ross: Do I have to be politically correct about murderers now too? Jesus Christ. She was a bitch, okay? She was a huge fucking bitch.

CHAPTER EIGHT

LUCY

The next morning, I go to see Grandma. I invite Mom, hoping she'll say no, but she grabs her crutches and hobbles out to my car.

"Has she sent you a picture of the house?" Mom asks as I navigate the streets of Plumpton. I remember them well, much to my dismay.

"No."

"God, it's awful. I'm so embarrassed."

It is not awful. It is, however, supremely weird.

I stand in front of it and cock my head. "Huh."

Mom grunts as she digs her crutches into the dirt and stops next to me. "She sold her old house—which was paid off, I'd like to add—to buy this . . . thing."

"It's pink."

"Yes."

"I feel like she should have mentioned that."

"She had them paint it that color on purpose. It was supposed to be brown."

"Huh."

"It's two hundred and fifty square feet. Who in the world wants to live in two hundred and fifty square feet?"

"Grandma, apparently."

"And why is it on wheels? Where is she going to take it? She's never left Texas."

That, I must admit, is a good point.

The tiny house is kind of cute, actually. It's basically a square box on wheels, but it has a certain charm, and it's not just the cheery pink color. There's a garden on the left side, and in front, two chairs and a small table. It's on a plot of land surrounded by trees, a much larger home barely visible in the distance.

The door opens, and Grandma steps out. She wears a loose, faded blue dress with white daisies dotting the hem. Her gray hair is pulled into a bun and her lips are a bright pink color that almost matches the house. I don't think I'll look that good when I'm eighty.

"Lucy!" She spreads her arms wide.

I walk across the grass to embrace her. She holds me at arm's length when I pull away.

"You're not just my favorite grandchild, you're also the most attractive one by a mile."

"*Mom.*" Mom stops next to me with a grunt. "I wish you would stop saying that. It's so rude."

"It's only rude if you tell the other ones." Grandma turns away, waving for us to follow. "Come in! I made iced tea."

I follow her inside, cold air blasting my face as I step out of the heat. Mom shivers. One upside of a tiny house—easy to keep cool in the summer. Or freezing cold, if you're Grandma.

For two hundred and fifty square feet, the house makes impressive use of space. There's a kitchenette to my right, and to the left, a sofa against the wall with a television mounted opposite it. For a moment, I wonder whether she sleeps on the sofa, until I see a rollout bed tucked into the wall. There's a bathroom in the far corner with only a curtain for a door.

"Sit down, Kathleen, you're making me nervous on those crutches." Grandma points at the couch, and Mom obediently sits. I put her crutches against the wall.

"See, I can just move the table around when I have company!" Grandma slides the small square table so it's in front of the couch.

I sit on one of the stools she pulls from underneath it. "It's very nice."

Mom shoots me a look like I shouldn't encourage her. Grandma pours tea from a jug into three glasses, and then plunks two of them on the table. They're stemless wineglasses, the kind you're supposed to use for red. I only know this because Nathan is insufferably pretentious about wine. I like to drink my wine straight from the can.

"I'm glad you think so. Your mother is extremely disapproving."

I take a long sip of tea and smile at her. Grandma doesn't ask if you want your tea sweet or unsweet. There's only one way iced tea is made, in her opinion—sweet enough to leave a nice coating of sugar at the bottom of the glass. (She is correct.)

Mom waves her arms around in a way that feels disapproving. "You had a three-bedroom house! And now you live in a closet!"

"Tiny houses are very hip. Millennials love them."

"You're not a Millennial."

She shrugs once, a shrug that would make Arya Stark proud.

Mom looks at me. Two matching vertical lines have appeared between her eyebrows. "Her old house was lovely. It had those big windows in the kitchen, and a sunroom in back."

She says this to me like I don't remember the house just fine. Like I didn't spend many evenings there as a kid to avoid the yelling and tension at home. Grandma and I would sit at the kitchen table, eating candy that would ruin my dinner, while staring out the huge windows at the neighbor who always had to chase her little dog down the street.

"The sunroom was too hot most of the time anyway," I say. Mom sighs.

Grandma nods in agreement, and then reaches into a cabinet to grab a bottle of vodka. She pours some into her tea.

Mom purses her lips. "Mom, it's not even noon."

"What's your point?" She pours a little more into the glass. "Lucy, you want some?"

"No, thank you." I try not to laugh.

"I seriously don't understand developing a drinking problem in your *seventies*," Mom says.

Grandma sits at the head of the table. "Why not? Way I see it, seems like the perfect time to develop a drinking problem. It's dull as hell around here."

I'm pressing my lips together hard to keep from laughing. Mom mutters something I can't understand.

"Let's give it a rest for today, shall we?" Grandma takes a long sip of her drink. "You can resume judging all my life choices after Lucy goes back to L.A."

Mom sighs heavily but doesn't argue. She adjusts the front of her pale green blouse, like having her neckline in order might fix this situation as well.

"How is L.A.?" Grandma asks. "How's Nathan?"

"Mmhhh . . . I think that's about to run its course." He still hasn't located his balls and officially dumped me, but I did get a *we should talk when you're back* text this morning that I haven't replied to yet.

Mom looks from me to Grandma, a tiny frown on her face. Mom didn't know about Nathan. It occurs to me now that Mom probably has no idea how often I talk to Grandma. Far more often than I talk to her.

Grandma has also noticed Mom's expression and now looks very pleased with herself. "And how is Plumpton? Different than when you left?"

"A little. There's a Starbucks."

Mom drinks her tea and makes a face. She puts it down, nudging it to the other side of the table. "Did you give some thought to what you want to do for your party?"

"Oh yes, I made a list." She jumps out of her chair—she moves like she's many years younger than eighty—and grabs a piece of paper from the kitchen counter. She hands it over to me. It's a list of people to invite, a few food suggestions, and a list of cocktails. At the bottom, in capital letters, it says "PIE."

"Instead of cake?" I point to the word.

"Yes. Several types of pie. But definitely pecan. And apple. And peach."

I laugh. "Okay. I'm sure Dad can handle that."

Mom nods. "Don makes an excellent apple pie."

Grandma looks at me. "You know that radio host is in town?"

"Podcaster, Mom. They call them podcasters now." Mom glances at me and then quickly away.

I rub the goosebumps on my arms. "Mom told me."

The very large bottle of vodka is still on the counter. I imagine smashing it into Mom's head.

A soft voice whispers in my ear, "*Let's kill—*"

"Has he ever tried to contact you?" Grandma asks.

"*Let's kill—*"

Not now. I shake my head, and the voice, away. "He emailed me."

Mom blinks. "About what?"

"About doing an interview."

"What did you say?"

"Nothing. I didn't respond."

She clucks her tongue. "That's rude."

"I never respond to emails about Savvy."

"Can't blame you," Grandma says.

Mom leans back in her chair. "He was perfectly nice."

"Of course he was; he wanted something from you." Grandma turns her attention back to me. "Are you going to go see people while you're in town? Any of your old friends?"

I snort. "What friends?"

Listen for the Lie Podcast with Ben Owens

EPISODE TWO—"SHE WOULD NOT HESITATE TO CUT A BITCH"

When Lucy moved back to Plumpton after college, she moved to a neighborhood referred to as "the Block." The Block is actually several blocks that form a square. It's an area within walking distance of the main downtown strip, which had once been run-down, a spot that hadn't kept up with the rest of Plumpton's growth.

About twenty years ago, they tore down many of the old homes and renovated some of the old ones. It quickly became a popular spot for young, well-off couples to buy homes, and is now one of the most exclusive areas of town.

Matt and Lucy bought the Hampton House, which caused a stir in the neighborhood. I spoke with Joanna Clarkson, who was one of the first people to move to the neighborhood, with her husband.

Joanna is a whirlwind of a woman, bustling around her bright, enormous kitchen, trying to make me snacks before I can finally get her to sit down and talk to me.

Joanna:	Hampton House was this big, beautiful house built in the early twentieth century. It was turned into a museum in the seventies, which shut down in the nineties, and then was boarded up for years, when that area went downhill. When they started redoing the area, they didn't tear that house down. They gutted it and turned it into this gorgeous, charming home. Wraparound porches and huge windows . . . have you seen it?
Ben:	I dropped by there earlier, actually.
Joanna:	It's so nice. I think there was some talk about turning it into a bed-and-breakfast for a while? But I guess those plans changed, and it was sold to Dale, at first—he was the mayor. He and his wife lived there a few years, and they put it on the market right when Matt and Lucy were moving here. There were multiple offers, but Dale chose them because of Lucy.
Ben:	He knew her?
Joanna:	He knew her parents. Everyone did. It just felt right that

it should go to her, considering her family's history with the town. I remember thinking that Lucy really lucked out, marrying a guy who came from money. She never would have been able to afford that house otherwise. People thought that Lucy lucked out in general with Matt, actually.

Ben: Yeah? He was well liked around here?

Joanna: Oh yeah. Are you kidding? People *loved* him. And it just . . . it goes to show, doesn't it?

Ben: What?

Joanna: Men. I'm sorry, hon, don't take this personal, but with Matt and Lucy, it really seemed to prove that men only care about looks. Because Lucy, well, she's beautiful, but . . .

Ben: But?

Joanna: Well, I guess you don't have to be nice when you look like that, do you?

Ben: She had a lot of friends, though? By all accounts, she was pretty social.

Joanna: I guess.

I also spoke with Nina Garcia, who was one of Lucy's best friends in high school. Nina is a nurse at a nearby hospital, and she's still wearing her pink scrubs when I arrive at her home, her dark hair falling out of a clip.

Nina: Sorry, twelve-hour shift. I'm scattered. What were you saying?

Ben: Were you surprised when Lucy moved back after college?

Nina: No, not at all. Lucy's family, on her mom's side, has been here for like . . . ever. Like I think they were one of the original families who settled here. And even though she wasn't the cheerleader type like Savvy, she still embraced small-town life. She said we were a cool small town, like Stars Hollow.

Ben: I don't know Stars Hollow. Where is that?

Nina: From *Gilmore Girls*, Ben. You need to brush up on your early-2000s television.

Ben: I will get right on that.

Nina: Except with more wine. We're Stars Hollow, but with more wine and cowboy boots. Anyway, Lucy and I grew apart a little in college—we went to different ones—but I was excited when she texted me that she was moving back with Matt after the wedding. She said he'd fallen in love with the town when they visited her parents, and he wanted to open a brewery/restaurant thing. Thought it would be perfect, since we have so many tourists. Figured he could get the husbands who weren't into wine. Didn't work out, I guess. It was only open a few years.

Ben: So, you two reconnected when she moved back?

Nina: Ehhh . . . sort of? I mean, that was the plan. But we had both changed, and it was kind of hard. I was about to give birth to my first, and she wasn't even thinking about kids yet, so we didn't really have a lot in common. And my ex was . . . well, he preferred for me to be home. And then Lucy started hanging out with Savvy and some of the women in her neighborhood. The friendship just fizzled. High school friendships don't always transfer to adulthood, you know?

Ben: Sure.

Nina: And Lucy and Savvy . . . they had one of those intense, obsession-like friendships, you know?

Ben: I don't.

Nina: I guess it's mostly women who do it. But sometimes you meet a girl who is just, like, your soulmate. Not in a romantic way, but in a friend way. Which can almost be more intense. You could tell that Savvy and Lucy were in one of those intense friend-soulmate relationships.

Ben: An intense relationship usually has pretty serious ups and downs. Did they fight?

Nina: I don't really know. I didn't hang out with them much.

Ben: I've heard that Lucy has a temper. Did you ever see that?

Nina: I mean . . . I don't know. Would people say she had a temper if she was a man? They'd say she stood up for herself when it was needed.

So that's what I'm going with. Lucy wasn't afraid to stand up for herself.

CHAPTER NINE

LUCY

I don't realize it's Saturday until I step into the grocery store. I have no sense of time without a job.

But, apparently, it's Saturday, so the entire town of Plumpton is out shopping for groceries. There are two large grocery stores in town, but the other one is shitty and gets whatever produce was left over.

Still, I should have gone there.

Because, from the moment I walk in, I can tell that people recognize me.

No one in Los Angeles has ever recognized me. Pre-podcast, I was only famous to a tiny murder-obsessed corner of the internet. There are far more exciting people to see in Los Angeles. A guy from one of the cop shows shops at the grocery store near my house. No one is going to notice a maybe-murderer when the dude who has been looking mildly annoyed by his gorgeous partner for eight seasons is squeezing avocados in the produce section.

But there are no avocado-fondling actors in Plumpton. *I* am the biggest celebrity in town.

I push my cart past a large bin of toilet paper, trying to pretend that a woman with a helmet of gray hair isn't openly gawking at me. I wonder whether I should know who she is. I've tried my very best to block out all my memories of the people in this town, except for Savvy. Savvy is the only memory I want, ironically.

Mom made a list—some general stuff they need like eggs and bread, plus a few things for the party. I push my cart through the aisles as fast as I can. Mom didn't put buttermilk on the list, but I grab it anyway, hoping it will encourage Dad to make biscuits. And chocolate sheet cake. If I have to be here, I'm at least going to eat some of Dad's food.

I pile the food into my cart, grab several bags of candy (sugar is my main weakness, unless you count my inability to stop murdering people in my head), and make my way to the very long checkout lines.

"Lucy?" The baffled, familiar voice rings out loud enough for at least half the store to hear.

I try not to wince as I turn to find the source. Nina Garcia stands in the next checkout line over, her mouth literally hanging open.

"Wow. Hi." She plants her hands on her hips, which are a bit wider than last time I saw her. She's curvier all over, actually. She's the sort of woman who looks nice in those dresses that cinch at the waist. I look terrible in those dresses. Like a stick wearing a sack.

"Hi, Nina." I try to smile. I haven't seen or spoken to her since before Savvy died. If I'd run into her two days ago, I might have still been bitter about that.

After listening to the podcast, I'm finding it harder to hold a grudge. And I'm usually so good at holding grudges. It's one of my best talents.

"Well come here, girl, give me a hug!" She steps forward and wraps her arms around me before I can react. Her long, wavy dark hair smells like fake coconut.

I don't know what to do with this friendliness from Nina. It could be a Texas thing, I guess. The fake-friendly "pretend everything is fine even though I hate your guts" thing that Texans do didn't apply to me last time I was here. But maybe five years is too long to keep up that level of hostility. Texans are nothing if not polite (to your face).

But on the podcast Nina actually didn't sound like she hated my guts. She wasn't passionately defending me, but she wasn't throwing me under the bus either. There are plenty of high school stories she could have told that would have made me look terrible.

I don't know what to do with that. I'd be much more comfortable if she'd shouted "*I hope you get hit by a truck!*" at me from across the store.

But hugging? Hugging is weird.

I pat her on the back and try not to look uncomfortable as she pulls away.

"I heard you were coming to town but I honestly didn't believe it." She points her finger up and then down my body. "You look great, by the way. How's Los Angeles?"

"It's . . . good. You know, sunny."

"Oh, I bet. I visited there once. Did the whole tourist thing, saw the handprints and all that." Her eyes flick to something behind me, and I turn to see two women staring at me. One glares when our eyes meet.

She's standing next to a rack of scissors, and I imagine ripping the plastic off and jamming it into her throat.

"If you slice it like this there's so much blood, let's kill—"

Shit. The voice is back. Shit.

I'd hoped that by pretending it wasn't happening, the voice would fade away again. It had been so quiet since I left Plumpton.

"Let's kill—"

"How's your mom doing?" Nina asks. "I heard it was a bad break."

I turn away from the hostile ladies, and the voice quiets. "She's good, I think. You know how she is."

"I sure do." She laughs. The woman in front of her moves forward, and Nina pushes her cart up and then turns back to me. "Are you just here for your grandma's birthday or . . . ?"

"Why else would I be here?"

She looks flustered. "Oh, well, I just thought that with Ben back in town . . . you know about him, don't you?"

My stomach dips to my feet at the mention of the smug podcaster. I take a swift glance around, like he might be lurking.

"Yeah, my mom told me he was around."

Nina chews on her lip, and then looks relieved to move her cart forward again. She leans around the rows of snacks and lip balm. "Let's get together soon, okay? I'll call the house. You have to come by, see the kids."

There's no way she actually wants me to see her kids. I am not child appropriate. She really is just being polite this time. "Sure."

She smiles. "I'll talk to you soon, Lucy."

Listen for the Lie Podcast with Ben Owens

EPISODE TWO—"SHE WOULD NOT HESITATE TO CUT A BITCH"

I spoke to many of Lucy's former friends and people she grew up with, and a theme emerged in our talks.

Jill: Lucy had a temper. She would not hesitate to cut a bitch.

That's Jill Lopez. It was actually her wedding that Lucy and Savannah attended the night of the murder, a fact that she doesn't appreciate me bringing up.

Jill: Yes, it was my wedding. And yes, I'm pissed at Lucy for ruining that memory for me forever. I didn't even know her all that well. I shouldn't have invited her, but my mom wanted to invite like, all of Plumpton.

Ben: But you knew Lucy well enough to know that "she would not hesitate to cut a bitch"?

Jill: Everyone knew that.

Ross Ayers, a high school classmate, personally got a taste of Lucy's temper.

Ross: See that? Right there?

Ben: Your nose?

Ross: That bump? That's Lucy. She broke it senior year.

Ben: She broke your nose?

Ross: Yep. I wish I could have testified at a trial, tell everyone how crazy she was. I wasn't even the first guy she hit! She decked a dude at the CVS a few months earlier.

Ben: What happened? When Lucy hit you, I mean.

Ross: We were in the parking lot after school—me and some friends—just hanging around, waiting for our rides, when Lucy comes out. Lucy sees me and she just totally freaks out. This chick has murder in her eyes. Some guys nearby had just come from playing basketball, and she snatches the ball out of their hands and chucks it at me. From like only a few feet away. Hits me right in the nose. Then she screamed something—I don't even remember what she said—*punches me*, and leaves. Well, no, she didn't leave. A friend dragged her away.

Ben: Why did she do that? Had you two interacted before?

Ross: Barely! Some in class and stuff, but I don't think we'd ever even had a conversation. She just lost it. I don't know why.

I then spoke to Emmett Chapman. Emmett was one of Lucy's closest friends in high school.

Emmett: Lucy and I were friends . . . forever? I can't actually remember school without Lucy. Back in elementary school our teachers would make us line up alphabetically, and Lucy was always right behind me. Chapman and Chase. And she started sticking up for me all the time, so we became friends.

Ben: Sticking up for you?

Emmett: Yeah, I was bullied a lot in elementary school. I was tiny and just an easy target in general, so I dealt with a lot of shit. But Lucy was always kind to me. She wasn't afraid to be loud. I was such a shy kid. She yelled at people for me.

Ben: So, she had a temper? I'm hearing that a lot from people.

Emmett: Um, I don't know if I'd say that. No, I wouldn't say that.

Ben: Did you guys stay in touch after high school?

Emmett: Yeah. We both went to UT, but we didn't hang out as much after freshman year. We just fell in with different crowds and did our own thing. But we both came back to Plumpton after graduation, and we became good friends again. I actually hung out with Matt and Lucy all the time, with the woman I was dating back then. They were our couple friends.

Ben: Were you friends with Savannah too?

Emmett: Yeah, definitely. Not in high school, but later, when we all moved back, yeah.

Ben: Were you two close?

Emmett: No, I was better friends with Matt and Lucy. But Savvy was always really nice to me. Savvy was nice to everyone.

Ben: How would you describe Lucy and Savannah's relationship?

Emmett: They were close. I don't know what else to say. People always seem to want me to uncover some big hidden secret, or say that I could tell they secretly hated each other, but I didn't see any of that.

Ben: What did you think, when you heard that Lucy was the prime suspect in Savannah's murder?

Emmett: I was shocked. Never in a million years did I think Lucy would hurt Savvy.

CHAPTER TEN

LUCY

Sunday evening, Grandma sends me to pick up dinner for the two of us at Plumpton Diner. On my way out, Mom informs me that their salads are disgusting and warns me against ordering one.

"Who orders salad at a diner?" I ask, one foot out the door, the sticky humidity and chilly air-conditioning mixing together in a weird, unpleasant way.

She sniffs. "Well, everything else there is dripping in grease."

"Sounds delicious."

I escape before she can invite herself along.

The diner has been around since I was a kid, and it looks exactly the same on the outside. On the inside, the seats have been upgraded from cracked red plastic to a much nicer shade of blue. It's cleaner than I remember.

I walk to the counter and ask the red-haired teenager standing there about our order. Judging from the bored look on his face, he doesn't appear to recognize me.

"It's not ready yet." He looks down at his phone, scratching at a pimple on his cheek. "You can sit wherever while you wait."

I slide onto an unsteady stool at the counter, glancing around at the other diners. It's early for dinner—five o'clock—and the place is pretty empty. There's a couple in the corner. A mom with her two kids at a table nearby.

And a dark-haired man by himself in a booth by the window, staring at me.

I recognize him right away. Ben Owens. Smug podcaster.

He lifts one hand. He's waving at me.

I almost laugh.

And then, I imagine getting back in my car and ramming it into the side of the diner. Straight through the window. Ben's body sprawled out on my hood.

"*Hitting him with your car is bo-ring,*" the voice whispers in my ear. "*Put your hands around his neck until you can feel the life drain out of him. That'd be fun, right? He probably deserves it. They always deserve it. Let's kill—*"

Shut up, I tell the voice calmly.

It can't be a good sign that I've started talking back to it again.

Ben doesn't move, but he tilts his head slightly, an expectant look on his face. It's an invitation, maybe.

I imagine that he'll just get up and walk over to me if I decline the invitation.

I slide off my stool and walk across the diner.

"*Such a lovely throat you have there, sir,*" the voice says. "*It would be a shame if something happened to it.*"

He smiles, flashing his perfect, white teeth. Braces and regular whitening. Those teeth did not happen by accident.

I suspect that nothing about Ben Owens is an accident.

He extends his hand. "Hi. Ben Owens."

I ignore the hand. "I know who you are."

He gestures to the seat across from him. There's a half-eaten sandwich on the table next to a laptop, which he closes and pushes aside. He also flips over a small notebook so I can't see what was written there.

"Please, sit."

I'm still standing next to his booth like an idiot, and I guess I didn't come over just to say hi.

I slide into the seat. He drops his pen on the floor and has to get out of his seat to retrieve it. He's flustered.

I imagined him a lot smoother. Confident. Working a room.

He settles back into his booth. His dark eyes meet mine briefly, and then his gaze is anywhere but at me. I don't know whether he's nervous or embarrassed or just really high-strung.

"I'm speaking to you off the record right now," I say. "I don't want to have a conversation if any of this is going in the podcast."

"Do you have something you want to tell me?" He plays with the edges of the notebook paper, like he's itching to turn it over and write something down. His fingers are long, the nails neatly trimmed, and I quickly look away.

"No, nothing in particular. I just wanted to make it clear that this isn't me consenting to an interview."

"Okay. Off the record."

"Okay."

"I heard you were in town. How's your mom?"

"She's fine, thanks. I heard you were in town too. Why?"

"Because you're here."

I cock an eyebrow. At least he's honest.

"Thought I might change my mind about an interview once I saw your charming face in person?"

The edges of his lips twitch. "Maybe."

"You've already gotten some good ones."

"You've been listening?"

"Yes."

"What do you think?"

"Riveting."

"Thank you." He apparently didn't notice—or chose to ignore—my sarcasm.

I slouch down in my seat, propping up the soles of my shoes on the booth next to him. "So what's the verdict? Did I do it?"

He rubs the edges of the notebook paper more determinedly, giving me an amused look. "I've heard you're direct."

"It's one of my many charms."

"I'm collecting evidence and presenting it, not making judgments."

"Bullshit, you totally weigh in with your opinions eventually. I've listened to the first season."

"Thank you for that. And eventually, yes, I'll bring my own opinion into it, but not right now." He leans forward, both arms on the table. "Let me interview you. No one ever gets your side of things."

"My side of things is just going to be a fucking disappointment to you, Ben. I still don't remember anything."

"Not that. I mean, yes, if you suddenly remember what happened that night, by all means, call me right away—"

"You'll be my first call for sure," I say dryly.

"—but you can give your side of things on so many other issues. Your relationship with Savannah, Matt, what happened at the wedding . . ."

"I am not putting my relationship with Savvy out there for everyone to judge again. I hated doing it the first time and I'm not doing it a second time."

I glance over at the counter. The teenager has disappeared.

"I enjoyed your books," Ben says.

My gaze snaps back to his face. "What?"

"Your books. The Eva Knightley books."

I drop my feet from the booth and straighten. He looks smug again.

"How did you even?" A pit begins to form at the bottom of my stomach.

"Let's kill, let's kill, let's kill—"

"My PI is very good." Smug, smug, smug.

"Listen, those books . . ." I clasp my hands together, cracking my knuckles. "I can't write under my own name. I mean, no one wants to read romance novels from the girl who allegedly bashed her best friend's head in."

He looks startled by that.

"And I've managed to keep that name a secret so far, and I would really appreciate it if you—"

"Relax, Lucy, I'm not going to tell anyone." He smiles. Smugly.

I hesitate. "If I give you an interview?"

"What? No. Jesus, Lucy, I'm not *blackmailing* you. I really did like the books."

"You read romance novels?"

"Well, no, these were my first, but maybe I should read more, because they were very exciting. I liked the one with the couple that pretended to be married best."

"Why?"

"Apparently I enjoy a good fake-marriage trope. This is something I've just discovered about myself recently."

I barely resist the urge to laugh, but my lips twitch. Fuck. "No, why did you read my books?"

"I was interested. And I did consider putting it on the podcast, honestly. Read some passages. But I can't really see how it's relevant. Paige—my assistant—said that putting it on there would just be a dick move, and I have to agree."

"I like your assistant."

"She's smarter than me."

"Ma'am?" The teenage boy at the counter has reappeared, and he's talking to me, holding a large plastic bag full of takeout containers. I know that everyone calls women *ma'am* here, no matter their age, but it still makes my eye twitch. I've been in Los Angeles too long.

I start to slide out of the booth.

"Just one question." Ben reaches forward like he's going to touch me. He doesn't. He presses both palms flat to the table. "Off the record."

"You can ask, but I may not answer."

"How well did you know Colin Dunn?"

I sigh. Colin Fucking Dunn.

"You think Savvy's boyfriend did it. How original. Why didn't anyone else think of that?" I deadpan.

Literally everyone has thought of that. It's always the boyfriend or the husband.

Except, in this case, it wasn't.

"How well did you know him?" he asks again.

"Not well." Colin's face flashes through my mind—he had a great face. A strong jaw, and a slightly crooked smile. Savvy loved his smile.

"You really think Colin went straight home that night? Why'd you guys leave him and Matt at the wedding?"

I slide out of the booth. "This is more than one question, Ben."

"I never was a rule follower."

God, he's the worst.

He grabs my hand and presses a card into it. "Call me if you want to talk about Colin after tomorrow's episode."

CHAPTER ELEVEN

LUCY

"**G**randma, what the fuck?"

I drop the takeout containers on the table and turn to face my grandmother, who is sprawled out on the couch in the center of her tiny house, watching one of the *Avengers* movies.

She blinks at me with wide-eyed innocence. "What?"

"You sent me to the diner because you knew that podcaster bastard was there."

"Well . . . yes."

"Please . . ." I pause, closing my eyes briefly as I gather myself. "Please tell me that you didn't plan this entire party just to get me here to talk to that podcaster."

"I don't know why you're asking. It's pretty obvious that's exactly what I did."

"Oh my god." I drop into a chair and put a hand on my forehead. "Why would . . . what in . . . *Why?*"

She stands, adjusting the bun that's wobbling on the top of her head. She walks over to the table and pulls the food out of the bag. "Have you *seen* him?"

"You sold me out to a podcaster because he's *cute?*"

"He's not just cute. My god. He even looks better than that—that guy, who is that?"

I drop my hand from my forehead to see her pointing at the

television. "Chris Evans." I roll my eyes. "He is not cuter than Chris Evans."

"Well, agree to disagree." She puts my burger and fries down in front of me. "But, no. I did not sell you out because he's cute. I'm just saying that it might have helped when he showed up at my door with that smile."

"Smug smile," I mutter.

"Oh yes, very smug. That boy is extremely impressed with himself." She laughs and walks to her minifridge. Her loose green dress swishes around her calves. "Do you want a beer?"

"No, thank you."

She cracks one open for herself and then sits down at the table. She pops a fry into her mouth. "I think that he's your best shot."

"Best shot at what?"

"At figuring out who killed Savannah. We spoke for a long time, and he was very straightforward with me. He wants to find out the truth, not just hang you out to dry like everyone else."

I take a bite of my burger to avoid having to reply to that. I don't want to tell her that the idea of Ben finding the truth terrifies me.

She points at me. Her fingernails are bright pink, the color chipped at the ends like she's been picking at it. "Don't get that look."

"What look?"

"Like you've decided you're guilty and have something to hide."

"*Let's kill—*"

I take another bite of my burger.

"I told him I'd convince you to let him interview you," she says.

"Bold of you to think you could actually do that."

"Lucy, let's not pretend that you're not going to do this for me." She pats my hand.

Dammit.

"You need him," she continues.

"I do not need that idiot."

"Yes, you do. People believe men. Especially men who look like that. If he says you didn't do it—if he even casts enough doubt—people will actually believe him. Look at that Ronan Farrow fellow. No one believed that movie man assaulted all those girls until he said it was true."

I sigh, because she's right.

Of course, that also means that if Ben decides I did it, I'm extra fucked.

"He solved a cold case on the first season of the podcast," Grandma says. "He's going to figure this out, and you're going to help him."

"The Harpers hired three different PIs and came up empty. How is Ben going to suddenly solve this?"

"He said he was going to find information that no one else had."

I grab a fry. "How exactly is he going to do that?"

"Well, for one, you're going to help him. And two, he already has."

I stop with my mouth half-open, ready to take a bite. "What?"

"Colin didn't go straight home from the wedding."

Listen for the Lie Podcast with Ben Owens

EPISODE THREE—"MATT WAS TOO GOOD FOR HER"

Colin Dunn had been dating Savannah for a few months when she was killed. I'll let him introduce himself, in his own words.

Colin:	I was a real shithead. [*laughter*] Yeah, man, I was just not into that whole small-town life. I hated every second of it, and I hated myself for not being brave enough to just hop a bus out of there. I sort of took that out on Savvy a lot.
Ben:	Took it out on her? How?
Colin:	I wasn't that nice to her. I know I probably shouldn't admit that, or I should, like, try to make myself look good, but, whatever, man. I just feel like I should be honest about it.
Ben:	Take me back a bit. How'd you guys meet?
Colin:	At the bar where she worked. I wasn't old enough to drink but I had a fake ID—yo, can I say that? Am I like admitting to a crime?
Ben:	You're fine.
Colin:	Yeah, so I was nineteen or twenty or whatever, and I had a fake ID. I don't think Savvy knew it was fake. No, she definitely didn't know. I always felt like I was a bad influence on her. She was just the nicest, sweetest girl, and I was *not* the nicest guy. I think if I had met her a few years later, I could have been a better guy for her, but . . . well, she got murdered. Which is a bummer.
Ben:	It is indeed a bummer.
Colin:	Anyways, we met at the bar, and hit it off right away.
Ben:	This was when?
Colin:	That was early in the year, like January. So, like four months before she died.
Ben:	And you dated up until she was killed?
Colin:	I mean . . . I don't know if *dated* was the word. We weren't . . . uh, yeah, you know, let's just say we dated. Yeah. Savvy was a nice girl. Nicer than me, that's for sure.
Ben:	Did you know her friends?
Colin:	Uh, sort of? Some of them?

Ben:	Did you know Lucy? Had you met her before the wedding?
Colin:	Yeah, I'd met her once or twice. She was in the bar once, and she'd been over at Savvy's place once when I dropped by. So, I knew who she was, but like . . . we weren't buddies.
Ben:	Did you have any particular impression of her?
Colin:	Uh . . . she was hot?
Ben:	Anything else?
Colin:	Not really.
Ben:	Did you know Matt?
Colin:	Not until the wedding.
Ben:	And you hung out with him and Lucy at the wedding?
Colin:	Yeah. We were at the same table.
Ben:	What did you think of them?
Colin:	Lucy didn't really talk to me. Not in a rude way, just in a "we have nothing in common" way. Matt and I talked about basketball some—it was during the NBA finals. Matt was a good time. He came to have fun at that wedding. Well, you've heard.
Ben:	And you saw that?
Colin:	Oh yeah. He was definitely wasted.
Ben:	How was he acting? Was he a happy drunk, was he angry . . . ?
Colin:	Pretty happy drunk, from what I remember. He was dancing a lot, laughing . . . completely ignoring Lucy, who seemed pissed about something.
Ben:	At him?
Colin:	I don't know, man. I asked Savvy about it and she said Lucy was fine. "Don't worry about it," she said. Like it was none of my business. And it wasn't. I didn't really care.
Ben:	Savvy drove you to the wedding, but she left without you. What happened there?
Colin:	Lucy and Matt had a fight, I think. I don't know what it was about. But Savvy seemed upset about it, and she asked her brother—Keaton—to take me home. I didn't go with him, though. I didn't live far, so I just walked.
Ben:	You walked straight home?

Colin:	Yeah.
Ben:	By yourself?
Colin:	I . . . yeah.
Ben:	A guest at that wedding says she saw you getting into a car with a woman.
Colin:	What guest?
Ben:	Just someone who wishes they'd spoke up earlier. Did you get in anyone's car that night?
Colin:	I . . . um . . . look. I sort of . . . started talking to someone after Savvy left and one thing led to another . . .
Ben:	And you left with her?
Colin:	Yeah.
Ben:	So, your alibi, that you told the police. That you went home and were there all night. That wasn't true?
Colin:	I mean . . . I was home by like three a.m.
Ben:	The coroner put Savvy's death somewhere between midnight and three a.m. So you were actually out and about during the time she was killed.
Colin:	It sounds bad when you put it like that. I wasn't *out and about*. I was with this woman, and then I went home.
Ben:	She could vouch for you?
Colin:	Not . . . I mean, she wouldn't.
Ben:	Why not?
Colin:	She wasn't exactly . . . single.
Ben:	She was in a relationship.
Colin:	Yes.
Ben:	You went to her house?
Colin:	No . . .
Ben:	Where'd you go?
Colin:	Just her car. She drove it a little bit down the road and we just . . . I don't think anyone at the wedding even noticed we were gone. They definitely didn't notice *I* was gone, anyway. If her husband was suspicious, I don't know.
Ben:	And then she drove you home?
Colin:	No, I walked. She had to get home.
Ben:	You walked home, alone, at what? One a.m.? Two? In the rain?

Colin:	It's a safe town, man.
Ben:	I'm just trying to clarify the timeline here. You were out, alone, during the time Savvy was killed. But you lied to the police and said you walked home right after she left.
Colin:	I didn't kill her.
Ben:	But this is the correct timeline now?
Colin:	I didn't kill her.
	Yo, can we start again? I feel like I messed this up.

CHAPTER TWELVE

LUCY

Did you call Ben?

I glance down at the text Grandma just sent me.

"You're sure you don't want roses? Your mom said pink roses." The florist frowns at me suspiciously, like I've come into her shop with the intention of ruining my grandma's birthday party.

I press the *call* button on my phone and put Grandma on speaker. She picks up right away.

"Hello?"

"Grandma. Opinion on pink roses?"

"Tell your mother I will vomit on her pink roses."

I raise my eyebrows at the florist. She purses her thin, red lips, like she's very insulted on behalf of pink roses everywhere.

I take Grandma off speaker and press the phone to my ear. "Party planning is going terribly and your birthday is going to be a disaster."

"Can't wait. Have you listened to today's interview with Colin? Did you call Ben?"

"I'm still thinking, traitor. I'll call you later, okay? I have to stop this pink roses disaster."

"Oh yes, please do."

I press *end* on the call and return my attention to the red-faced florist.

"Gerber daisies. No roses of any color."

I return to my parents' house to find Mom trying to sweep the floor with one hand while holding on to a single crutch with the other. I drop my purse on the kitchen table and take the broom from her.

"Thank you, hon. The girls are coming over in about ten minutes and I can't have this place looking like a pigsty." She fluffs her hair, which is already fluffy enough to make most southern women proud.

"Who are *the girls*?" I sweep some crumbs out of a corner and into the pile.

Mom hobbles over to the couch. "Just some friends. They come over every other week for tea. We do a book club sometimes, but not today. We just did a book last week."

"Which one?"

"Oh, I don't know. I never read them. Who has the patience for reading anymore?"

I snort as I sweep the dirt into the dustpan. She twists around to look at me.

"You stopped by the restaurant to look at the room?"

"Yes. It's very nice."

"And approve the menu?"

"They gave me a sample of their meatballs. Highly recommended." I dump out the dustpan and return the broom to the closet.

"I heard from Janice today that she and your uncle Keith are all booked at the inn, so no need to worry about that. Ashley and Brian too."

"I was definitely not worried about that."

"Your aunt Karen too," she says, ignoring me. "All set. No one needs rides; they're driving in from Houston."

I was definitely not going to offer a ride to the family members I haven't spoken to in years.

"Did you talk to the florist about the flowers?" Mom asks.

"Yep."

"She's going to do centerpieces with pink roses?"

"She sure is." I head to the stairs. "I should make myself scarce for this, right?"

"Goodness no! I told them you'd be joining us. Don't embarrass me."

"Way too late for that, wouldn't you say?"

"I meant don't embarrass me by going to hide in your room when I said you'd be joining us."

"All right. It's your funeral."

"I've never understood that saying and I'd prefer that you not explain it to me."

The doorbell rings. Mom fluffs her hair one more time and waves for me to answer it.

I walk over to the front door and pull it open.

I can see immediately that *tea* means *wine*.

Four ladies stand on the front porch, each armed with a bottle of wine. Two white, two red.

I try very hard not to imagine murdering them by grabbing a bottle and smashing it across their skulls, but it's difficult when they bring their own murder weapon.

I smile instead and invite them in.

Three of them I know—Marian, a pleasant woman with (fake) bright red hair and a smile that freezes in place every time our eyes meet; Betsy, who has a helmet of curly gray hair and tells me exactly how many calories are in the brownies she brought (285 per square—"*these are* not *diet brownies!*"); and Peggy, a very short woman who follows me into the kitchen, tells me which wineglasses to pull from the cabinet, and then washes them even though they look perfectly clean to me.

Janet's new. She'd moved to town five years ago, so we never had the pleasure of meeting. She looks nervous as she shakes my hand. I can't blame her.

Marian does actually make tea—very good tea—but it's obvious that the wine is the main attraction here. She gives us all a mug, and then Peggy hands out the wine in the now extra-clean glasses.

I take a glass of wine when it's offered to me but take only tiny sips, because I'm a lightweight. I don't need to get day drunk with these ladies.

Mom is on the couch with her broken leg stretched out in front of her, and Peggy settles down on the other end. Janet and Betsy take the love seat, and I sit in a chair from the kitchen table with Marian.

Peggy frowns as she sips her wine. "I can't remember—is Lucy short for Lucille?"

I shake my head.

"It's just Lucy, then?"

"Yes."

Peggy raises her eyebrows like she disagrees with my parents' naming choices. I glance at Mom, but she's smiling pleasantly. I grab a 285-calorie brownie from the coffee table and take a bite. It's a damn good brownie.

"These are amazing," I say. Betsy beams.

Marian looks at Mom. "How are plans for the birthday party going?"

Mom sighs dramatically. "Oh, it's fine, I guess. Mom's no help, though. She just keeps asking what kind of cocktails we'll be having."

"A woman after my own heart," Janet says, and drains her wine. Betsy refills it for her.

"It's been quite an ordeal calling everyone in the family and getting them here on such short notice," Mom continues. "I'm wondering if this whole shindig was a bad idea."

"Of course it wasn't!" Janet says. "It will be lovely to have your whole family in one place again."

"You're helping your mom, aren't you?" Peggy asks me accusingly.

"Lucy's been very helpful," Mom says quickly. "But she couldn't help with the calls. Some of my family would be very startled if Lucy called them up suddenly."

"I can't imagine why," I say dryly.

Janet looks horrified. Betsy shifts, clearly uncomfortable. Peggy appears delighted.

"Oh stop." Mom takes a long sip of her wine. "We're all thinking it, so we might as well say it."

"Why not?" I grab another brownie.

"Those are two hundred and eighty-five calories," Betsy says.

"I know."

"I just thought you might have forgotten."

I take a bite. "I didn't."

"Are you one of those women who can eat anything they want and not gain weight?" Marian asks. She looks extremely offended by this. More offended than when my mom not-so-subtly brought up my being a suspected murderer.

"She's genetically predisposed to be thin." Janet gestures at Mom.

"She runs like ten miles every morning," Mom says.

"Not *ten* miles. Not every day, anyway. But, yeah, I can eat whatever I want and not gain weight." This is not true, but I enjoy the sour look that comes over Marian's face as I say it. I take another bite of the brownie.

"Anyway, I think Lucy could take over some of the planning, even if your family will be startled to hear from her," Peggy says.

I shrug. "I'm fine with it."

"See? She's fine with it."

Mom rolls her eyes. "Lucy is always fine with startling people."

"She has a point." I polish off my brownie.

Betsy cheerfully bounces her hands off her thighs. "Let's change the subject! Lucy, you live in—"

"Have you met that boy?" Peggy interrupts. "The one doing the podcast? What's his name?"

"Ben," Janet says.

"Right, Ben. He's certainly good-looking, isn't he? Not sure what he's doing in radio. Should have been an actor."

"He looked like a baby to me." Marian tugs on a lock of red hair. "Younger than my son. Is he even out of college?"

Mom takes a brownie, clearly influenced by my good decisions. "He's about twenty-five, I think."

"Twenty-eight," I correct. Everyone turns to look at me.

"You've listened to the show?" Peggy asks.

"Yes."

"There's a new episode today," Janet says. "It's very well done, isn't it?"

"Who do you think cheated on her husband with that Colin boy?" Peggy whispers loudly, and then cackles.

I've only listened to half of today's episode, but I've always thought that Colin is too dumb and lazy to kill anyone. I decide not to share that, since I'm the only other suspect at this point. "I'm riveted. Can't wait to find out if I did it."

Janet's mouth drops open.

"Lucy, stop trying to shock people," Mom says pleasantly.

"I don't really have to try, Mom."

"*Anyway.*" Peggy clears her throat. "Kathleen, how's your leg?"

CHAPTER THIRTEEN

LUCY

I try to avoid going by Hampton House. I tell myself that I do not need to see it, and that I *really* don't need to risk running into Matt, who is living there with his new wife.

But I end up driving across town anyway. No one has ever accused me of making good decisions.

The sun has just slipped away when I arrive, the streetlamps clicking on. The lawns are still perfectly manicured, and there isn't a single car parked on the street. The homeowners association is always watching.

I pull up to the curb in front of the house and turn off the engine.

It looks the same. The flowers I chose to line the front of the house are still there. So are the misters above the porch, my best effort to make the porch comfortable in the summer months (it didn't work).

Through the front windows, I can see the white wood shutters I chose, shut tight. I guess it doesn't make sense to get rid of custom shutters, but I'm still surprised she didn't trash them. I might have worried they were cursed. I might have burned everything in a house where my new husband's murderous ex-wife used to live.

I enjoyed decorating the house, even though I hadn't really even wanted it. Matt was the one who was enchanted by it, by what it would say about us.

"*That house will make us the stars of that town*," he'd said. "*Everyone will be talking about it.*"

He was right, of course. The whole town was buzzing about it. Matt's right about everything, though. Just ask him.

I'd been reluctant to take money from Matt's parents, the only way we could afford the house. He'd dismissed that concern. They'd put aside money for his first house years ago. He said it like, *Obviously they did that. Who doesn't put aside nearly a million dollars for their son's first house? Obviously!*

I'd never gotten the hang of the rich-person lifestyle. There was so much *guilt* involved. Every time his parents would come over there were little jabs thrown everywhere. Remarks about upkeep and resale value. A snide comment about the brewery (which they also paid for). I'd rather be broke in an apartment with a foot-fetishist landlord than deal with that.

A car turns onto the street, and I quickly turn the key in the ignition, turning my head so the driver can't see my face. I watch it get smaller in my rearview mirror, and slowly let out a breath.

A knock on the window makes me jump.

I turn to look out the passenger's-side window.

It's Matt.

Listen for the Lie Podcast with Ben Owens

EPISODE THREE—"MATT WAS TOO GOOD FOR HER"

Stephanie: I'm sorry, but Matt was too good for her.

Ben: Why did you think that?

Stephanie: It wasn't just *me* who thought that. It was a pretty common sentiment.

I spoke to a lot of people about Matt, including Stephanie Gantz, who was friends with Matt and Lucy, and lived in the same neighborhood. She squeezes in an interview with me between shuttling her teenagers to soccer practice.

Stephanie: Matt was just so friendly. So easy to be around. He came over and had a beer with my husband the first day he moved in. I didn't meet Lucy until a few days later—I'm from here, but I'm a good ten years older than Lucy, so I didn't know her when she was younger—and it was just like . . . okay. Not the warmest lady you'll ever meet. It's weird that she and Savvy became such good friends, actually.

Ben: Why is that?

Stephanie: Because Savvy was a sweetheart. Bubbly, and charming, just the whole package. She would have been a better match for Matt, if you want to know the truth.

Ben: But you and Lucy became friends eventually?

Stephanie: Acquaintances, I guess. I lived down the road, and we're a tight-knit bunch here. Lucy never quite fit in, though. She was so young. Me and the other ladies . . . I probably shouldn't say this, but, oh well. We all used to joke about Lucy being Matt's first wife. We always knew a second would be coming.

Ben: Because they were young, or something else?

Stephanie: Because they were young, for sure. At that age, it seems fun to have someone who is your opposite. Later, you realize that it's exhausting. You want someone who brings peace to your life, not someone you're always at odds with. Matt and Lucy were at odds.

Ben: Do you mean that they fought a lot?

Stephanie: Oh, they definitely fought a lot. You could tell when you saw them together; they'd be doing that thing where you're trying to subtly fight but hope no one notices. But you could hear the yelling coming out of their house. It was that loud.

Ben: Who was yelling? Matt or Lucy? Or both?

Stephanie: Both.

Ben: Was that ever cause for concern? Did anyone ever call the police?

Stephanie: Oh goodness no. Of course, knowing what I know now, I might have feared for Matt's safety a bit more back then. And, of course, I feel so bad for Matt now, with everything.

Ben: You mean with Savannah's murder?

Stephanie: Well, no, I mean Kyle. Kyle Porter. You know about him, of course.

Ben: I've heard some things.

Stephanie: You should talk to Kyle.

CHAPTER FOURTEEN

LUCY

I roll down the window, like an idiot.

Matt leans into the car, casually resting both forearms against the bottom of the window, his hands hanging over the passenger's seat.

He has great hands. Long fingers, and nails that he keeps perfectly trimmed. I have a thing about hands. I once ghosted a guy after one date because his nails were long. That was it. He was really nice, and cute, and we had a great time. But I wanted to hurl every time I thought about those fingernails.

He's wearing his dark hair much shorter these days. I wonder whether he's starting to lose it. The petty part of me hopes so.

His eyes were the first thing I noticed about him—blue and bright—and they're hard to look away from, even now.

"Hi, Luce," he says.

This is a real shit stain of a situation I've gotten myself into here, so I say nothing.

I imagine closing the window, trapping his neck, hitting the gas, and dragging him down the street.

"Let's kill—"

"Were you going to knock, or just sit out here all night?" he asks.

I sigh. "I was just driving by."

"You're parked."

"I was curious to see how the house looked."

He glances back at it, and then at me. "Since you're here, do you want to come in?"

I give him a truly baffled look. "I don't think your wife would appreciate that."

"We're getting divorced. She moved back to Houston."

I try not to smile. I swear to god, I try not to be the asshole that I am, but I utterly fail.

If he sees the twitch of my lips, he pretends not to.

"Come in," he says. "Have a drink." He's got that glint in his eye, the one that means he's already debating whether to have sex in his bed or on the kitchen table. He loved having sex on the kitchen table. We picked out a very sturdy one specifically for that purpose. I wonder whether he still has it.

No. Shit. No. I am not doing this again.

I look out the front window. "You sure you want to be alone with me?"

"Lucy." He sighs heavily. It's his "Lucy is being ridiculous again" sigh.

"*Lucy, just go to your parents'. Please? Just for a few days. I need to think.*" He stood near the front door as he said those words to me, nervously cracking his knuckles. I remember thinking he was poised to make a quick escape.

He'd looked terrified. Of me. I'd been home from the hospital for less than twenty-four hours. The police hadn't started seriously questioning me. The media hadn't even turned on me yet.

But Matt? Matt was sure I was guilty. My husband was too scared to be in the same house with me.

"Maybe some other time." I put the car in drive, and he steps back onto the sidewalk.

I don't look in the rearview mirror as I drive away.

CHAPTER FIFTEEN

LUCY

I spot Ben as soon as I walk into the diner, sitting at the same table as last time, typing on a laptop.

He looks up and smiles at me. Grandma was right about one thing—he's got the smile of a superhero. No need to panic, ma'am, this extremely handsome gentleman is here to help. That's Ben's energy.

The friendliness has to be an act, his way of trying to get me to do an interview, but it's a good act. I'll give him that. He actually looks pleased to see me.

I walk to the booth and slide in across from him. The sticky plastic squeaks against my bare legs.

"I didn't actually think you'd reach out," he says.

I shrug. I'd emailed him last night asking to meet this morning. "Is this our official meeting place now?"

"Well, I'm here most days, so it's my official meeting place, yes."

"You come here and work? Don't you have a hotel room or something?"

"I do. But I like working in coffee shops or diners. And Vince said he didn't care because I don't come during busy times. Plus, I order lots of food." He grabs his menu and holds it out to me. "Do you want something? The burger is good. The pesto chicken sandwich is really good. I don't recommend the tuna melt."

"I'm fine."

"Are you sure? It's on me. They also serve breakfast all day and the French toast is great."

I hesitate. I haven't actually eaten much today, except for a banana after my run. And it smells like grease and syrup in here. My stomach rumbles.

"You totally want that French toast, don't you? Good choice." He straightens, looking in the direction of the kitchen, where I can see the top of a head. "Hey, Vince! Add a French toast to my order!"

"*Bacon?*" a voice responds. Ben looks at me and I nod.

"Yeah!"

"*You got it!*"

"Thanks."

"Sure." He closes his laptop. "How are things going with the birthday party?"

"My mom told you about that?"

"Your grandma did."

"They're fine, I guess."

"You guess?"

"Do you actually want to talk about my grandma's birthday party?"

A piece of dark hair falls across his forehead, and he shakes it back. "No. I was being polite. Making small talk."

"I'm not good at small talk."

"I noticed."

"Some people think that means I'm just an asshole."

"Not being good at small talk makes you an asshole?"

"Apparently. That's what some people say." My mom is always subtle about it, though. "*Polite people chat with each other, Lucy! They ask how your day is going.*"

"Are you an asshole?" he asks.

"Kind of."

"Well, that's honest."

"I try."

He drums his fingers on the top of his computer, and I try not to watch. He's amused. By me, I suppose.

"I see we're moving to the 'cheating whore' section of the podcast," I say.

He blinks, clearly taken aback. "I . . ."

"It's fine. I'm used to it. Not exactly new information, though, and contrary to popular belief, I do actually want you to solve this, Ben."

"Melting flesh smells like barbecue, and then there's no body. Win-win!"

I clench my jaw, willing the voice away.

"Let's kill—"

"Why don't we work together?" Ben asks.

"I'm really not interested in getting into the podcast game."

"I don't mean with the podcast. Not directly, anyway. I'm not going to pay you."

"This offer sounds irresistible already."

"Work with me to figure out who murdered Savannah."

"Besides me, you mean."

"Or you. Full disclosure, if you did it, I'm going to tell everyone."

There's that fucking superhero smile again. He's one of the annoying ones. The type complaining that they can't have a girlfriend because they care about her too much. Too tortured for a girlfriend. He's that superhero.

"That's fair," I say.

"Let me interview you. And work with me on background."

"What do you think I'm going to tell you?"

"You knew Savannah better than anyone. And in all this information, I barely have anything directly from you. Tell me your side. Tell me your theories. I have theories coming out my ears and I need to know how off base some of them are. Help me out here."

Vince appears with my French toast and Ben's sandwich. Vince frowns down at me, and then looks at Ben.

"Do you know who that is?" he asks him.

I roll my eyes. "Why would I be sitting with him if he didn't know who I was?"

Vince's frown deepens. He holds the steaming plate of French toast closer to his chest, like he's not sure he wants me to have it.

"Thank you," Ben says earnestly. "It all looks great."

Vince relents, plunking the plate down in front of me and sending the glob of butter on top sliding down the side of the bread.

I watch as he walks away. "I don't think he likes you anymore." I grab the syrup from the end of the table. "This is what happens when you hang out with me, by the way. Get used to more of that."

"Does that mean you'll help me?"

I take a bite of the French toast. Ben was right, it's very good. "Fine."

He brightens. "Really?"

"Yes."

"Including an interview? On the record?"

"Yes."

Now he's positively delighted. "Seriously?" He picks up his phone and begins typing.

"Why do you look so surprised? My grandma planned an entire birthday party just to get me here for this. You didn't think she'd convince me?"

"Honestly, no."

"I'm going to tell her about your lack of faith. She won't be pleased."

"Too late, I'm already texting her." He glances up briefly from his phone with a shit-eating grin.

"You're texting my grandma?"

"We talk often."

"Jesus Christ."

"Beverly loves me," he says smugly.

"I'm well aware."

"The feeling's mutual." He glances up at me. "You're wrong, by the way."

"About what?"

"New information. Kyle coughed up some."

Listen for the Lie Podcast with Ben Owens
EPISODE THREE—"MATT WAS TOO GOOD FOR HER"

Kyle Porter lives in Austin, and I meet him downtown, in the conference room of a trendy hotel. He's on his way to get drinks with a colleague, and he looks like the main character of a sexy legal drama. Stylish, effortlessly cool.

Kyle:	I think Lucy had been living in Plumpton for about a year when I met her? After she moved back as an adult, I mean. I was in Plumpton a lot for work, and I ran into her and Savvy at the bar one weekend. Lucy would hang out there sometimes during the day, when it was slow, and write.
Ben:	Write?
Kyle:	She was writing a book. She'd bring her laptop to the bar, which looked kind of funny. I saw her sitting there, typing away, so I just went over and said, "Are you drinking or working?" And she told me she was writing a book, which I thought was cool. We got to talking.
Ben:	And then what happened?
Kyle:	I think it was the third weekend I was in town. I could tell that third time that she'd been waiting for me, and she was just . . . looser. There's a hotel next to that restaurant, and after a couple glasses of wine I took a chance and asked if she wanted to get a room.
Ben:	Did you know she was married?
Kyle:	I saw the ring. But I was single, and honestly, I wasn't looking for a relationship anyway. A married lady seemed like a kind of ideal situation, actually.
Ben:	What was your impression of Lucy? Did she seem happy?
Kyle:	*Happy* is not the word, no. Lucy was complex. Layered. She wasn't interested in making other people comfortable, which I really liked about her. Not a common trait in a woman.
	She seemed older than her early twenties. A real old soul. A deep thinker. She was writing that book, but she'd just get so stuck in her head. I'm not surprised that she never managed to publish anything.

Ben: Did Lucy talk about her marriage with you?

Kyle: Not at first. But our . . . tryst went on for months, nearly a year, and eventually she did talk about him a little.

Ben: Did you get the impression it was a happy marriage?

Kyle: I got the impression it was complicated. Most marriages are, though. Right? I've never been married. But that's what I'd always thought. It seemed dramatic, to be honest. She was so young. I'm a good fifteen years older than her, and I remember thinking that it didn't sound like either of them should have gotten married.

CHAPTER SIXTEEN

LUCY

I gave my number to Ben before leaving the diner yesterday, full of French toast and regret. I've never given a journalist my phone number (though some found the old one anyway), and I can't shake the feeling that I made a serious error.

I've actually been wondering whether I've made a whole slew of serious errors lately. My entire fucking life for the past few days is a serious error, starting with my decision to fly across the country for my traitorous grandmother. My traitorous grandmother who spends about 80 percent (conservative estimate) of her day drunk. Her judgment clearly can't be trusted.

My phone buzzes the next day, as I'm sitting in Mom's office, staring at the poster above her desk that says *Make Today So Awesome That Yesterday Gets Jealous.* I look down to see a text from Ben.

Are you free this afternoon?

I am currently spending my days staring at a motivational quote that borders on toxic positivity, thinking up ways to write kissing scenes without using the word *lips* fifteen times on one page. Of course I'm free.

I type a one-word response: Why?

Want to meet my assistant? She's in town.

I spin around in Mom's desk chair. I do, surprisingly, want to meet his assistant. She sounded smart on the podcast last season. She called Ben out on his shit.

Okay. Where?

        We're in my room at the Plumpton Suites. Room 226.

Now?

        Whenever you're ready. We'll be working for a while.

So, I put my laptop in my room and carry on with my terrible life decisions by driving across town to the nicest hotel in Plumpton.

Ben answers the door, dressed casually in jeans and a faded gray T-shirt.

"Hey." He steps back so I can walk inside. The room is a basic suite with a kitchen and a small living room, two laptops on the coffee table. A pretty Black woman with a head of long, thick curls and a friendly smile, sits on the couch.

"Thanks for coming," Ben says. "Paige didn't believe that I actually got you to agree to an interview."

Paige stands. "You cocky little shit. This is not going to help your ego at all."

"Paige, this is Lucy. Lucy, this is my assistant, Paige. She hates me."

"Sorry." She's addressing me now, her hand extended. "It's nice to meet you."

"You too."

"Please sit down and tell me how he got you to agree to talk to him."

I sit down in the chair in the corner of the living room as Paige takes a seat on the couch again. Ben stays standing in the kitchen, leaning against the counter.

"Can I get you anything?" he asks. "Water? Or coffee? That's all I have. Oh, and whiskey."

"I'm fine, thanks."

Paige is studying me with such intensity that I wonder whether she's trying to memorize my face so she can paint it later.

"Paige," Ben says.

"What?"

"You're doing that thing again."

She blinks. "Right. Sorry. Is it rude to say you look different than the photos I've seen of you?"

"No." I lean back in my chair. "The only photos that got around were the ones where I looked devious."

"That's what it is." Ben snaps his fingers. "I kept thinking there was something about you that was surprising."

"My lack of deviousness?"

"Or the expression, anyway. Your level of deviousness remains to be seen."

"I suppose it does."

Paige is staring at me again.

"Paige," Ben says.

She doesn't look away this time. "I can't *believe* you're sitting here talking to us. Do you listen to the podcast?"

"Yes."

"Okay. Okay." Paige scoots forward on the couch, pressing her palms together in a prayer pose. I can feel the excitement rippling off her. "I don't know where to start."

"Paige, she's not here for an interview," Ben says. "I just asked her to drop by to say hi."

He's buttering me up for the interview. If I'm comfortable with him—and with Paige—I'm more likely to open up. Give him the good stuff.

I have no idea what the good stuff would be, but I suppose he can hold out hope.

"I know." Paige drops her hands. "Just one, though. I have to know, because I have a theory."

"Sure." Why not? Fuck me up, Paige.

"I've never killed a woman, but I'm willing to try anything once."

I shift, trying to ignore the voice. It's getting louder lately.

That can't be a good sign.

"Why did you punch Ross Ayers in high school?"

I blink, startled. I don't know which question I was expecting, but that wasn't it.

"Should have just fucking killed him. That would have been much more satisfying."

"No one knows. We asked everyone," Paige continues.

No, only Emmett knew, and he was always good at keeping a secret.

"He was taking up-skirt photos of a girl in one of our classes," I say.

"I knew it." Paige makes two fists like she's either victorious or getting ready to punch someone. "I knew it was something like that."

Ben looks startled, like this isn't a theory she had shared with him.

"I think he saw me telling the teacher, because the photos were gone when they checked his phone," I say. "I didn't tell people because the girl he'd done it to begged me not to. She was embarrassed. So, I figured since he wasn't getting punished, I'd take matters into my own hands."

"Paige—"

"I know, call Ross to see if he'll do another interview." She's typing on her phone.

"He's just going to deny it."

"Emmett knew, right?" Paige asks. "He got shifty when I asked him about it."

Jesus. I can see why these people actually solved a case last season. They're actually really good.

I don't know whether I'm relieved or terrified.

"I have an idea—"

"I didn't tell him who the girl was, but, yeah, he knew," I admit, silencing the voice.

"I get the feeling Emmett is keeping a lot of your secrets?" Paige cocks her head. It's more of a challenge than a question.

"I haven't spoken to the man in five years."

"Why not?" Ben asks.

"Shockingly, people stop calling when you've been accused of murdering a mutual friend."

I think of the missed calls on my phone, the texts from Emmett that I ignored.

Paige is staring at me like she knows I'm lying.

I look away.

"Are you in touch with Matt?" Ben asks.

"I wasn't, but I just saw him recently."

"Are you going to see him again?"

I shrug. "He asked to get together, but I haven't texted him back. Why?"

"He won't do an interview. I thought maybe you could put in a good word."

I lift an eyebrow. "Seriously? You want *me* to try to get Matt to do an interview?"

"Why not?"

"He thinks I did it."

"Is he right?" Paige asks.

I shoot her an amused look to try to cover the swell of panic I feel. "You know what? Fine. No promises, but I'll try."

Listen for the Lie Podcast with Ben Owens

EPISODE FOUR—"THE AMNESIA DEFENSE"

Reporter (news broadcast): Breaking news tonight—a local wedding took a tragic turn when one of the guests, twenty-four-year-old Savannah Harper, was found dead in the woods not far from the festivities. A second young woman was found wandering nearby, also injured in the apparent attack, and is currently in stable condition at the hospital. Police are asking that anyone with information . . .

Savannah was pronounced dead at the scene after Gil—the jogger—found her. The coroner later determined that she died from a blow to the head. Two blows to the head, actually. Someone hit her with an unknown object twice, and then left her there to die.

Lucy was initially thought to be a second victim, not the perpetrator. She'd also suffered significant injuries.

However, police found no evidence of a third person at the scene. An autopsy showed that the scratches on Savannah's arms were from Lucy's fingernails, and the bruising appeared to be in the shape of Lucy's hand. When witnesses began to come forward with what they'd seen at the wedding, the narrative around Lucy changed.

I spoke with Nina Garcia about what she saw between Lucy and Savannah that night.

Nina: A bunch of people saw Lucy and Savvy fighting at the wedding, yeah.

Ben: What do you mean by fighting? Can you describe what you saw?

Nina: I came out of the bathroom and Lucy and Matt were making out in the hallway. Savvy looked *pissed*.

Ben: Savvy looked pissed about Lucy kissing her own husband?

Nina: Yeah. And Savvy, like, cleared her throat, and they stopped. Then Lucy tried to say something to Savvy and Savvy let her have it. I couldn't hear what she said, but it was super tense.

Ben: You didn't hear anything at all?

Nina: No. And I didn't see it, but I heard that later, when Savvy and Lucy left together, Savvy was still angry. People saw her yelling at Lucy and slamming her car door. There was clearly a situation happening there.

Lucy has insisted, from the very beginning, that she has no memory of Savannah's murder. In fact, she claims to not remember anything from the night of the wedding at all.

Here's Colin Dunn again, Savannah's date to the wedding.

Colin: Yeah, Lucy says she doesn't remember anything after leaving her house that day. She doesn't even remember arriving at the wedding, I guess.

Ben: So, what does she remember? From what you've heard.

Colin: She remembers getting in the car with Matt to leave for the Byrd Estate. But then nothing else? I didn't even know amnesia was a real thing. I thought they made that up for TV.

Ben: It's a real thing.

Colin: Weird, man. Anyways, yeah, they had me go talk to Lucy a couple days after she got out of the hospital.

Ben: Why?

Colin: They were like, trying to get Lucy to remember what happened that night. Matt had told her some stuff, but he was really wasted. I can hold my booze. My memory was all right.

Ben: Were you okay with that? With going to talk to her?

Colin: Yeah, whatever. I felt bad about—well, you know. The whole thing with that woman in the car. That wasn't cool.

Anyways, I went over to the Chases', because Lucy was staying with her parents. I asked her to tell what she *did* remember, and she said, "We met in the parking lot and we all went in together and found our table," and I was like, "No, we didn't." And then she just started sobbing, which was really weird.

Ben: Sobbing?

Colin: Yeah, so apparently someone else had seen Matt and Lucy talking to another couple in the parking lot, and they'd thought it was me and Savvy. They'd told the police that, because at the time, they were trying to put everything together, so it was all important, you know? But that person got confused or was like also wasted or something because we actually got there later. Lucy and Matt were already sitting at the table when we walked in.

Ben: That upset Lucy?

Colin: Like, for real upset. Totally freaked me out. I thought she was going to pass out or something. Kathleen and Don told me later that Lucy had said she remembered walking into the reception, with Matt and me and Savvy. Like she had created a whole new memory around the bad information? I think everything went to shit after that. Lucy couldn't tell what was real and what she was creating to try and remember.

Ben: Did you believe her, when she said she didn't remember anything?

Colin: I don't know, man. She was putting on a hell of a show if she was lying. I sort of believed her after people told me that amnesia wasn't just a TV thing.

The thing I don't really get is—wouldn't she remember *something* eventually? Like after the head injury healed? That's suspicious to me, man.

Something stuck out to me during my conversation with Colin—he said that he went to see Lucy just two days after she got out of the hospital. He went there specifically to try to help her re-create the night her friend was murdered, which seems like a huge amount of stress to put on someone who just suffered a head injury.

In fact, not many people talk about Lucy's head injury at all. It's been reported that she suffered a "moderate traumatic brain injury," which is actually a very serious injury. I spoke to a doctor who preferred to stay off the record since he never treated Lucy Chase, but he confirmed that yes, amnesia is a real thing that happens with brain injuries. In fact, it's not that people who have suffered a brain injury *forget* what happens, it's that their brain stopped making memories at all. The memory doesn't exist.

So, to answer the question that a lot of you have been asking—yes. The amnesia defense *is* a real thing. Given the extent of Lucy's injuries, it's possible that she really doesn't remember what happened that night.

But is that the truth? And why is everyone in Plumpton so convinced she's lying?

CHAPTER SEVENTEEN

LUCY

I think we should break up.

I see Nathan's text as soon as I wake up. It was sent at two in the morning Texas time. Midnight in California. I wonder whether he was drunk.

Why???? I laugh as I push *send*.

I wonder what finally pushed him over the edge. Maybe he made it to the episode about my cheating with Kyle. He could excuse murder, but he drew the line at my cheating on my husband.

It's only six in the morning in Los Angeles, so I don't expect a response right away. Or ever, maybe.

Mom's gym agreed to let me use her pass while I'm in town, and I get on the treadmill, until *run run run* is the only thought going round and round in my brain.

Nathan hasn't texted back by the time I get home and shower, but Matt has.

Every part of my body tenses when I see his name on my screen.

Hey. Meet me for lunch. Please?

I want to ignore it, like I ignored every single other text he sent me over the years.

But I think of Ben's request. Of Grandma's request. Of Savvy.

I was never good at convincing Matt to do anything, but maybe things are different now. Maybe I'm different now.

Maybe I'm just an even bigger idiot.

Sure, I reply.

Matt's waiting in the booth of the Mexican restaurant when I arrive, scrolling through his phone. He looks up and smiles when he spots me walking toward him.

A waitress passes me, holding a tray of sizzling fajitas. Oh damn. Those hot plates could do so much damage if pounded into a human skull. I'd have to be careful not to burn myself in the process, though.

"Let's kill—"

Nope. No. I do not have the energy for the voice right now. Let's focus, brain.

Matt stands as I approach, and he's hugging me before I can react. He smells familiar—a hint of cedar in his aftershave, mint from his Tic Tac habit.

I avoid looking at him as we pull away, because I'm repeatedly bashing a fajita plate into his face.

I slide onto the red plastic, noting that Matt has a margarita in front of him and has ordered one for me as well. I'm not a huge fan of day drinking, or of salt on the rim of my glass, and he knew both of these things at one point. I'm not sure he cared back then either.

My phone buzzes, and I nudge it out of my purse to see that Nathan has replied to my last text.

We're just going in different directions.

I guess that's fair. I'm possibly headed to prison, and he is headed back to the dating apps to find a new girlfriend.

Another text pops up.

I'm sorry. I'll pack up your stuff. Tell me when you want to come get it.

I drop my phone back in my purse and look up at Matt. Ex-husband in front of me, ex-boyfriend texting me to pick up my shit. I am positively on fire.

"Thanks for coming." Matt intertwines his fingers, sliding them across to the middle of the table. He clearly remembers that I like his hands.

"Sure." I take a tiny sip of my margarita because I actually would like to take the edge off this day, and because he'll comment on it if I don't drink it. I'm good at avoiding pissing off Matt.

Mostly.

I carefully put my drink back down. It's a colorful Mexican tile table, the type that might topple your drink if you put it down on the edge of one of the tiles. Matt hates it when I spill things.

"How are you doing?" His brow is furrowed in concern. "It must be hard, being back."

"It's all right."

"Are you listening to the podcast?" he asks.

"Yeah. I'm in touch with him, actually. Ben."

He stops with his margarita almost to his lips. "What?"

"I ran into him at the diner. He asked for my help."

"Your . . . help?" He says *help* like it's the weirdest thing he's ever heard in his life.

"Yeah, he wants an interview. I figured what the hell?"

"Are you serious?" He puts the margarita down. It wobbles on the uneven tiles.

"Yes."

"Lucy, that is not a good idea."

"Why not?"

His eyes widen slightly, like I should already know the answer to that question.

Because you murdered her, Lucy.

"He's not on your side," Matt finally says.

"No. He's not."

"Then . . . ?" He's exasperated. I'm very familiar with this emotion from Matt.

"No one's on my side. But he doesn't seem to be on anyone's side, so that's really the most I can ask for."

He lets out a long sigh and takes another drink of his margarita. I'm still getting used to his shorter hair. It's cropped so short I can see his scalp. Something about it makes him seem hostile. His scalp is angry.

"He said that you didn't do an interview."

"Of course not."

"I don't care if you do one. Just, if you said no because of me."

"Jesus, Lucy, of course I said no because of you." His exasperation is growing. "*You could show a little gratitude, dammit!*" he had screamed at me as I stuffed my clothes into garbage bags. I still don't know what I was supposed to be grateful for. I guess that he wanted to stay married, even though he thought I murdered my closest friend?

I can't muster up any gratitude for that, even now.

"*I have an idea!*" the voice yells.

"I think you should do it." I dip a chip into the salsa and pop it in my mouth.

"I literally can't think of a worse idea."

"I'm doing an interview. Kyle's already told the whole world that you were cheating on me. You don't want to share your side?"

"I wasn't cheating on you."

"*I HAVE AN IDEA!*"

I manage not to snort-laugh, which is a real accomplishment. "Then you *really* should do the interview and tell Ben that."

He leans back in the booth, working his jaw in a way that used to make me nervous. I pull the napkin off my silverware and imagine stabbing the knife in his eye.

"You know what? Fine." He's got me now. That's his "I'll show her" tone. "Tell Ben to call me again. I'll do it."

Listen for the Lie Podcast with Ben Owens

EPISODE FOUR—"THE AMNESIA DEFENSE"

When the news about Savannah's death first broke, it was widely believed that there was a third person who killed Savannah and injured Lucy. But when police were unable to find evidence of anyone else on the scene, and when Lucy continued to insist that she remembered nothing about that night, the narrative began to change.

Remember Joanna Clarkson? One of Matt and Lucy's neighbors from the Block? She spoke to me again about how suspicion started to shift to Lucy.

Joanna:	Well, the scratches and bruising on Savvy's arms were concerning, for sure. But I was still skeptical until I heard about them fighting at the wedding. And then right after that, Matt threw Lucy out of the house, and it just doesn't get any more suspicious than that.
Ben:	He threw her out? Do you know that for sure?
Joanna:	I know for sure that he asked her to leave.
Ben:	And this was immediately after she was released from the hospital, right?
Joanna:	Right. And that is just weird timing. You do not kick your injured spouse out of the house after suffering through a trauma like that unless you think she did it. I'm sorry, I know Matt, and that is the only reason he could have done that. The only reason.
Ben:	At this point, did most people you knew think that Lucy was the one who murdered Savannah?
Joanna:	Everyone I knew thought that.
Ben:	But the police never arrested her for the murder, correct?
Joanna:	They never did. Something about not having a murder weapon, or a solid case. I don't know. I think they were in over their heads. No offense to the Plumpton PD, but they're used to corralling drunk tourists, not investigating murders.
Ben:	But didn't it give people pause, that there wasn't enough evidence to arrest Lucy?

Joanna:	Sure, I thought about that some. But our justice system needs evidence, witnesses. Just because someone doesn't go to jail for something doesn't mean they didn't do it.
Ben:	What about self-defense? Lucy was badly injured. Were there conversations about how Lucy might have had to defend herself?
Joanna:	From Savannah? That's just nonsense. That girl was a little sweet thing. But here's all I need to know about the situation—one of those girls is dead, and the other one immediately traipsed off to California and claimed to have acquired a convenient case of amnesia. I'm on the side of the one who ended up dead, all right? I'm on her side.

But what about a motive? Why would Lucy suddenly kill her best friend? Why were Lucy and Savannah fighting at the wedding?

Nina seemed to imply that there might have been something happening between Savannah and Matt. Was it jealousy that could have driven Lucy to murder?

I spoke to Kyle Porter about this theory.

Kyle:	Lucy told me she was pretty sure Matt was cheating on her too. I've hesitated to say that before, because I thought that maybe she was just justifying our affair to herself. But she told me once that she thought Matt had probably been making his way through the neighborhood.
Ben:	Like, sleeping with women in their neighborhood?
Kyle:	Yeah. I really don't know if she was just trying to make herself feel better . . . maybe that was it. But I heard some stuff about Matt's second marriage ending pretty quickly too, and I started to feel bad about not believing Lucy.

Lucy actually said some stuff about Matt that I've been reevaluating lately. Like, one time Matt texted her while we were together and she got this weird look on her face. I asked what was up and she said, "Just my husband telling me what an idiot I am." And another time she said something like, "Matt prefers I don't talk when we hang out with friends." I sort of just brushed those off, thinking she was exaggerating, but I think the guy was kind of a jerk. Savvy actually said something to me once. |

Ben: About Matt?

Kyle: Yeah. She knew about me and Lucy, and she said, "You can probably get her to leave Matt, if you want. That would be best for her."

Ben: Did you? Try to get her to leave Matt?

Kyle: No. I really wasn't looking for a relationship, especially not with a twenty-two-year-old or however old she was then. I actually ended things not long after that. Seemed like shit was getting complicated.

Ben: How did Lucy take it?

Kyle: She didn't seem upset at all. I was almost . . . [laughs] I was almost insulted that she didn't seem to care. She just shrugged and said, "If that's what you want." Lucy never showed much emotion, though. I think that's why I brushed aside the stuff about Matt. Because she never seemed that upset about it.

Ben: Did you ever see her or Savannah again?

Kyle: Never Lucy, but I saw Savvy once, about a month later. She was on the street, talking to Matt.

Ben: Do you know what they were talking about?

Kyle: No, but I remember thinking it looked intimate. He had a hand on her arm, and she was standing close to him. And I was like, "Oh, that makes sense. Savvy told me to convince Lucy to leave Matt because she's sleeping with him." But that was just speculation.

I swear to god though, man, it looked like something. And Lucy said that Matt was sleeping his way through the neighborhood . . . She might have known something was up with Matt and Savvy.

Most of the people I talked to were skeptical of the jealousy theory, but none more than Emmett Chapman.

Emmett: Jealous? Of what?

Ben: Some people have speculated that Savannah and Matt were having an affair.

Emmett: Dude, that's ridiculous.

Ben: Why?

Emmett: I never saw any evidence of that. But even if they were,

	why would Lucy *murder* Savvy for that? I don't think Lucy even liked Matt that much.
Ben:	You don't think Lucy liked her own husband that much?
Emmett:	Uhh . . . shit, maybe I shouldn't have said it like that. I just mean that their relationship was getting a little rocky.
Ben:	You don't think that Lucy might have been angry about a close friend sleeping with Matt?
Emmett:	I don't know. Maybe? She would have been mad at Matt too though, right? And he's still alive.

CHAPTER EIGHTEEN

LUCY

Emmett Chapman is one of those "he was right there, dumbass," guys.

The kind of guy you don't notice until you're too old and fucked up to appreciate him. Until you're murdering people in your head (and maybe in real life, who knows?) and decide that, for his own safety and mental health, he should probably stay far, far away.

That was my rationale for not calling or texting him back after Savvy died.

It was also my rationale for not sleeping with him, back when I noticed that he might be interested. I mean, the rationale back then was technically that I was married and I'd only *just* stopped cheating on Matt with Kyle, but it feels similar. Using my high school best friend as an excuse to leave my husband, probably fucking Emmett all the way up in the process, is a bridge too far, even for me.

I drive downtown, park on the street, and stare at the front of the art store for several minutes. The words *Creativity Is Good for the Soul!* are written in big, cheerful bubble letters across the glass storefront, with little flowers and hearts painted around it.

That's probably Emmett's art. He was always doodling constantly growing up—in his notebooks during class, on the sidewalks with chalk, on his own skin when he was bored. He used to come hang out with me at the bar where Savvy worked and draw on napkins while I wrote.

He would draw something for each of us, sliding one napkin across the bar to Savvy, and another to me. Sometimes it would be a sketch of me hunched over my laptop, or a cheerful cartoon version of my face, or just whatever random thing was in his mind that day.

"You should really try to make it as an artist," I'd told him one day, after he'd presented me with a napkin drawing of a dragon humping a car.

"Yeah, real high-quality stuff there," he'd said with a snort.

"It is! Whatever happened to moving to New York and trying to work on graphic novels?"

"Well, it turns out you can fail at that from anywhere."

"Seems like it'd be more fun to fail at it in New York."

He'd barked out a laugh and bumped his shoulder against mine. *"We should have gone together, after college. Like we used to talk about."*

I'd looked away then, because I didn't want to think about what my life would look like if I'd gone to New York with Emmett after college instead of marrying Matt. I'd returned my attention to the dragon.

I think I still have those napkins, stacked neatly in a box in the corner of Nathan's apartment.

I stare at the storefront.

I don't even know whether Emmett is working today. I'm going to have to actually get out of the car to check.

Any minute now.

It takes another few deep breaths, but I finally step out of the car and into the sticky air.

I immediately regret my decision.

I'd been so focused on the store that I'd failed to look over my shoulder, a few doors down.

A group of men stand beneath a green and white awning outside a restaurant, their laughter echoing down the street. One of the men is looking in my direction, the smile slowly fading from his face.

Keaton Harper. Savvy's older brother.

He has a beard, and a belly, but I'd recognize that death glare anywhere. One of the men notices Keaton's gaze and lets out a loud "oh shit" when he spots me.

I quickly turn away. Emmett is standing in the window of the store, and he lifts a hand in a tentative wave.

I'm tempted to bolt back into my car, but I've been spotted from all sides.

Emmett points to the door, which I realize now has a *Closed* sign on it. I nod and walk to it. Behind me, I hear angry murmurs.

Emmett smiles as he opens the door. I sometimes catch myself picturing the kid I knew growing up—skinny and awkward, with a frizzy helmet of blond hair.

But he hasn't looked like that since we were teenagers. He's tall and solid now. His blond hair is wavy instead of a frizzy mess, cut and styled in a way meant to convey ease but that probably took a little work. He has a dusting of beard growth on his jaw.

Like I said. *He was right there, dumbass.*

I step inside. The art store is decently sized, but so jam-packed with crap that it feels claustrophobic. Every inch of wall space is covered by a brightly colored poster or intricate, handmade wooden signs. I stare at the giant wall of wooden *Welcome* signs to my left and think that you could probably do some real damage by smashing one into a face.

I blink and return my attention to Emmett. "Hi."

"Hi." He looks intrigued, but not exactly happy to see me. No one can blame him.

He clears his throat, and a bigger smile suddenly breaks across his face. "Sorry. I knew you were in town, but I'm still sort of stunned to see you."

"Sorry to just drop by like this."

"I'm glad you did." He smiles again, and I'm more relieved than I want to admit. I try very hard not to care that everyone in this town thinks I'm a murderous hag, but I'd be lying if I said I wasn't relieved to hear Emmett at least sound like he was a tiny bit on my side.

"You're in town for a family thing?" he asks.

"Yeah, just popped in to ruin my grandma's birthday party."

He cocks his head in this way that makes my chest hurt a little. It's his "Lucy is being ridiculous again but it amuses me" expression.

He gestures at the aisles of paint. "Uh . . . did you need some art supplies for the party?"

"No. I actually just came to see you."

He looks startled, and also a bit delighted.

"I'm sorry that I never returned your calls or anything back then. I was just . . ."

"Traumatized?" he guesses.

I bark out a laugh. "Yes."

"It's all right. I—"

A *bang* on the window makes me jump. I turn to see Keaton with both hands on the glass, face twisted with anger.

"Emmett, what the fuck?" He hits both hands against the glass again. He's right beneath a cluster of little painted hearts on the window, like they're growing out of his head, which should be funny, but I can't find the humor in any of this right now.

"I'm sorry. I should have just called." I take a step toward the door, toward Keaton, and wonder whether anyone will help if he jumps me. Emmett might call the cops, at least.

I'm sure the cops would take their sweet time showing up. And they wouldn't be on my side when they got here.

"No." Emmett reaches for me, like he's going to stop me, but his fingers only lightly touch my arm. "It's okay. You can stay."

Keaton stomps away, and I let out a slow breath. "I think it's best if I bolt before he comes back."

"Yeah, okay." Emmett looks disappointed, but he walks to the window and peers out. "He's going into the restaurant with his buddies."

I pull open the door and take a step out. Emmett follows me, quickly glancing down the street to where Keaton had been. Still clear.

"Nina's been meaning to call you and invite you over for dinner," he says. "Why don't we do that soon? I'd love to catch up."

I turn, confused. "Are you and Nina . . ."

"Oh! Yes." He smiles. "We're dating. For a few months now."

Of course they are.

I force a pleasant expression. "Sure. Dinner would be great."

If he notices that I'm disappointed, he doesn't let on. "It was great to see you, Lucy."

I turn away before I embarrass myself further. "You too, Emmett."

Listen for the Lie Podcast with Ben Owens

EPISODE 4—"THE AMNESIA DEFENSE"

Lucy went to stay with her parents after she left—or was kicked out of—the home she shared with Matt. Joanna walks me through those couple of days after the murder, because I'm still unclear about why everyone became convinced Lucy was the one who killed her friend.

Ben: So it was Matt throwing Lucy out that made people think that Lucy was the one who murdered Savannah?

Joanna: That started it, yeah. But it was the stuff with her parents that really sealed the deal for most people.

Ben: What stuff?

Joanna: I don't want to say too much, because I love Kathleen and Don. They're good people. But, listen. Kathleen was telling the entire town that Lucy would never hurt anyone right after it happened, and then a couple days later she completely changed her tune.

Ben: How so?

Joanna: She started getting weird and cagey. Completely stopped defending Lucy. Apparently she said some *very* weird stuff to Savannah's family. And Don refused to talk to anyone. Still won't.

Ben: He won't talk about Lucy at all?

Joanna: Nope.

I heard this from several people, so I started to ask around about the Chases.

William: Yeah, we got a Starbucks a few years ago, which is fine, I guess. But only go there for coffee. Don't buy any of those stale muffins or breads or whatever they sell. Go over to Daisy Street Bakery for any of that.

That's William, one of the bartenders at the bar Norma recommended to me. It's a quiet night, and William, who has lived in Plumpton for every one of his fifty-three years, is happy to talk to me. He's a tall, broad man, with a gray beard that extends several inches past his chin. He would be intimidating if not for the friendly smile.

He tells me all about Lucy's family. Her grandmother, Beverly Moore, was born and raised in Plumpton. She had three children—Keith, Kathleen, and Karen. Keith and Karen both live in Houston now, but Kathleen returned to Plumpton after finishing college. She brought her fiancé, Don Chase, with her. They got married, had Lucy, and opened a bakery together—Daisy Street Bakery, which numerous locals have mentioned to me.

William: You talk to them yet? Kathleen and Don?

Ben: Not yet, no.

William: You should. Don don't talk to no one about Lucy, but Kathleen will talk to you for sure. She'd be happy to.

Ben: You think so?

William: Oh yeah. Kathleen's real chatty. She ain't got nothin' to hide.

Ben: What about Don?

William: What about him?

Ben: Does he have something to hide?

William: Welllll . . . listen, this is just town gossip, but you're trying to get to the bottom of this, and I respect that.

A lot of folks think that Don knew more than he let on. He was shifty back then, let me tell you what. And I don't blame him one bit. If it had been my daughter, I would have protected her no matter what.

Ben: You think Lucy remembered something and told him?

William: I don't believe the amnesia defense for a minute, first of all. But, yeah. She told her daddy, and he did what he had to do. That's what I think. That's what a lot of folks think. And, well, there was the thing about Kathleen and Savvy's mom, Ivy.

Ben: What thing?

William: I probably shouldn't say anything, but someone's got to tell you. Apparently, Kathleen basically told Ivy that she knew Lucy was the one who killed Savvy.

CHAPTER NINETEEN

LUCY

The mood in the house this evening can only be described as *hostile flailing*.

I can tell the exact moment when Mom starts listening to episode four, because she's suddenly calling everyone in town. I can only make out a few words as I creep past her bedroom door and down the stairs, wincing at every creak—"*irresponsible*" and "*outrageous*"— but the constant chatter never ends.

"*I don't know!*" Mom's voice is really loud now. "*He was so nice when I spoke to him, and now he's acting like Don and I know everything. I did an entire interview with him months ago, told him anything he wanted to know, and he hasn't aired a word of it!*"

I grab my purse from the counter and slip out the door. I need to be elsewhere just in case she realizes who's really to blame for all of this (me).

Dad is strolling up the front walk, sweat wilting the collar of his white shirt, and I almost run smack into him.

"You're in a hurry." He looks . . . amused, which is unexpected, given Mom's mood. Even if he's not listening to the podcast, there's no way she didn't immediately text him upon starting today's episode.

"Sorry." I step around him and say, "I'm going to Grandma's," even though I hadn't actually decided on that. But it was what I always did, as a kid. Run away before the screaming gets too loud to ignore.

"Lucy."

I stop and look back at him.

"If you've remembered something, and you want to talk to someone, you can still talk to me."

I open my mouth, but nothing comes out. I'm not sure what I expected, but that wasn't it.

"I . . ." He sighs and slides his hands into his pockets. He looks sad, which is an emotion I haven't seen in him in a long time. I've forgotten what he looks like when he's not just a little bit scared. "Maybe I didn't handle things right. I don't know. But I meant what I said back then. It's okay."

"*It's okay.*" I could still see Dad, five years ago, tears in his eyes as he gripped my shoulders. "*If you remember something, you only tell me, okay? Whatever it is, it's okay. I promise. But you can only tell me. Understand?*"

I remembered looking at him, at the hard set of his mouth, at the wild desperation in his eyes, and realizing that he thought I killed Savvy. He was *sure* I killed Savvy, actually.

I guess five years hasn't restored his faith in me. And who can blame him, honestly?

"*Do you ever imagine bashing your parents' brains in? I thought about that a time or two. That's normal, right?*"

"You'll be my first call for sure," I say, and turn to walk to my car.

Listen for the Lie Podcast with Ben Owens

EPISODE 4—"THE AMNESIA DEFENSE"

Savannah's mother, Ivy Harper, hadn't mentioned anything about Kathleen Chase confessing to her that Lucy had killed Savannah in our first interview, so I went to talk to her again. I asked her about those days right after the murder.

Ben: Thanks for sitting down with me again.

Ivy: Sure.

Ben: I'm trying to understand how Lucy became a suspect in Savannah's murder. Can you walk me through it?

Ivy: I can try.

Ben: Did you see Lucy after Savannah died?

Ivy: Oh yes, of course.

Ben: When?

Ivy: We were at the hospital within ten minutes of her arriving. We wanted to find out what had happened to Savvy. They didn't let us in, though. Not that day. We had to wait until the next day.

Ben: What happened when you went to see her?

Ivy: I begged her to tell me what had happened, but she just kept saying she didn't remember. She was crying and crying . . . I felt bad for her at the time, but I was also incredibly frustrated. This was the only person in the world who could tell me what happened to Savvy, and she was just blubbering.

Ben: I— Right. So. Did you ever see her again after that?

Ivy: Many times.

Ben: Many times?

Ivy: I thought that it was best for me to keep going over there, keep pushing and letting her see how upset I was.

Ben: You already thought she did it at this point?

Ivy: I had my suspicions. There were the scratches on Savvy's arm and the bruising that Lucy couldn't explain. Then people started coming forward saying they were fighting at the wedding. And every time I went over to talk to Lucy, she was just . . . weird.

Ben: Weird?

Ivy: Hysterical. Just crying and shaking. It was odd, given that she's a pretty stoic girl most of the time.

Ben: Did you get the impression that she was having any problems from her head injury?

Ivy: What kinds of problems?

Ben: With traumatic brain injuries, people often have trouble creating memories in the same way. Especially short-term memories. It can last for a long time after the injury.

Ivy: I really don't know.

Ben: Did Lucy seem confused? Did she keep forgetting things? Besides the incident, I mean.

Ivy: Hmmm . . . she did, actually. I'd go over there and she'd start telling me all the things she'd told me last time. I thought she just really wanted me to know.

Ben: But at the time, you didn't think that the injury could account for Lucy's odd behavior?

Ivy: Maybe. I can't recall exactly. But, honestly, it doesn't matter either way. It was after I saw how Don and Kathleen were acting that I knew for sure it was Lucy.

Ben: How were they acting?

Ivy: Suspicious. Don would hover while I asked Lucy questions. Kathleen left us alone, but Don acted very weird every time I went over there. He was outright hostile at first.

Ben: Hostile?

Ivy: He told me I was upsetting Lucy, that she'd been hurt too and I needed to wait to talk to her. Kathleen convinced him, but he would linger in the doorway and listen to everything. He never left us alone. I actually told the police about that.

Ben: About him lingering?

Ivy: Yeah. It struck me as . . . someone trying to make sure that his daughter doesn't say the wrong thing. He was treating her like she was a child again. I started to think that Lucy had told him something and he was trying to protect her by making sure she didn't tell anyone else. And then I think that the guilt got to Kathleen, and she said something.

Ben: What did she say?

Ivy: [*long sigh*] You know, I've kept this to myself, because I don't blame Kathleen and Don. I really don't. But once, when I went over to their house, Kathleen followed me outside after I finished talking to Lucy. And she gave me this really long hug, and when we pulled away, she was crying, and she said, "Just wait a little longer, okay? I'll make this right."

CHAPTER TWENTY

LUCY

"Are you trying to imply that I'm crazy?"

Ben is sitting in his usual spot at the diner, leaned casually back in the booth. His laptop is closed in front of him, his notebooks piled neatly on top. He's done for the day, or taking a break, or saw me coming and put everything away.

He squints at me. "What?"

I slide into the booth across from him. The redheaded kid behind the counter is staring at me. Someone must have clued him in as to who I am.

"Those questions you asked Ivy. What were you getting at?"

"What do you think I was getting at?" One side of his mouth lifts in an aggravating smirk.

"That I'm crazy. That a blow to the head and the stress of being accused of murder got to me and made me completely bonkers."

"That is not what I was getting at."

"Then what?"

"I'm just trying to get a clear picture of what happened right after the murder. The attention seemed to be very intensely focused on finding out who murdered Savvy. How many days did you have to recover before Savvy's mother came to ask you questions?"

Zero days. I could still see Mrs. Harper standing in the doorway of my hospital room, tears streaming down her face. She'd held my hands and begged me.

"*Please, Lucy*, please. *We need to know something. Anything.*"

"I just think it's strange that your mother was so willing to give Mrs. Harper immediate, unfettered access to you." Ben lifts an eyebrow.

"I said it was fine. At the time. I could make my own decisions."

"I didn't say you couldn't."

I pause and then blurt out my next words. "I was invested in figuring out who murdered Savvy too. And I never told my parents I did it." Not that I remember, anyway. The days after the murder are very fuzzy.

"Listen, when the urge to murder someone strikes, sometimes you just gotta go with it."

The voice is loud, and clear. I actually jump a little and glance around, like someone might be standing next to me.

He cocks his head. "I know."

"I'm just saying, I had no problem with Ivy coming over and asking me questions. I wanted to help."

"I'm sure you did."

"What's that supposed to mean?"

"Oh my god, Lucy, it means that *I'm sure you did.*" He's amused now, and I'm startled to discover that I genuinely care whether or not he thinks I killed Savvy. How fucking annoying.

"Do you always think that people have nefarious intentions, or is it just me?" he asks.

"It's just you," I lie.

"I'm just saying, that if it were *my* child, and she'd just experienced a major trauma and a serious, life-threatening injury, I wouldn't let anyone near her. I'd build her a pillow fort and guard the doorway. Even if she was a twenty-four-year-old woman claiming that it was fine." He arches an eyebrow. "But that's just me."

I don't know what to say to that, so I look over at the teenager who is now furiously typing on his phone, tongue poking out one side of his mouth.

"Did you know that Beverly invited me to her birthday party?"

My attention snaps back to Ben, my lips turning up in amusement. "She failed to mention that."

"Is it okay with you if I go?"

"It's her party. You don't need my permission."

"I feel like I do." He leans back in the booth, tossing his hair out of his eye with a sort of easy sexiness that makes me uncomfortable.

"Why? Is it against the rules to go to a birthday party with the family of the woman suspected of murdering the subject of your podcast? Are there podcaster ethics?"

"I don't . . ." He cocks his head, like he's considering. "It's not against the rules. I've always considered the podcaster ethics to be the same as journalism ethics."

"Sure."

"I won't go if it'll make you uncomfortable."

"You're the one who's going to be uncomfortable."

"You think so?"

"My mom did not appreciate episode four, since you lightly implied she was a bad mom for letting Ivy talk to me and is also maybe involved somehow."

"I have a high threshold for awkward." That damn hair is in his eyes again.

My smile widens. "I believe that."

"Does that mean I should go?"

"You absolutely should go. I suspect Grandma will be very disappointed if you're not there."

"You think so?" He looks flattered.

"Absolutely."

"Okay then. I will be there tomorrow."

"Can't wait."

"And we're doing our first interview on Monday?"

"Our *first* interview? We've talked several times."

"First interview where we really get into things. Your grandma said you'll be here through next week?"

I let out a long sigh. "She did, did she?"

"Is that wrong?"

"No. She's right." She'd bought me a one-way ticket, which should have been a sign that she'd planned on my staying longer than she let on. I could book my own and hightail it out of here, but I'm invested now. I can't stop thinking about what Grandma said—that Ben is actually going to figure this out.

I feel like I owe it to Savvy to stay until he does.

Not to mention that I have nothing to go back to. I'm still fired, my boyfriend is now my ex-boyfriend, and I've yet to sign a lease on a new apartment. I might as well be here, even if *here* makes me want to punch myself in the face.

"Good," he says. "I'm starting this new thing next week, changing up the podcast format. I'll be dropping a bunch of miniepisodes instead of just doing two a week, so we can get stuff out in real time. I think people are really going to like it."

"Great," I say dryly.

He cocks an eyebrow.

"Fine. Whatever. Monday," I say. "First interview. I'll be ready."

"*I'm always ready,*" the voice sings. "*Let's fuck someone up!*"

Listen for the Lie Podcast with Ben Owens

BONUS EPISODE 1

Hey, guys. I know that you weren't expecting a new episode until tomorrow, but I need to update you about what's going on with the show. First of all, I am currently back in Plumpton, Texas. And second, I am in contact with Lucy Chase.

I know that a lot of you already know this, because you saw the picture of us together at the diner. To answer the question that approximately ten thousand of you asked on Twitter—Yes, Lucy has agreed to an interview.

In the interest of full disclosure, I wanted to let you guys know that I've always been counting on getting an interview with Lucy. Her grandmother assured me that she could get Lucy to do it, and she wasn't wrong. According to Beverly, it didn't even take that much convincing. So far, Lucy has been direct with me.

And, to be totally frank with you guys, I've had to scrap or totally rework some of the episodes I had planned for the rest of this season. Lucy being back in town has completely changed things, and we've learned a lot of new information recently.

Want to know what some of that new information is? Tune in tomorrow to hear an interview with Matt Gardner.

Yes, *that* Matt Gardner. Lucy's ex-husband, giving his first interview ever.

And keep an eye on your podcast app, because I'll be releasing some quickie bonus episodes—like this one—to keep you fully updated on everything that's happening over here.

For now, I leave you with this interview with Nina Garcia.

Nina:	Yeah, of course I know Mrs. Chase. Or—Kathleen. I always called her Mrs. Chase in high school, when I'd go over to Lucy's house. Hard habit to break.
Ben:	Are you two friendly?
Nina:	I mean, I say hi when I see her around, but we're not friends or anything.
Ben:	Do you remember seeing her at the wedding?
Nina:	Sure, vaguely.

Ben:	The whole time? Later that night?
Nina:	I couldn't say. It's been too long.
Ben:	What about Colin Dunn? You know Colin?
Nina:	A little, yeah, back when he lived here. Why?
Ben:	You heard on a recent episode about Colin having sex in a car with a married woman after the wedding?
Nina:	Yes.
Ben:	I have several sources who claim that Kathleen and Colin had an affair.
Nina:	. . . What?
Ben:	Did you know about that?
Nina:	What? Who said that?
Ben:	They've asked to remain anonymous. Though I was able to verify it.
Nina:	Colin? Colin Dunn?
Ben:	Yes.
Nina:	She's like thirty years older than him.
Ben:	Thirty-two years, yes.
Nina:	I . . .
Ben:	I was told it was a bit of an open secret here in Plumpton.
Nina:	Seriously? No one told me. But I guess . . .
Ben:	What?
Nina:	Well, now that you mention it, I remember him saying once that he liked older women. I thought he meant Savvy, because she was like four or five years older than him. I guess he meant like . . . *older.*
Ben:	It's a bit weird, isn't it?
Nina:	Sleeping with a woman thirty years older? I don't know, whatever does it for you, I guess.
Ben:	No, that everyone knew that Kathleen had an affair with Savannah's boyfriend, and no one thought it was important to mention.
Nina:	Well, it wasn't while he was with Savvy, was it?
Ben:	No, according to my digging, they actually did overlap. And like I said, mystery married woman in the car . . .
Nina:	. . . Oh. Then, yeah. That's kind of weird.

CHAPTER TWENTY-ONE

LUCY

I fully expect Mom to cancel the party.

I listen to Ben's miniepisode in disbelief the first time, and with more than a little amusement the second.

I didn't know Mom had it in her.

I should maybe be a little miffed on Savvy's behalf, but she was never that serious about Colin, and I honestly think she'd be amused as well.

I wait, clenched, for Mom to explode.

But she doesn't. The next morning, I come downstairs to find her cheerfully sewing lace onto a baby blanket she made for one of the girls from church.

Denial always did work well for her.

So, I say nothing, send Ben a text message that just says *damn, son*, and pretend like nothing happened.

Mom insists we get to the restaurant an hour early so we can micromanage the employees in charge of setting up the party. They don't seem particularly put out by this, like they're used to women in loud flower-print dresses fussing over the exact placement of mason jar candles.

Mom missed her calling as a wedding planner. She would have been so good at projecting a happy image for one day.

We're in a large room for special events at the back of the restaurant. They've set up a long picnic-style table, with said mason jar candles and flower arrangements dotting the middle.

Mom doesn't mention the daisies. Probably because they look so nice. Or she's totally forgotten that they were supposed to be pink roses.

Grandma arrives right on time, escorted by Ashley and Brian (my cousins, the asshole grandchildren). They're both younger than I am—early twenties—and neither of them look particularly happy to be there. Brian barely looks up from his phone to say hi.

Their parents, Keith and Janice, follow them inside. My aunt Karen, the youngest of my mom's siblings, sulks in after them, the usual sour expression on her face. She has an unfamiliar man in an ill-fitting suit with her.

I don't know when they all got into town. Mom mysteriously disappeared a few times over the last couple of days, so I assume they've been here for a while. No one had any interest in seeing me early, apparently.

They all glance at me and then quickly away. Except for Ashley, who looks me up and down and then squints, like she disapproves.

I look down at my dress. It's black, which is out of place with the rest of the colorfully dressed guests. It also has a plunging neckline, which would be more exciting on someone with bigger boobs. Still, the waiter circling the room, offering appetizers, seems to appreciate them. I do what I can.

Grandma hustles over to me, her purple sequins hustling with her. The birthday dress is very flapper-like, with a nod to a Vegas showgirl.

She squeezes my arm. "Everything looks lovely."

"You know Mom did most of it."

Uncle Keith and Aunt Janice appear behind her and give me loose hugs and tight smiles.

"Lovely to see you, Lucy," Uncle Keith says, rubbing a hand over his beard.

"I'm surprised you haven't gotten remarried," Aunt Janice says with a frown.

"Well, it wasn't so great the first time." I laugh. She doesn't.

"Wow," Ashley says. Her hair, which was light brown last time I saw her, is dyed a really nice auburn color, and I might have complimented it if she weren't staring at me like I was an alien.

"Hi, Lucy." Brian looks up from his phone long enough to glance at my boobs.

"Brian, you're looking so handsome!" Mom is just telling outright lies now, I guess. She pushes his shaggy brown hair out of his eyes, and he reels back like this is the worst thing to ever happen in his twenty-one years.

The smile on Mom's face fades to open-mouthed horror as she spots something behind me.

I turn. It's Ben, holding a present with a giant pink bow, wrapped much too nicely for him to have done it himself. He's wearing a blue button-up shirt, the sleeves rolled up to his elbows, and I notice that Ashley doesn't disapprove of anything she sees there.

I can't blame her, honestly.

"Ben!" Grandma exclaims at the same time Mom says, "What are you doing here?"

Ben lifts one hand in a wave. If he's surprised that Mom didn't know he was coming, he doesn't show it.

I can't help but think that he could have saved the miniepisode for tomorrow. He posted it before the party, when he knew he would see her after it went up.

I am both impressed and a little scared.

"Kathleen, don't be rude," Grandma says, waving a hand at Mom. "I invited him."

"You invited him?" Mom practically screeches, and then looks at me, like I should also be horrified by this.

I smile at her, and then walk to him. I pluck the present from his arms. "Ben. You're looking smug as usual."

He lets out a short, startled laugh. "Thanks?"

Mom gapes at me as I deposit the present on the table with the rest. Keith, Janice, and their offspring look confused.

"Everyone, this is Ben Owens," Grandma says loudly. "He's the host of that podcast. You know the one."

Ashley's mouth falls open. Brian starts furiously texting. Keith and Janice look like they're still waiting for the punch line.

I steal a glance at Dad. He's glowering in the corner. Karen rushes over to Mom and whispers something in her ear.

A group of older ladies with matching poufy permed hairdos appear at the door, and Grandma walks over to greet them. Mom joins her, pointedly avoiding looking at Ben.

Everyone else is staring at him, so I stroll over to stand beside him. Usually everyone is staring at *me*. Us being next to each other makes it easier for them.

We're both silent for a moment.

I point to the small bar set up on the far wall. "Drink?"

"God, yes."

An hour later, I'm sitting in the middle of the table with Grandma on one side and Ben on the other, an arrangement Grandma insisted on. ("It's my birthday, I get to decide where we sit!" she'd gleefully declared, ignoring Mom's protests.)

I'm on my second glass of wine and the room is pleasantly blurry around the edges.

They squeezed every possible chair they could up to this table, and my arm keeps brushing against Ben's. He is not blurry. In fact, he is in too sharp a focus, and I do my best not to look at him at all.

I'm suddenly reminded that it's been at least a month since I had sex, since Nathan and I had been in a dry spell pre–murder revelation. It's been much longer since I had really *great* sex (thanks for nothing, Nathan).

The waiter stops behind me and refills my nearly empty wineglass.

Well, that's not going to help me stop thinking about sex.

I reach for the glass, and then change my mind. Instead, I use two fingers to push it away a few inches.

Ben watches me, and our eyes meet as I sit back in my chair. I quickly look away.

Betsy is across from us—the friend of Mom's who brought the excellent 285-calorie brownies to tea/wine—and she's openly staring at Ben. He's pretending not to notice.

"Bruce," Betsy says.

"Ben," I correct, and reach for my water.

"Ben. You know that saying, he had a face for radio?"

I laugh mid-sip, nearly choking on my water.

"Betsy!" Mom exclaims.

"What? We were just talking about it the other day!"

"I've heard that, yes." Ben looks amused.

"You don't have that. In fact, I'd say it's a damn shame you decided to work in radio."

Laughter rises up from the table. Even Dad chuckles.

"Thank you." Ben reddens like he isn't often complimented on his good looks. Like he hasn't visited r/Podcasts on Reddit and seen the threads discussing how cute he is.

"How did you get into that?" Keith asks. "Podcasting?"

"I loved podcasts. I was obsessed with them, actually. Especially true crime. So, I decided to try one myself."

"Just like that?" Karen asks. "You weren't even a crime reporter before, were you?" I can tell she doesn't actually need him to answer this question. She'd googled him extensively earlier. Probably made it all the way to page five.

"No, I covered mostly lifestyle and entertainment as a journalist.

True crime was more like a . . . hobby of mine. I actually had a bunch of cases that I'd dabbled in over the years, participated in those sites online where amateur sleuths try to solve stuff. When I decided to do my first case, I picked the one that I had the most information on already, just to try and make it easier on myself."

"Did you solve it?" Keith asks.

"Of course he did." Janice bats his arm. "I told you all about it."

Keith frowns like he has no memory of that conversation, or maybe most things his wife has said to him.

"I did," Ben says.

"You remember," Janice says to her husband. "The teenager who was killed on prom night out in South Carolina. They found her body in the trunk of a teacher's car, but the guy *swore* up and down he didn't do it? Plus he had no motive *and* an alibi."

Keith shakes his head, still clueless. "Did he do it?"

"No," Ben says. "The girl's boyfriend did. He put her in the trunk because he thought she was flirting with the teacher and maybe something was going on. There wasn't, as far as I could tell."

"That was easy though," Ashley says, eyebrow cocked in a way that seems flirty. "It's always the boyfriend or the husband."

Her eyes flick to me and then quickly away.

Always the boyfriend, except when it's the best friend.

"I have an idea!"

Not now.

"I did have a feeling, going in," Ben admits.

"Got a feeling this time, Ben?" I ask. "Think you're going to solve it again?"

"Oh, good, dinner is here," Mom says loudly. Two waiters walk into the room, plates in arm.

I meet Ben's gaze. His lips twitch up but he says nothing.

I eat quickly, because the wine really is starting to go to my head. A waiter hovers, ready to refill my glass again at a moment's notice.

The wine is flowing freely, actually, and I hold mine but don't drink it as I glance around the table. Keith's cheeks are red. Ashley is laughing loudly.

I think this is supposed to be fun. Or, perhaps, it *is* fun. For everyone else. They could take a photo and put it on Instagram—#dinnerparty #sofun #lovemylife—and it wouldn't be a lie.

"Are you going to write a book, Ben?" Grandma asks, apparently continuing a conversation I wasn't paying attention to.

"A book? No." He glances at me. "Someday, I might, but I don't have any plans right now."

"People are saying you're going to."

"Which people?"

"You know." She waves her hand. "Twitter."

"Grandma, you're on Twitter?" Brian looks so startled that I wonder suddenly what kind of shit he's been posting on Twitter. Something he doesn't want his grandma to see, clearly.

"You're a good writer," Janice says. "I read some of your pieces in the *Atlantic* and *Vanity Fair*."

"Thank you," he says.

"Lucy, didn't you want to be a writer once?" Keith peers at me as if I've disappointed him, this relative I barely know. "What ever happened to that?"

I wasn't that good, I guess, is what I should have said. People love that sort of shit—humility and honesty, tied together to make everyone feel more comfortable after a rude question.

I smile. "Well, you know. No one wants to read a book from a murderer."

Keith reddens. Dad rolls his eyes.

"Lucy," Mom says wearily.

"Why didn't you ever write a memoir?" Ashley's clearly been waiting all night to ask that question.

"Bit hard to write a memoir about something you don't remember."

"You could write about everything else."

I shrug.

"Let's kill—"

"You never tell your side of the story," Ashley presses.

I've told it more times than I can count. No one believed me.

"I'm telling it to Ben." I take a sip of my wine.

Dad's head pops up. His eyes spark with anger and questions.

"You're telling it to Ben?" Mom says the words so slowly. Perhaps they're even interpreted as calm by the rest of the table.

Maybe they *are* calm. I take a quick glance around and no one else seems nervous.

I shouldn't be nervous. I'm a grown-ass woman free to give interviews to whichever smug podcaster I choose.

"I have an idea. Let's kill—"

I clench my fingers into a fist and will the voice away. "Yeah. I'm doing an interview with Ben soon."

"We already talked about a few things," Ben adds.

"That's an interesting decision, Lucy," Dad says.

Ashley snort-laughs and then claps a hand over her mouth. Others giggle nervously as well.

"Everyone has extremely high expectations of Ben." I'm trying to sound casual. "Just trying to help where I can."

"I appreciate it." Ben is also trying to sound casual. I'm better at it.

Dad opens his mouth like he has more to ask, then seems to think better of it.

"It seems like Lucy should tell her own story instead of me telling it for her, wouldn't you say?" Ben asks.

"That's true," Ashley says with wide-eyed sincerity.

"What a load of shit."

The voice in my head is so loud that I barely stop myself from jumping.

"Let's kill her."

I eye my knife, but I'm too buzzed to kill Ashley. For real or otherwise.

"Or him?"

I shift in my chair. The conversation has moved on without me, and Mom is staring at me.

"Right?" she says.

"What?"

"I have an idea!"

"The truth," Mom says. "That's all any of us have ever wanted. To just find out the truth."

"Yes." I nod. "The truth."

I take a long sip of my wine, which I should *not* do, but I want to quiet the voice. It works.

"And the truth involves digging up people's personal lives?" Keith's face is even redder. Anger and alcohol coming together to make one very crimson man.

"Keith," Janice says quietly, putting a hand on his arm.

He shakes her off. "I'm sorry, but why are we all acting like this man is welcome here? He—"

"You're very welcome, Ben," Grandma interrupts, patting his arm.

He looks at her in amusement.

"Mom!" Keith throws his hands up. "For god's sake. He went on that podcast and he said that—"

"Keith," Mom snaps.

"—Kathleen slept with a twenty-year-old in a car!"

"Wow," Ashley says.

"Oh my god." Brian actually puts down his phone.

"Dammit, Keith," Dad says.

"What? It's not even true!" Keith points a furious finger at Ben. "You just get on that little podcast of yours with your fake news, and you spout these accusations from '*anonymous sources.*'" He does finger quotes around *anonymous sources*.

"Maybe it's time for the pie?" Mom asks.

Keith ignores her, his attention locked on Ben. "Who are these sources?"

"I'm sorry, I can't reveal that."

"Or presents?" Mom suggests.

"Of course you can't! Because they don't exist!"

"Or more wine?" Grandma suggests, holding up her glass. A waiter scurries over to refill it.

Betsy leans across the table. "Maybe I should go," she whispers.

"Are you kidding? Things are just getting good!" Grandma exclaims gleefully.

Keith has both hands on the table, ready to fight. "And you implied that she and that boy—"

"Colin," I supply.

"Wow," Ashley says.

"—that *Colin* boy killed Savannah! We all know who did it—"

I raise my hand. Betsy's mouth drops open.

Grandma pulls my hand down. "Not the right crowd for that kind of joke, hon."

"No offense, Lucy," Keith says.

"Really, Dad?" Brian asks.

"But we all know who did it, and you're throwing around lies and telling people Kathleen killed her!"

"I'm just trying to get a handle on everyone's alibis." Ben seems remarkably unrattled.

In fact, his lips are twitching. The smug bastard might be enjoying this.

"That is not—"

"Oh, for fuck's sake!" Mom yells. Everyone freezes. "Yes, I had sex with Colin in my car the night of the wedding! Are you happy, Ben? You got me! I slept with the twenty-year-old, and to be honest, I enjoyed it."

"Wow."

"So that's where I was when Savvy was murdered," Mom finishes calmly. She smooths a hand over her perfectly coiffed hair, and it barely moves. "He's my alibi."

Uncle Keith gapes at his sister like he just realized she knows how to have sex. Dad lets out a long-suffering sigh.

"Oh, give it a rest, Don," Mom says. "Like you have any room to talk."

I try so hard not to laugh, but a snort-giggle escapes my lips.

Neither of my parents has ever been all that discreet about their affairs. Dad used to leave his laptop open on the kitchen table and walk away while it dinged with messages, until Mom would scream for him to come answer his girlfriend. Mom, I'm pretty sure, only started sleeping around to get back at Dad, but it sounds like she's enjoying the hell out of herself now. Good for her, I guess.

I'll never understand why they're still married. I thought for sure that they were just waiting for me to move out before they split, but it's been over a decade since I left for college. I guess they've decided that tormenting each other for the rest of their lives is preferable to divorce.

Grandma puts down her wineglass and reaches across the table for Mom's hand. "Kathleen, I just want you to know that I mean this sincerely—I'm deeply proud."

We eat pie in near silence. Grandma's friends try to liven things up again while she's opening presents, but we're all still stuck on "*I had sex with Colin in my car.*"

Everyone scurries out as soon as they can, and I help Grandma into a sleek black car that has shown up to whisk her away. It's another mystery man, this one at least ten years younger than she is. His fancy car smells too strongly of cologne, but his smile is friendly as he nods at me.

Grandma pats my cheeks as she settles into the front seat.

"I told you I'd ruin your birthday," I say.

"My dear, you made it the best birthday ever."

I shake my head in amusement and close the door. She waves as they drive away.

I trudge back into the restaurant. It's nearly empty, the wait-staff clumped together around the hostess stand. They abruptly stop talking as I walk by.

I head to the back room to grab Mom's mason jars and the rest of the cake. I hear murmured voices as I approach, and I slow as I reach the door.

Dad stands near the end of the table with Ben, his arms crossed over his chest. Smoke from a recently extinguished candle billows up next to them. I stand back, out of view, absolutely shameless about eavesdropping.

"I know you don't care about this, but I implore you to consider what's best for Lucy," Dad says.

"How do you mean?" Ben asks. He drank far less wine than the rest of us. His voice is much clearer than Dad's.

"She's told her story several times. It doesn't need to be repeated." Dad's already frustrated.

"She's never told her story."

"Of course she has."

"Not directly. It was always filtered through the police or you and her mom or her lawyer or the media. No one has ever heard directly from her."

"But why do you think that was?"

"Because you were protecting her?"

"Yes!"

"And that's what you're doing now?" Ben asks. I wonder whether Dad hears the skepticism in his voice.

"Of course."

"I'd love to interview you, if you'd like to go into more detail," Ben says.

"I'm not doing an interview," Dad snaps. He starts to turn, and I quickly backtrack a few steps. I wait until he's coming out of the room to start down the hallway again. He frowns as he passes me.

Ben is typing on his phone as I grab a box and head to the table for the mason jars.

He looks up, and then walks over to grab a few of the jars. Our eyes meet as he puts them in the box.

My story is still being filtered through him. I wonder whether he realizes that. Savvy's story is being filtered through him. Through everyone he's interviewed who has sanded off the edges of the real girl to present the world with a perfect victim.

"I'll see you Monday," he says softly. He heads to the door but pauses, looking over his shoulder at me. "You know I'm only interested in finding the truth, right? For Savannah."

"I know."

He nods and starts to walk away.

"Wait, Ben."

He looks back at me.

"That's what I want too," I say. "The truth."

In my head, the voice snorts.

"To figure out what happened to her," I amend. "I'm going to help you figure it out, no matter what those dumbasses say." I gesture vaguely to the table, where the dumbasses (my family) were seated a few minutes ago.

Ben smiles. "I'm glad to hear it. We'll figure out the truth together, Lucy."

I swallow nervously as he waves, then turns and walks away. I listen to his footsteps fade.

The truth.

"*The truth doesn't matter.*" The voice—Savvy's voice—is so clear now, clearer than it's been in years.

It's always been Savvy talking to me. Since the first few days after she died, when her screams were so loud I thought my head was going to explode, to later, when she quieted to a murderous constant companion.

To now, when she's apparently had enough of me ignoring her.

"Let's kill—"

I close my eyes, willing the memory away, but it won't go. She's been there for days now, on the edge of every thought I have, yelling at me to notice her.

The memory forms, bright and clear, like it sharpened over the years instead of fading.

LUCY

FIVE YEARS AGO

"I know the truth doesn't matter," I said. I was sitting at the empty bar, the sounds of laughter from the staff coming distantly from the kitchen. The restaurant had just opened, and the dining room was deserted. It was just me and Savvy.

She stood across from me on the other side of the bar, leaning her forearms against the counter. She was in a tank top that showed her tattoos—flowers on one arm, and Harley Quinn on the other. She had a thing for supervillains. No one ever mentions that. Maybe they think it's not important.

She was beautiful—big, downturned eyes, and dark blond hair tied up in a messy bun. Her eye makeup was nearly always smudged. I was pretty sure she rarely remembered to take it off at night. She just touched it up the next day and called it good.

A guy once said to her, "You look like the fun kind of mess." Rude, but not wrong.

I, on the other hand, was a mess and not even a little bit fun.

I had a bruise on my cheek. It was small. I could easily cover it with makeup, but I'd wanted Matt to see it and feel bad. He hadn't. Instead, he pointedly held up his hand to show where I'd scratched him.

Savvy was right. It wouldn't matter if I said I'd scratched him because I was defending myself. That he started it.

Well, no, he'd dispute that. Matt would say I started it, by scream-ing at him again. "Don't start shit you can't finish," he'd always say.

"He said he'd tell my parents about me pushing him down the stairs if I went to stay with them," I said.

"You didn't push him down the stairs," Savvy said.

I hadn't, but I was fairly certain that Matt actually thought I had. He'd said the lie so many times he'd started to believe it himself.

Hell, I was starting to believe it. The (fake?) memory of me vio-lently shoving him now plays next to the (true?) memory of me flailing out my arms in anger and of him tripping because he was drunk again.

"But the truth doesn't matter," she said again.

"I should have controlled my temper," I said softly. I should have just cried. Taken the hits and crawled away to show my scars. I should have been a better victim. The truth doesn't matter if you fight back.

"I have an idea." Savvy leaned closer to me. She met my eyes. Her mouth was set in a hard line, her gaze steely and serious. "Let's kill your husband."

CHAPTER TWENTY-TWO

LUCY

Nina calls me the day after Grandma's party.

"You seriously invited Ben to your grandma's birthday party?" she says, by way of greeting.

I stretch out on my bed. The sun filters in through the blinds, already high in the sky. I'm hiding from my parents in my room like a teenager. "My grandma invited him. Wait, how did you know that?"

"Three different people called me and told me that he showed up at the birthday party and caused a scene."

"He didn't so much *cause a scene* as sit there and enjoy the chaos that his presence caused."

"Oh, dear lord."

"Honestly, I'm sad I didn't film it."

I would have liked to replay that smug little smile of Ben's. That wasn't a superhero smile. That was the grin of a man who liked to watch shit burn.

"You're really going to do an interview with him?"

"Yeah. I'm helping to fill in some gaps for him."

"I'm not sure if that's brilliant or stupid, Lucy."

"Same."

She laughs. "You want to come for dinner tonight? Emmett wants to join us, and he doesn't work on Sundays."

"Sure." I need an excuse to get out of the house.

"Great. I'll text you the address."

Nina Garcia lives in what I'd always considered to be the most boring part of Plumpton. A builder had quickly erected a clump of homes on the northwest side of town, all of which looked vaguely similar. Driving down the street is like the beginning of a horror movie. It's too perfect to be real.

I park my car on the street and climb out.

I guess I was wrong about Nina—she actually meant it when she said I should come over to see her kids. She always was just a little bit too nice for her own good.

A small, dark-haired child with something blue smeared across his mouth opens the door after I knock.

"Hello," I say.

He says nothing. He just stares. I've always admired the way kids unabashedly stare at you. They don't care whether you're uncomfortable. Kids have zero fucks to give about your feelings.

"Mijo, go find your brother." Nina appears and ushers the giggling child away. "Sorry. He loves answering doors. He's been obsessed with it lately." She steps back, sweeping her arm out. "Come in, come in."

She's wearing a casual green dress, her soft curls loose around her face. I'd never noticed Nina and Emmett taking much romantic interest in each other when we were younger, but I can see why they've hooked up now. They're both just very pretty.

I can't help but think that Nina is here to torture me. She's the living embodiment of what I could have been, if I'd had an hourglass figure and a touch more common sense.

I walk into the house and through a surprisingly neat living room. All the toys are stacked nicely in bins in the corner.

From the back of the house, a child lets out a shriek. I jump, but Nina looks unfazed.

Emmett walks into the room, a child hanging off either arm. The blue-mouthed one who opened the door is upside down, giggling. Emmett smiles at me. His dark blond hair is mussed, like there was a playful struggle back there with the kids. The kind of hair that's begging to be touched again. Maybe pulled a little.

Jesus Christ. I'm such an idiot.

"Is it just me, or did he get really hot?" Savvy's voice is in my head suddenly. I let her back in and now she won't leave.

A memory of a random day with her in the restaurant takes shape, almost against my will.

"I've always thought Emmett was cute," I said, glancing over to where he was standing by the door to the restaurant.

"Yeah, but he's like 'shove you up against a wall and fuck you' hot now," she said, and then laughed at the expression on my face. "You're ridiculous, you know that?"

"I didn't say anything."

"You blush like a schoolgirl every time I bring up sex. I wish we'd hung out in high school. I would have had the most fun corrupting you." She reached across the bar to pat my hand. *"But I'm glad I have the opportunity now. Better late than never."*

"What's better late than never?" Emmett asked as he slid onto the stool next to me.

"For me to corrupt this angel," Savvy said sweetly.

Emmett barked out a laugh as Savvy walked to the other side of the bar to help a group of guys.

"You and Savvy Harper are friends now, huh?" Emmett gave me a deeply amused look.

"Yeah, I didn't see that one coming either."

"That's what you get for moving back to your hometown. Eventually, you end up becoming friends with the former prom queen cheerleader."

"I heard that!" Savvy called as she grabbed a glass. "And I was homecoming queen, not prom queen. We didn't have a prom court."

"The fact that you even know that," Emmett said incredulously.

"Some of us didn't pretend to be too cool for everything." She gave us a meaningful look.

"Hey." I swung an arm around Emmett's shoulders. "We weren't pretending. We actually were too cool."

"No, we weren't," Emmett whispered.

I shot him a grin. "No, we weren't."

Savvy winked at me. "Good thing you're hanging out with me now."

Emmett is staring at me. I try to look like a sane person who isn't being bombarded by past memories. I don't think I succeed.

Nina grabs the upside-down child and sets him on the ground. Emmett puts down the other, taller one.

"This is John and Chris," Nina says, pointing to the little one, and then the bigger one. I've met the older one before, but she correctly assumes that neither of us remembers it all that well. "This is Lucy."

I wave awkwardly. I'm never around kids. I don't know how to act with them.

"Lucy is an old friend," Nina says to them. Neither of them look like they give a shit. The smaller one—already forgot his name—is staring at me again, though.

The doorbell rings again, and the older one shrieks. "Abuela!"

"Come on," Emmett says, casting an amused glance at me. He ushers the boys out the door.

"I asked my mom to watch them tonight so we could actually have some adult conversations," Nina says.

"They're cute," I lie (all kids look the same to me).

"Oh, thanks." She smiles. "They're a handful."

Emmett returns, minus the kids. He walks to Nina, slipping an arm around her waist. She leans into him with an easy familiarity. The sort of couple that's been together for a while but still remembers casual affection.

When we were in high school, Emmett used to talk about leaving Plumpton. Of the three of us, he was the one who seemed the most restless, the most eager to explore the world.

I wonder whether he's disappointed he never got out. Or whether he's jealous of me, for up and moving to Los Angeles.

But I didn't really get out. I wasn't here physically, but in a way, I've spent every day of the last five years here. Other people moved on with their lives. Look at Nina and Emmett.

I'm still defined by everything that happened to me in my hometown. By my first husband, and the life I had in my early twenties. I'm like the football jock who never gets over peaking in high school, except I'm the tragic murder version.

Fuck, that's depressing.

Emmett gives me a concerned look, like he can read that emotion on my face, and I quickly look away and pretend to be fascinated by the family pictures hanging on the wall.

"Can I get you a drink?" Nina moves toward the fridge, covered in papers with scribbles that are supposed to be art, and Christmas cards of smiling children, even though it's August. "Emmett and I don't drink alcohol much, but I can offer you a Topo Chico."

"Sure, thanks." I don't need any alcohol after yesterday's extravaganza. My head still hurts a little.

She opens the glass bottle of mineral water and hands it to me. "I'm really glad you came."

"Well, I'm not exactly flush with invitations, if you want to know the truth."

Emmett leans against the counter, crossing his arms over his chest. "Are people nicer than when you left?"

"Maybe. Less hostile, at least."

He half smiles. "Folks have had some time to think about it."

"And what conclusion have they come to?"

Emmett and Nina exchange a look, and I know exactly what conclusion people have come to. The same one they always come to.

"I think some people are realizing they were quick to judge," Nina says. "The DA would have tried you if they had enough evidence."

I suppress a smile by taking a drink of my water. Nina says it like she's trying to convince herself. She's been lying awake at night, staring at the ceiling, coming up with logical excuses why I might not have done it.

"We always had our doubts," Emmett says quietly.

"I appreciate that."

They're both quiet for a moment, exchanging another look I can't quite pin down. Nina grabs a towel from the counter and twists it nervously in her hands.

"I still don't remember anything, if that's what you wanted to ask," I offer helpfully.

Nina twists the towel so hard I think she's going to rip it in half, and then turns away to open the oven a crack. "Hope you like lasagna!"

And then Savvy's standing next to Nina, grinning with her smudged eyeliner, dark blond hair piled on top of her head in a messy bun.

I freeze. She's a horrible, perfect hallucination. Everything I've been shoving into the deep recesses of my mind for five years come back to life to haunt me.

I want to force her out again. She shouldn't be whispering to me, and she sure as shit shouldn't be standing here with that familiar smirk on her face. Nothing good will come of it.

Of course, desperately pushing her away for five years hasn't gotten me anywhere at all. My first therapist, the one I saw right after moving to Los Angeles, would barely be holding back an "I told you so" if she were here. She told me that ignoring Savvy's voice wasn't the solution. "She'll come back," she'd said. "You can't ignore the past forever."

The therapist was right, I was wrong. What else is new.

"*Lucy doesn't like lasagna,*" Savvy offers helpfully. "*This woman continues to be the fucking worst, Luce. No surprise there.*"

I wince. Emmett looks concerned again.

Savvy saunters over to him. *"He's still super hot, though."*

"You okay?" Emmett asks quietly.

Next to him, Savvy sticks her tongue in her cheek like she's giving him a blow job. She doesn't look the way people always describe her now. They talk about her on the podcast like she was an angelic blond angel. Gliding through life with a halo shimmering around her head.

The Savvy in front of me is the real version. Highlights grown out, makeup half-assed, frayed red bra strap sticking out from her tank top.

I clear my throat and force a smile at Emmett. "Yeah. Fine. Great."

I am not okay. Letting myself think about Savvy again has brought her back to life, and I don't think she's going to leave until I figure out what happened to her. I will be haunted by my friend and her murderous musings for the rest of my life unless I get my shit together.

Savvy lets out a long, disappointed sigh. *"Are we going to kill a dude or what?"*

"Why don't you sit down?" Emmett gestures to the table.

"Yes, please sit!" Nina says. "Dinner is almost ready."

I force a smile as I slide into a chair, and brace myself as the memory of that day with Savvy forms again, as clear as ever.

LUCY

FIVE YEARS AGO

"Yeah, sure, let's kill my husband," I said with a laugh. "How should we do it? Knife him while he's sleeping? Push him into traffic? Wait, I know. Poison in the liquor bottle. Matt sucks down those drinks so fast he'll be dead before he realizes the taste is off."

I laughed again, but Savvy didn't. She cocked an eyebrow. My smile slowly faded.

"Savvy." I shifted on the barstool as I realized that I was the only person kidding around. "I can't kill him. I can't kill anyone."

"Why not? He deserves it."

I opened my mouth to argue.

"Don't you dare say he doesn't." She wrapped a warm hand around my arm. "I've seen bruises on you so many times, and I know you're not even telling me the worst of it."

I wasn't. The worst of it was too much to recount. It wasn't even that it was humiliating, I just couldn't bring myself to put together words to explain how he'd choked me until I blacked out. Or when "things had gotten out of control" (as he always liked to put it) and he'd dragged me by my hair from the kitchen to the living room and then slammed my head repeatedly into the hardwood floors until I saw stars.

"He deserves it," I confirmed quietly. "But even if I wanted to kill him—"

"We," Savvy interrupted. "Even if *we* wanted to kill him. I wouldn't make you do it alone."

I huffed out a laugh. "Damn, Savvy, I knew you were ride or die, but that's next-level."

She tossed her hair over her shoulder with a grin. "I'm the best friend in the world, you can say it. And as the best friend in the world, I would be delighted to help you off your dickhead husband."

I stared at her, still convinced she must have been kidding.

She cocked an eyebrow. "What do you say? Are we going to kill a dude or what?"

Listen for the Lie Podcast with Ben Owens

EPISODE FIVE—"A MYSTERY WOMAN"

Today, for the first time, you're going to hear from Lucy's ex-husband, Matt Gardner. Matt has declined to speak with the press since Savannah's death, and only agreed to talk to me now because Lucy asked him to.

He comes to my hotel room in Plumpton first thing in the morning. He looks older than the photos I've seen of him, and tired. I ask him if he agreed to this interview because of Lucy.

Matt: Yeah, she mentioned that I should talk to you.

Ben: Why?

Matt: I don't know, I guess she likes you. Or . . . she wants to know who killed Savvy.

Ben: Let's talk about your relationship with Lucy. You two stayed in touch after divorcing?

Matt: No. I hadn't spoken to her at all since she left town five years ago. But she came by the house a few days ago, and then we also had lunch recently.

Ben: She reached out to you, then?

Matt: Yeah. She just showed up one day.

Ben: How would you describe your relationship when you two were married?

Matt: Mmmhh . . . passionate. We were really in love, but we also fought a lot. We probably got married too young. But I was crazy about her. From the moment I met her, I was smitten.

Ben: What did you fight about?

Matt: Normal marriage stuff. Money, in-laws, work. We probably should have gone to therapy. I realize now that we just weren't very good at communicating with each other. I take some responsibility for that. I wish we'd worked on it instead of giving up.

Ben: You wish you'd stayed married?

Matt: I guess I don't mean that exactly . . . it's hard to know what would have happened. But with the benefit of hindsight, I can see a world where we took a step back and tried to see the good in each other.

Ben: After Lucy was released from the hospital, she went to her parents' almost right away instead of home. Several people I've talked to said that you asked her to leave. Is that true?

Matt: That's true.

Ben: Why?

Matt: It was just a lot to handle at the time. Savvy—*our* friend, not just hers—was dead, and the police were already asking questions that . . . it was a lot.

Ben: The police were asking questions that made you suspect your wife had killed her friend?

Matt: Well . . . I don't know. They were asking questions that made me uncomfortable. I shouldn't have sent her away. I feel bad about it now.

Ben: Did you go see her while she was at her parents' house?

Matt: Uh, once, yeah.

Ben: How was Lucy doing then?

Matt: I . . . think she was about the same. Sad. Confused.

Ben: What did you do while Lucy was at her parents'?

Matt: What do you mean?

Ben: Just, in general. It must have been strange, having your wife out of the house, right? What did you do?

Matt: The normal stuff. Went to work. I worked more, actually. The local media would sometimes pop up at my house so I stayed there a lot.

Ben: Did you stay with any friends?

Matt: I think I crashed on a buddy's couch once or twice, yeah.

Ben: How about any women? Did you stay at the homes of any women? Or have them over?

Matt: I mean . . . it's been five years. Like I said, I crashed on some couches. Maybe some were women.

Ben: I have two people who say they saw you regularly coming in and out of the house of a woman I'm choosing not to name here, for her sake.

Matt: Like I said, I stayed with some friends occasionally. Got away from the media.

Ben:	They say the two of you had been sleeping together since before Savannah died.
Matt:	I don't know who these anonymous people are, and I don't know why they think they know what I'm doing behind closed doors.
Ben:	They also said that the woman started spending some nights at your house very soon after Lucy left.
Matt:	Again, I don't know why these people think they know my business.
Ben:	So they're wrong? Or they're lying?
Matt:	Yes, they're wrong. And what does it even matter? How is it even relevant?
Ben:	Good point. Let's move on. How did you get home from the wedding?
Matt:	I drove.
Ben:	Even though you were, by your own account, pretty drunk?
Matt:	Listen, it wasn't a great decision. But yeah, I did. And I'd sobered up a bit by the time I left.
Ben:	When was that?
Matt:	Not long after Lucy and Savvy left.
Ben:	But you didn't see them?
Matt:	No, they took the back road. I took the main road, like they told us to.
Ben:	And you went straight home?
Matt:	Yeah.
Ben:	And you were alone the rest of the night? No one came and picked you up, later that evening?
Matt:	You know what, I actually think I'm going to leave. This was a bad idea.
Ben:	A neighbor confirmed to police that they saw you come home.
Matt:	[*muffled noises*] I'm done.
Ben:	That neighbor has since reached out to express regret about lying. They saw you, but another car showed up shortly after. They said it was a woman, and you two had an argument in your driveway.
Matt:	[*muffled noises, banging*]

Ben: They didn't know who the mystery woman was, but apparently you were shouting at her, and then she left. And then you got back into your car and drove away. So, you told the police you were home all night, but you were actually out during the time Savvy was murdered.

And that's the end of the interview, folks. Matt left then, and I haven't been able to get in contact with him again since.

CHAPTER TWENTY-THREE

LUCY

I agree to go out to the woods with Ben, to the spot where Savvy was found. It's not what I expected for our first interview, but I don't have a good reason to say no.

And I really tried to think of a good reason to say no.

So now I am marching to the door of Ben's hotel room, about to drive with this smug, lying podcaster to the scene of the crime.

"Hello." Ben greets me at the door of his hotel room with a smile.

"Hello, asshole."

Behind Ben, Paige lets out a cackle. She sits on the couch, bare feet casually propped up on the coffee table. I wonder whether the two of them are sleeping together.

I hope not, and then I hate myself for it.

Ben's smile widens, like he relishes being called an asshole. "It's so nice to see you too, Lucy."

"When were you going to tell me that Matt left with some mystery person the night that Savvy died?"

I called and texted Matt several times since listening to the episode last night. Shockingly, he seems to be avoiding me.

"*Let's kill him before he kills you,*" Savvy says in my ear. "*Didn't I tell you how good I am at that? I can make a man wish he never laid eyes on me, much less hands.*"

It wasn't the plan, to kill him the night of the wedding. We were still just talking about it.

Did the plan change? Did we run into Matt that night?

I think of him standing near the front door, genuine fear in his eyes. The man who once sneered at me, *"You call that a punch? Hit me again. HIT ME AGAIN!"*

"You found out eventually, didn't you?" Ben says, pulling me back to the present.

"I thought we were working together here. I don't get a heads-up?"

"No," Ben says.

"No," Paige echoes behind him.

"Not really feeling the trust here, Ben."

He laughs. "Do you trust *me*?"

Not even a little bit. "Fair point."

He grabs his bag and steps out of the hotel room, pulling the door closed behind him. "I'm going to turn the mic on once we're in the car, okay?"

"Okay." I turn away, in case my face betrays my nerves.

I follow Ben to his car. "Are there more interview bombshells coming?"

"Of course." He opens the door and smiles at me over the hood. "Ready?"

"Have you been out here since it happened?" Fifteen minutes later, Ben is worried. He frowns as he says the words, taking his eyes off the road for so long that I actually point out the windshield to remind him that he's driving. He faces forward.

We're on the narrow road that leads to the Byrd Estate. There are two roads that go to the venue—a main one, nicely paved and less dangerous, and this one, narrow and bumpy, with thick trees on either side. The latter is a much faster way to get to the highway, and it's the one where they found Savvy's car parked, abandoned.

"Yes." I slump down in my seat. My heart is thumping too fast, and I try to pretend that it's just a sugar rush from the cookies I ate before leaving the house. The cold air blasting out of the vents is finally starting to cool the car down, and I focus on the feeling of it against my face.

I haven't seen Savvy again, but her voice is in my head constantly now. Just an endless stream of "*Let's kill your husband!*"

"When?" He glances at me again, but only for a moment this time.

"My mom brought me out here after the police opened the area back up. We walked around, hoping it would spark a memory." I speak a little slowly, considering my words before I say them. I'm Podcast Lucy now.

I am not "I was planning to kill my husband with my friend" Lucy. She needs to stay buried deep inside.

"It didn't." It's not a question.

"*Get up, Lucy. GET UP.*" The memory of Mom yelling at me as I collapsed, fingers gripping the dirt, came roaring back. I try to push it away.

"*This is not how innocent people act. You know that, right?*" she said to me as we drove away, me sobbing in the passenger's seat.

I hadn't known that. How would an innocent person have acted? I'd always meant to ask.

"Lucy." Ben's concerned again.

"No, it didn't work."

He parks in the dirt on the side of the road. The buzz of crickets grows louder as I open my door.

He holds his digital recorder as we begin walking into the trees. They're thick, providing ample shade, but it doesn't help much. It's after six, the sun still blazing, the air thick with humidity. Sweat is already rolling down my back, and we've been out of the car all of two minutes.

I thought the microphone would bother me more. I thought that visiting the scene of the crime after all these years would bother me less. Everything is still upside down, and I feel off-balance. I wish I'd said no to this. No, Ben, interview me indoors, in air-conditioning, like a normal fucking person.

We're following a thin dirt path, and I focus on it. Try to breathe.

"The police had this area roped off for what, a week?" Ben asks.

"Yeah, I think so."

"And how long after that did you come out here?"

"I don't remember exactly. A couple days, maybe."

"What was that like for you? To visit the scene again, I mean."

I bite back my first response—*It was a fucking party, Ben, what do you think?* I'm Podcast Lucy right now. Innocent people don't make sarcastic comments.

"*Innocent people don't plot to kill their husbands.*" That wasn't Savvy. She never said that. But I hear the words in her voice anyway.

"It was rough," I say.

He nods and is quiet for several moments.

"What about before? You're a runner, right? Did you ever come out here for a run? That trail is nearby."

I don't know how he knows that I'm a runner, but it's entirely possible that Ben knows more about me than I know about myself at this point.

"I didn't start running until a few years ago. And I hate running outside, so, no. I'd never come out here for a run. Especially not in this heat." A bug dive-bombs my face, and I barely stop myself from screaming a curse. I flap my hand in front of my face a little too vigorously. I look as crazy as I feel.

"But you knew about the trail, right?"

"Yeah, of course. It's not a big town, and the sign for the trail is right off the road. I passed it a million times."

We're still walking, and I realize I don't know exactly where Savvy's body was found. Everything looks the same out here. Just a dirt path looping through identical trees.

Would an innocent person have remembered? Maybe an innocent

person would have come out here every day, desperately searching for the memory. I visited twice and dissolved into hysterics both times.

I can actually sort of see Mom's point, now that I think about it.

I catch Ben staring again, eyebrows drawn together. He must know where Savvy's body was found. He would have planned all this out beforehand—the route, the questions. Maybe he even practiced that concerned look he keeps giving me.

He points. "It's right up here."

I wonder whether he read the expression on my face. The thought makes me uncomfortable. I turn away from him.

My heart is thumping too loud in my ears and sweat is pouring down my back. It's not even that hot today, by Texas standards. I feel a little dizzy.

I spot flowers in a small pink vase in front of a tree and I stop. Yellow roses. Savvy's favorite.

"Her mom comes out here regularly," Ben explains, noticing my gaze. I nod mutely.

There's no evidence of where Savvy was found, of course—it's been too long—but I remember now. The police showed me photos of the body, half-covered in dirt, her dress ripped in several places.

I stared at the torn strap of her dress, hanging on by a thread. I knew how that happened. I knew, but I couldn't remember.

Or I just wanted to remember so badly that I tried to create a memory. Hard to say now.

"Are you okay?" Ben asks.

"Yeah."

"Does being out here make you feel any particular way?"

I stare at him. Marvel at the stupid question.

"You've seemed out of sorts since we got out of the car. Is it hard for you to be out here, at the spot where she died?"

"Of—of course it's hard." I take a breath, but it doesn't help.

Savvy appears behind him. She's in a short black dress that she wore often—cotton, casual, clinging to her body in a way that made everyone take a second glance. She grins as she mimes strangling him. I blink and she's gone.

I need to get out of here. My mind is swimming, and I can't be Podcast Lucy when I can't think straight. I might say something awful or dumb or—

This is not how innocent people act.

"Can you talk about why it's so upsetting for you to be out here? Is it just because it's the spot where Savvy died, or does it bring up other memories as well?"

A bead of sweat rolls down the side of my face. It's too hot to breathe. The air is thick and horrible.

The edges of my vision go black. My legs go numb. There's a loud buzzing in my ear and I don't know whether it's all the goddamn bugs or that my brain has given up. I wouldn't blame my brain cells for peacing out. I'm surprised they made it this long.

"Oh shit." Ben's voice sounds far away, but when I sway, I hit him instead of the ground.

He slows my fall but we both still end up in the dirt. I don't think he's caught very many swooning ladies. He's not very good at it.

I don't want to be down here, so close to where Savvy was, but all I can manage is to sit up, butt in the dirt.

"Hey. Lucy. Look at me." Ben is on his knees next to me, one hand on my back and the other on my arm, like he's worried I'm going to fall over.

I mean, I guess that's fair.

"Are you okay?"

He's full of stupid questions today.

"Can you . . . I don't know what to do. Should I call an ambulance?" He's already got his phone out. I catch sight of the microphone, on the ground not far away.

I shake my head.

"Do you want some water?"

I shake my head again.

"Jesus. I'm sorry." He speaks softly, and his hand goes a little firmer on my arm. "I'm so sorry."

I blink twice. A breeze ruffles his hair, and it provides a tiny moment of relief from the heat.

"For what?" I ask.

He looks startled. "For bringing you out here. For pressing you."

His expression is soft, like he's found a wounded puppy to take care of, and I don't like it. I pull my arm away and slowly get to my feet. He reaches out to make sure I'm steady but doesn't touch me again.

I turn away. "I'm going back to the car."

CHAPTER TWENTY-FOUR

LUCY

Ben doesn't take me back to the hotel.

I don't realize where we are until he turns onto the road, and I can see the tiny house up ahead. Grandma steps out as he slows to a stop, hands on her hips.

"What are we doing here?" I ask.

He unbuckles his seat belt. "I didn't want to just leave you alone after that, and your parents are assholes."

"Wow, tell me how you really feel, Ben."

He gives me a look like "you know it's true," and I almost laugh. I hate how delighted I am that he thinks my parents are assholes.

I need a drink. At least we've come to the right place for that.

"I texted Beverly and she said to come over." He steps out of the car.

I follow him, wondering how often he's texting my grandma, and how many times he's been out here. He knows my parents are assholes, and he's chummy with my grandma. He already knows so much more than I ever wanted him to.

"*Murdering your husband can be our secret,*" Savvy whispers. "*But then you're stuck with me for life. There's no dumping a friend once you've committed a felony together.*"

Grandma waggles a finger at Ben. "I told you."

He lifts both hands in surrender. "I know."

I trudge toward her. My legs are heavy. "What'd you tell him?"

"That you're not as tough as you act." Her dress today is white with yellow daisies, and there's a small reddish-brown stain on one boob that is probably red wine, but my first thought is *blood*. Savvy giggles in my head.

"Hey." I mean to sound insulted, but it comes out tired.

"Did you eat anything besides sugar today?" Grandma asks, like I'm still ten years old.

I consider. "Not really."

"Come on. What do you like on your pizza, Ben?"

An hour later, when I'm full of sausage and mushroom pizza, the world feels steady again. Grandma made me a vodka tonic, and I think the pleasant buzz is the only thing keeping me from feeling the full embarrassment of fainting on Ben earlier.

We're sitting on her porch in creaky plastic chairs, a fan blowing hot air around us as the sun sets. Grandma emerges from the house with two drinks. She hands one to Ben.

"You getting any writing done in between all this?" She sits down, propping her feet up on the grungy wicker ottoman as she sips her drink.

"Not really. I haven't felt much like writing happy people in love."

"But you're so good at it!" She reaches over and whacks Ben's shoulder. "Isn't she?"

"You are." He glances at me with a half-smile. He's on his second drink (and Grandma pours them strong), legs stretched out in front of him, fancy microphone forgotten in the car. He looks more relaxed than I've ever seen him, and I wonder again how many times he's been here.

"I acted dumb when he asked me about your books, by the way," Grandma says. "But he told me you guys talked about it."

"I know." I sigh. "It's only a matter of time before it comes out."

"Ben said he's not telling people!"

"I'm not," he says quickly.

"Yeah, but if he can figure it out, other people can too. And now everyone is thinking about me again." I cast an annoyed look in Ben's direction, which he ignores.

"Maybe not." She pauses. "I hope people really are having sex like that in their twenties the way they are in your books."

Ben laughs mid-sip, and then presses the back of his hand to his mouth as he coughs.

"We were all so repressed in our twenties," Grandma continues. "Just focused on marrying the first jerk who asked."

"Was Grandpa the first jerk who asked?"

"Yes."

"Ah." I barely remember the man—he died when I was a kid—but I'd guessed from the way she never spoke about him that he wasn't particularly missed.

"The world seemed so dangerous for women back then," she says.

"We're sitting here with a man who investigates women's murders, so I wouldn't say it's safe now."

"Oh sure." Grandma waves dismissively. "But you know what I mean. I never could have left my husband and moved to Los Angeles by myself, like you did. I was supposed to get married and stay married, so my husband could protect me. I needed to be transferred straight from father to husband, or something terrible might happen to me."

She takes a long sip of her drink. "My life vastly improved once both those men were gone. Men don't protect us, not really. They only protect themselves, or each other. The only thing men ever protected me from was happiness."

"Oh shit," Ben murmurs under his breath.

"A little too much honesty there for you, Ben?" I ask.

"I would expect nothing less from you, Beverly." He smiles at Grandma with genuine affection.

"I wouldn't go so far as to call you one of the good ones, but you're not half bad," Grandma says.

Ben bursts out laughing, the sound echoing off the quiet porch. "I will take that compliment, thank you."

I lean my head back with a sigh. She's right. She's always right. She was right about me coming back, about her party, about Ben. I've been angry with Ben for dredging up the past, but it needed to be dredged up.

No one protected Savvy back then. The very least I can do is find answers for her now.

"You're not half bad," I repeat softly. One side of Ben's mouth turns up, and when our eyes meet, I have to look away.

Grandma squints, and I follow her gaze to a gray-haired man walking down the road in our direction, swinging a cane like some kind of dapper gentleman from the 1920s. "Oh, hold on." She gets up and struts toward him, glass in hand.

I watch her greet the man with a kiss. The vodka buzz is intensifying, and I actually feel a little jealous. I'm reminded again of how long it's been since I had good sex.

"That's a different man than the one who came by when I interviewed her," Ben says with a soft laugh. He pauses for a moment. "Do you agree with her about Matt?"

I look at him in surprise. "What about Matt?"

"Have you finished episode five?"

"No, I only got about halfway before I had to meet you."

"Oh." He's watching Grandma and her suitor. She laughs at something he says. "You should finish episode five."

"Why? What'd she say?"

He takes a long sip of his drink. "She thinks Matt killed her."

Listen for the Lie Podcast with Ben Owens

EPISODE 5—"A MYSTERY WOMAN"

If I'm being honest, Beverly Moore is the reason you're listening to season two of this podcast.

I reached out to her last year. I didn't even expect a reply to my email, but she called me up within hours of receiving it. Told me she'd be happy to talk to me about Lucy.

Ben: Mrs. Moore, I really appreciate you sitting down with me today.

Beverly: Oh, hon, you can call me Beverly.

Ben: Okay. Beverly. Can you tell me about your granddaughter? What was Lucy like when she was younger?

Beverly: She was a real no-nonsense girl. Just didn't have time for any shit, you know? I've always admired that about her. I was so concerned with whether or not everyone liked me at that age.

And people hate that quality in a young woman, don't they? They don't know what to do with a girl who isn't looking for their approval. They feel like they have to bring her down a peg.

Ben: You knew Savannah, didn't you?

Beverly: Of course. Lovely girl, and I'm not just saying that because she's dead. Some young people, they don't want to talk to us old folks, but Savvy was a real sweetheart to everyone. I used to help out at the bakery, and she'd come in a few times a week. She'd often stay and chat for a while.

Ben: Tell me about how you met Matt.

Beverly: Lucy brought him home . . . I guess it was the summer before her senior year of college. They'd already been dating for a bit.

Ben: What did you think?

Beverly: Well, I could tell that Lucy was madly in love. And I wanted to like him, for her sake, but . . . I didn't really. He was so charming, in that way that's always felt suspicious to me.

Ben: Can you elaborate on that?

Beverly:	Some men, they've got to put on a show when they're around women. It's like they don't actually know how to talk to us, so they choose over-the-top chivalry. "If I pull out her chair and make a big show of talking about how moms are heroes and women are actually the strong ones, they won't notice that I don't have any interest in listening to a single word that comes out of their mouths."

    Matt was like that.

Ben:	Did you tell Lucy your concerns?
Beverly:	Not at that time, no. She was twenty years old. No one wants their grandma weighing in on their boyfriend at that age. At any age, honestly. So, I kept my mouth shut until they got engaged.
Ben:	You said something then?
Beverly:	I did. Lucy called me all excited, telling me Matt proposed, and I said, "Honey, why don't you wait a bit? You're so young. Go to Europe. Buy an old van and travel the country. Don't get married. You have your whole life to be married."

    She didn't like that, of course. And when she asked if I didn't like Matt, I told her, no, I didn't. I said that I got a bad feeling from him, and that if he really loved her, he would understand that she wanted to wait a few years to get married. What kind of twenty-two-year-old boy wants to get married these days anyway? We're not Mormons, for Christ's sake.

Ben:	What was her response?
Beverly:	She was polite, but it was obvious that she wasn't going to take my advice. I can't blame her. I was the same way when I was her age. Stars in my eyes. Thinking about my pretty white dress and the chubby little babies who would look up at me adoringly.

    In the end, life is just sweatpants and children who resent you and all your choices. But no one wants to hear that.

Ben:	What about after they got married? Did you warm to Matt?
Beverly:	Goodness no. I hated him even more, and I don't care who knows it.

The act started to fade a bit, and I'd catch him sniping at Lucy. I'd see him roll his eyes at something she said. And he started to slip, say things that he really meant after I'd known him a few years. Men can only hide it for so long, you know?

Ben: Hide what?

Beverly: Who they really are. Matt's real, horrible self was shining through after a few years.

Ben: What kinds of things did he say?

Beverly: Well, let me tell you the one that really matters. I may be old, but I remember this word for word. We were out to eat at the restaurant where Savvy worked. We saw her over at the bar as we walked in, and Don leaned over and said something to Matt. I don't know what. But Matt goes, "*That little slut hates me.*"

Ben: . . . He said "little slut" in front of you?

Beverly: He sure did. He muttered it under his breath, and he looked a little embarrassed after, like he hadn't meant to say it. Don just laughed a little, like he was embarrassed too, and I don't think either of them realized I'd heard.

Ben: Did you tell Lucy?

Beverly: No. I considered it, but I didn't know what purpose it would serve. But I really started to worry at that point. If that was something he'd say to his wife's *father*, what sorts of things must he be thinking? Or saying to Lucy?

CHAPTER TWENTY-FIVE

LUCY

"Mom, you should have at least talked to me first." Mom greets Grandma at the door this way. From my spot leaning against the kitchen counter, I can see Grandma pull off her sunglasses to reveal an unamused expression. I pop another donut hole in my mouth.

Grandma steps into the house, waving off her daughter. "I don't need your permission to tell people my opinions."

"Ben isn't people, he's—" She stops with the front door half-closed, using the end of her crutch to prop it open. "Whose truck is that?"

"A friend's." Grandma plops down at the kitchen table.

"Which friend?" Mom closes the door and hobbles over.

"Just a friend."

"How many *friends* do you have these days?"

"I don't know, Kathleen, a few," Grandma says, exasperated. "I'm a likable person."

"Wouldn't know what that's like," I quip.

She puts a soft hand over mine. "Better to be interesting than likable, in my opinion."

Mom wrinkles her nose like she disagrees.

"Do you want some coffee?" I ask Grandma. "I just made a fresh pot."

"Yes, hon. Thank you."

I pour her a cup and drop the box of donut holes in the middle of the table. Grandma fishes out a powdered-sugar-covered one.

"Ben is not people!" Mom says, picking up her earlier complaint. "He broadcasted that interview to millions."

"I think it's *thousands* of people," I say. "Let's not pump up Ben's ego any more."

"Can you be serious for a minute, Lucy? Your grandmother could get sued."

"For what? Saying Matt's an asshole? He is. You can't sue people for telling the truth." I don't actually think that's true, but it sounds good.

"She implied that he killed Savvy. He can sue for that." Mom starts fussing with the napkin holder in the middle of the table, lining up all the purple napkins so they're perfectly straight.

"No, he can't." Grandma waves her hand dismissively. "I didn't accuse him of anything. I just told everyone about the horrible things he said. If he didn't want them out there, he shouldn't have said them."

"Men say shit," Mom says, and I reel back in surprise at the curse. We're a bad influence on her. "They talk and talk and sometimes it's horrible, but that's the way they are. It doesn't mean anything."

"Of course it means something," Grandma says. "They wouldn't say it if it didn't mean something. And I'm tired of this whole town acting like the sun shines out of Matt's ass. I knew they would all get on that podcast and say how wonderful he was, and that's exactly what happened. Someone needed to tell the truth."

"*The truth doesn't matter,*" Savvy whispers in my ear.

"I suspect Lucy will also tell the truth about him when she does her interview." Grandma looks at me expectantly. No, not expectantly. It's a challenge.

"I will," I lie. "For sure."

Grandma smiles like this lie satisfies her.

"I think you should be . . . selective in your truth," Mom says slowly.

My eyebrows shoot up. "Seriously? After all these years of you hounding me to tell the truth about what happened that night and now—"

"I didn't *hound* you. And of course you should be up front about everything with Savvy. I'm just saying, this podcast has gotten a little off track and, frankly, sex obsessed."

"Sex obsessed!" Grandma cackles.

"Did we need to know about Lucy's affair? Or Matt's? Or mine? Why is he constantly talking about it?" Mom sniffs.

"You're right, he should have mentioned all of Don's affairs if he was going to bring up yours," Grandma says.

"That is the exact opposite of my point, Mother. Lucy, please do not mention your father's constant rotation of girlfriends."

"Oh my god." I lean my head back with a moan. "I'm having high school flashbacks."

Grandma pats my hand again.

"You really care if I bring up Dad's affairs?" I ask Mom, even though I never had any intention of doing that.

"It's irrelevant."

I cross my arms over my chest as she determinedly avoids my gaze. She doesn't want me to talk about Dad's affairs, and she doesn't want Grandma to talk about Matt being an asshole. Mom is, as always, dedicated to protecting the men in her life above all else. I'm not sure she even realizes she's doing it. It's a habit at this point.

"Speaking of the truth," I begin, unable to resist making Mom even more uncomfortable. Both Grandma and Mom freeze, like I'm about to reveal something important. "Can we talk about Colin Dunn for a minute?"

Mom lets out a long-suffering sigh and plucks a napkin with a small dog-ear from the stack. "Don't change the subject."

"Oh yes, *let's* change the subject," Grandma says, brushing powdered sugar off her shirt.

"I'm not talking about Colin," Mom says, and then pauses. "Because there's nothing to say."

"At least tell me how that happened," I press. "Ben said it was an ongoing affair."

"I don't know why Ben thinks he knows my business."

"Is he right, though?" Grandma has a shit-eating grin on her face.

Mom takes a donut hole and breaks it apart. She puts a tiny bite on her tongue, and then drops the rest of it on the napkin. "No. It was just that night."

"That's too bad," Grandma says wistfully. "He's very cute, for a twentysomething." Mom rolls her eyes, but the edges of her lips twitch.

"Was the wedding the first time?" I ask.

"Yes." The lines between her eyebrows appear again when she looks at me. "He said that he and Savvy saw other people."

"They did."

"Then why are you looking at me like that?"

"I'm not looking at you! This is just my normal face!"

She frowns and breaks off another tiny piece of the donut. "It was years ago, and it was once, and—"

"Was it good?" Grandma interrupts.

"*Mother.*"

"What? Young men were *not* great at sex when I was—"

"Please don't finish that sentence," Mom says, face scrunched up like she's in pain.

"I'm just saying. Some things get better with age."

I snort-laugh. Mom crosses her arms over her chest and shakes her head.

I lean closer to Grandma. "Savvy had no complaints," I whisper.

She cackles. Mom's cheeks turn pink as she shoves the rest of the donut in her mouth.

CHAPTER TWENTY-SIX

LUCY

I sit in bed that afternoon, laptop propped up in my lap, and text Ben to ask when we're doing our next interview. The big one. The one where I'm supposed to tell all about Matt.

I still need to decide what "all" will be.

I'm not actually interested in sharing my sob story with the podcast universe. I was never all that interested in telling anyone except Savvy.

She understood that. She didn't take my hand and gently suggest we march down to the police station. She didn't ask, "Why don't you just leave?"

She said, "*That's usually when men kill the woman. When they try to leave.*"

And I said, "*I actually don't think Matt would do that.*"

"*Is that really a risk you want to take?*" she'd asked.

No. It wasn't.

And she knew. Right away, she knew that I didn't want to just leave.

I wanted fucking revenge.

"*Let's Thelma and Louise this shit,*" she'd said, and I'd laughed.

I can't very well tell my abused-wife sob story to everyone when I once laughed about killing my husband. That's not cool.

My laptop dings with a message from Ben.

Want to grab a drink tonight?

And do the interview?

No. Interview tomorrow, maybe?

I sigh and start to type, Can we just get this over with already? I quickly delete it. That's not something an innocent person would say.

Downstairs, I hear Mom laugh loudly, as if she's inside my head.

Ben saves me from having to type anything at all. Meet me in an hour at Bluebonnet Tavern?

I can feel that this is a bad idea by the way I glance over at my closet to see which dress I should wear. I'm relieved that I have an hour, so I have time to do my hair and put on makeup. There's danger here, and I should say no. *No, Ben, I'll see you for the interview. Text me then.* That's what I *should* send.

Sure, see you in an hour, is what I actually send.

I'm at Bluebonnet an hour later. I chose the purple dress, which I rationalized by telling myself that he'd already seen me in it. I'd been wearing it the day we met, at the diner. It's cotton, casual. Not a date dress. It's a "too fucking hot for pants" dress.

Bluebonnet is big and bright, the large windows at the front letting in plenty of the early evening sunlight. The floors and walls are wood, the latter covered in Texas decor so we won't forget which state we're in. There's a Texas flag, a *Don't Mess with Texas* sign, and a bulletin board advertising various Hill Country wine tours. A bright *Real Ale* sign flickers as I walk by it.

Ben is already sitting at the bar, wearing a blue button-up shirt with sleeves pushed to his elbows. It's a date shirt, I note. One that's too warm for this weather. I try not to read too much into it.

He smiles when he spots me. I slide onto the stool next to him.

"Hey. Thanks for coming."

I glance at his drink, which is pink. "Is that a cosmo?"

"Why do you say it like that? Cosmos are delicious. And they're the happy hour special."

"I didn't say it like anything."

The bartender, a pretty woman with dark hair cut into an angled bob, approaches and looks at me expectantly.

"I'll have one too." I point to his drink. I don't drink hard liquor often, and I ignore the voice in the back of my head that says I should take this purple dress home.

"You got it." She walks away to make the drink.

Savvy is on the other side of the bar in her place suddenly. I want to look away, but she looks so real. I have to remind myself that she's a product of my twisted, damaged brain.

She leans closer to me. Even in my hallucination, she smells a little like smoke. She only smoked when she drank, but, well, she drank a lot.

"*You know what I would do,*" she says with a grin.

I shift on my barstool.

"*I'd let him fuck me in the bathroom.*" She has a wistful look in her eye. "*And then probably out back behind the bar too. Remember that time you found me in the parking lot of the Charles? That guy had me bent over the hood of his car, my naked ass in the air, and you rushed over because you thought he was raping me? And I had to be like, oh no, honey, this was my idea.*"

Ben takes a sip of his drink. "Why do people judge men for ordering pink drinks? It's weird to gender drinks."

"I didn't say anything."

"*You're not wearing a bra under that dress, are you?*" Savvy asks. "*I approve.*" She winks at me and disappears. I let out a long breath.

"Men are lying when they say they don't like fruity drinks. That guy over there with a beer wishes he had my cosmo."

I laugh, which makes his face brighten. The bartender returns with my drink and I take a sip. It's strong, thank god.

A burst of laughter explodes from behind me, and I look to see a group of women at a corner booth, many empty margarita glasses in front of them. A waiter is putting new ones down.

A dark-haired woman on the end of the booth is draining the last of her margarita, and she barely takes a breath before she grabs the new one and takes a long sip. It's Nina.

She chugs half the margarita down in two gulps, and the other women explode into giggles again.

"You better go ahead and bring another one," she says to the waiter. He laughs and nods.

For someone who said she doesn't drink much, she sure is putting away those margaritas.

Our eyes meet as she puts the glass down, and she quickly looks away, like she hoped I hadn't noticed her. She hastily recovers, turning in the booth and waving at me.

She stands and walks to us. She's wearing skinny jeans that hug her curves, and no fewer than three men check out her ass as she passes them. I give them disapproving looks that not one of them notices.

"Hey, Lucy."

Ben turns around then, and Nina actually stumbles back in surprise. She blinks twice, and I swear she almost turns around and bolts. I can actually see the thought cross her face.

If Ben sees it, he pretends not to. He smiles and says, "Hi, Nina."

"Hi?" It comes out as a question, directed at me. "Is . . . everything okay?"

"Fine. How about you?"

She squints. "Uhh . . ." Her cheeks are pink, and I can almost see that huge gulp of margarita hitting her. "Good. Yeah. Good." She shakes her head. "I'm sorry. You seriously hang out with this guy?"

Ben laughs. "Tell us how you really feel, Nina."

Nina casts an irritated look at him. She sounded friendly on the podcast, but that look in her eyes is anything but. Something happened between her interviews and now.

"If you can't be friendly with the podcaster who's trying to prove you killed your best friend, who can you be friendly with?" I say it in an effort to lighten the mood, but both Ben and Nina look at me like I've grown a second head. *Shit.* That's not something an innocent person would say.

"I'm going to go back to my friends." Nina doesn't look at me as she turns. "Nice seeing you guys."

I don't think she means that. I watch as she heads back to the table of women who are now gawking at us. I wave. No one seems to appreciate that. I turn to face the bar again.

"I'm not trying to prove you killed Savannah," Ben says. "I'm trying to find out who killed her."

"That's the same thing to a lot of people."

"Not to me." He looks over his shoulder, and I follow his gaze to see Nina frowning at us.

"Did you guys get into it or something?"

"Not that I know of. But I offend a lot of people, so who can say?"

I laugh, and Nina's frown deepens. I put a hand on his arm. (Yes, it is unnecessary to touch him. Yes, I do it anyway.) "Turn around. She's going to think we're talking about her."

He smiles as he turns to face me again, and when I drop my hand from his arm, he catches my fingers, just for a moment.

"We are talking about her."

"We're supposed to be subtle about it. It's the Texas way."

"If you want to know the truth, I kind of love her and Emmett." He leans closer to me, so close that our shoulders touch.

"I hate to tell you this, but I don't think the feeling's mutual." I should move away. I don't.

"That's fine. I don't mind my one-sided love for them."

"And what is it about them that you find so lovable?"

"They're on your side."

I cock an eyebrow.

"I mean, the podcast would have gotten boring real quick if every single person I interviewed said the same thing. Nice of them to mix it up for me."

I smile. Ben's gaze flickers down to my lips.

I lean away a little, so that our shoulders aren't touching anymore, and take a sip of my drink.

"Have you talked to Matt since the last episode aired?" Ben asks. I wonder whether he's been waiting to ask that question since I walked in.

"No. He's been ignoring my texts. I could drop by his house again."

He looks at me. Looks away. Takes a sip of his pink drink.

"Is that . . . safe?"

Well, fuck. I wonder who told him. I wonder who even knows. I always thought that a couple of women from the neighborhood had an inkling, but I'm surprised they told him.

"Is it ever safe to confront a man about being a dick?"

"No." He says it like he has experience with this, which is unsurprising. "It's not."

I stay at the bar with Ben for two hours. He tells me about his family and his friends and how the east side of L.A. is the best side of L.A. I agree. It turns out we only live about fifteen minutes away from each other, which actually makes me a little uneasy. There's an upside to getting kicked out of Nathan's apartment.

I don't finish my second cosmo because I'm well on my way to tipsy. Maybe mostly on my way to drunk. Maybe already there.

I pull my phone out as we walk out of the bar and lean against the side of the building. He looks at me curiously.

"I'm calling an Uber."

He points. "Isn't that your car?"

"I'm too drunk to drive."

"Seriously? From two drinks?"

"I'm a lightweight."

"I guess so."

"It would probably be fine, but it doesn't seem worth the risk. I don't want to be the girl who murdered her friend *and* the girl who gets arrested for drunk driving. That's just embarrassing."

He laughs and pulls his keys out of his pocket. "Come on. I'll drive you home."

I slide my phone back into my purse. "Thank you."

"Do they even have Uber in this town?"

"There's one dude. Apparently he takes forever to show up."

"Not much incentive to be quick when you're the only game in town."

"*Hey, jackass!*" The screaming voice is familiar, and my fingers instinctively tighten into fists. I whirl around.

It's Matt, tearing across the parking lot like his ass is on fire. His face is twisted with fury, his whole body so tense I can see the muscles rippling down his arms.

But his anger isn't directed at me, which is a new experience. He's charging straight for Ben.

Ben dives into his car and I think he's going to make a run for it. But he emerges a moment later and tosses something small and black onto the hood of the car. His digital recorder.

"Hi, Matt," the smug idiot says.

"You son of a bitch, I should wring your neck." Matt comes to a stop in front of Ben and doesn't wring his neck.

He punches him in the face.

Ben stumbles but doesn't fall, his back hitting the car. Matt grabs him by the collar of his shirt. He's an inch or two shorter than Ben, but he's making up for it with sheer rage.

"I am going to sue you for every penny you're worth," Matt says through clenched teeth.

Ben tries to twist out of his grasp. "I'll give you my lawyer's number. Can you take your hands off me, please?"

Matt responds by gripping his shirt tighter and slamming Ben into the car.

"Matt!" I sound surprised, even though I'm not.

His head whips around to look at me, and then something behind me. I glance back. Half the bar is outside now, staring.

"Beverly is a fucking drunk, and that one is a fucking liar." Matt lets go of Ben's shirt to point at me, just so there's no confusion about who the fucking liar is. Matt is breathing heavily, eyes still wild like they always are when he loses control.

Ben's shirt is stretched out at the collar and hanging loosely around his neck, but he looks remarkably fine otherwise.

"I'd be happy to add your reply to the podcast, if you'd like to give one." Ben's voice wobbles, just a little.

"Go to hell, asshole. That's my reply." Matt turns and stomps away.

Ben lifts and lowers his shoulders, like he's making sure they're okay. Then he walks around to the hood of the car and grabs his recorder.

He looks up at me with a self-satisfied smile that should be more annoying than it is. "You want to come back to my hotel for a drink?"

CHAPTER TWENTY-SEVEN

LUCY

I'm sure it will surprise no one to learn that I made the stupid choice and accepted Ben's offer to go back to his hotel.

His suite is cold as I walk in, the AC up high. I shiver, and he pauses at the thermostat on his way into the kitchen.

"Sit," he says, pointing at the couch. His laptop and notebooks are stacked neatly on the table in front of it. Nothing for me to see there. I don't know whether I'd want to anyway.

"Whiskey?" he asks.

That seems like a bad idea. "Yes."

He pours two glasses, gingerly touching his cheek as he finishes. "Matt sure can throw a punch."

Yes. Well. He's had some practice.

He walks over to me, whiskey in hand, and holds one out to me. I immediately take a sip. It burns going down, but I lift it to my lips a second time because I would actually really prefer to be drunk again.

I glance at the digital recorder he left on the counter in the kitchen. The light is off. Not recording. He notices me staring at it.

"You recorded that? Matt yelling at you?" I ask as he sits down on the other side of the couch.

"Yeah, I turned it on just in time."

"Is that legal?"

"In Texas, you can record audio of people without their knowledge if there's no reasonable expectation of privacy. So, in a restaurant, or a bar, or . . ."

"If they're screaming in a parking lot."

"Yep."

"Were you recording in the bar?"

"No."

I don't know whether I believe him, but it doesn't matter either way. I didn't say anything to him that I'd mind being broadcast to thousands of true-crime fans.

"You could have just driven away," I say. "You had enough time to bolt."

His lips quirk up. "Where's the fun in that?"

I prop my bare feet up on the coffee table, cradling the whiskey against my stomach. "You're going to put that on the podcast, then?"

"Yes. Don't ask me not to."

"I wasn't going to." I watch as he takes a long sip of his drink. "You know everyone thinks you're hinting that he's the one who killed Savvy."

"I wasn't very subtle, was I?"

"Do you actually believe that?"

He looks at me with raised eyebrows. "It never occurred to you that Matt might have killed her?"

"Jesus Christ, Ben, I'm not an idiot. Of course it occurred to me."

His cheeks go a little pink. "Right. Sorry."

"I just . . ." I have nothing to say here.

Like I had nothing to say to the police. What could I say? *No, Officer, I definitely never would have killed Savvy, because actually we were planning to kill my husband together?* Not much of a defense.

I could have confessed that plan, and my suspicions that maybe, for whatever reason, we decided to go after Matt that night, and Matt killed Savvy in self-defense. And then he let everyone think that I did it as a giant *fuck you* to me.

I wouldn't blame him, honestly.

But, the fear. The look in his eyes when he asked me to go to my parents'. If that fear was because he thought I was going to try to kill him (again?), he would have told the police the truth. I can't think of any reason that Matt wouldn't go to the police if we'd tried to kill him that night. The truth would have mattered, for him.

Ben is staring at me expectantly.

"I wouldn't focus too much on Matt," I say, finally.

"Seriously?"

"I don't think he did it."

"*Seriously?*" It's the baffled word of someone who thinks I should know better. *Seriously, Lucy? He hit you!* He points to his cheek, which is red.

"It's your podcast, man, I'm just telling you what I think."

He lets out a long sigh. "If you want to know the truth, I can't figure out a motive. I think what Kyle said about them maybe sleeping together is bullshit."

"That is *definitely* bullshit."

He touches his cheek and winces. "Matt's still a dick, though."

"You should put ice on that."

"Meh."

I go to the fridge and pull a handful of ice from the freezer. I wrap it in a paper towel and walk over to him, holding it out.

"I think it's fine," he says.

I sit down next to him and put the ice to his face.

"Ow."

"Just for a couple minutes. Or are you hoping it swells so you can take a picture and put it on Twitter?"

A smile slides across his face, and I can't help the one that crosses mine as well.

He takes the ice from me and presses it to his cheek. We sit in silence for several moments that are not quite comfortable.

Then he tosses the ice on the coffee table, leans over, and kisses me.

I'm in his lap almost immediately, his hands under my dress and on my thighs. I can't remember why I thought this was a bad idea. This is a great idea. This is the best idea I've had since arriving in this cursed city.

He pulls my dress down around my waist, his hands on my breasts. I unbutton his pants. I'd like to blame the vodka for that decision.

And I'd like to blame the whiskey for letting him yank off my underwear so we can have sex right there on the couch.

But that would be a lie.

CHAPTER TWENTY-EIGHT

LUCY

I wake early, before the sun. Ben is asleep beside me on his stomach, his hair disheveled and falling across his eyes. My head hurts.

I sit up slowly. I'm in his bed, naked, because after having sex on the couch he pulled me into his bedroom and we had sex in here too.

An image of me smothering him with a pillow flashes across my vision. That's pretty standard for me waking up with men. It would be so easy to kill a sleeping man.

"*I still vote strangulation for this one,*" Savvy whispers. I shake the voice away.

I find my dress on the floor, and my underwear in the living room. It's ripped, so I toss it in the trash on my way out.

I'm outside before I remember that my car is still at the bar. I debate calling the one Uber driver, but he's probably asleep, and it's only about a mile down the road. I start down the sidewalk, hoping a strong breeze doesn't blow up my dress and expose my ass to the world.

It's hot, even just before sunrise, and sweat trickles down my back as I walk.

I wasn't nearly drunk enough last night to blame my choices on the alcohol, which was honestly shit planning on my part. Should have gotten wasted. Then at least I'd have an excuse.

But, no excuses. We didn't even use a condom, which is really just the icing on my bad-decision cake. I've had an IUD for years, so there are no smug babies in my immediate future, but who knows where Ben has been sticking that thing. He fucks like he gets around.

A little podcast souvenir. I should get a T-shirt: *I was the subject of a true crime podcast and all I got was this T-shirt and gonorrhea.*

My car is still, thankfully, in the parking lot, and I drive home to a dark, quiet house.

I walk upstairs and close my door softly, change my clothes, and climb into bed. Early morning sun is filtering in through the blinds, and there's a text from Ben on my phone. I ignore it and close my eyes.

My headache is gone when I wake the second time, and I'm starving now. I trudge downstairs. No sign of Mom, which is a relief. I don't need to add that to my hangover. I smear some cream cheese on a bagel and then hurry back upstairs.

There are more texts from Ben on my phone.

Hey. Did you get home okay?

You could have woken me up.

Seriously, just text me so I know you're not dead.

I perch on the edge of my bed, take a bite of my bagel, and text him back.

I'm not dead. I got home fine.

My phone rings immediately. Way to play it cool, Ben.

I swipe to answer it. "Hey."

"It's rude to leave a guy in bed, you know."

"Is it?"

"I think so, yes."

"Do you usually sleep with the murder suspect of your podcast?"

"The suspect in season one was a man."

"Is that a no?"

"It's a no." He sounds amused.

"Do you usually forget the condom?"

"No. Uh, I'm sorry about that, I don't—"

"It's fine, that's my fault too. I have birth control covered, I was just sort of hoping you hadn't been raw-doggin' it all over Los Angeles."

He lets out a short, startled laugh. "I have not been raw-doggin' it all over Los Angeles. Or anywhere. Usually."

Just with me, then. I don't know whether I feel special or insulted.

"I feel like your podcaster ethics have really gone to shit here, Ben." I mean it as a criticism, but he laughs.

"Whatever. No one ever accused me of making good decisions."

"*Questionable ethics, but you can't argue with the results!*" The words I read about Ben a couple of weeks ago float through my mind, and I have to work not to laugh. No one can say I wasn't warned.

In truth, no one ever accused me of making good decisions either.

"You want to get breakfast?" he asks. "I need to talk to you about something."

"I need to write. Talk to me now."

He pauses, and then clears his throat. "Uh, yeah. Okay. So, I'm putting together a bonus episode for tomorrow with the stuff I recorded with Matt yesterday. I want to send it to you first and let you veto it."

Veto it? I had sex with the man two times and I'm now apparently in charge of the podcast. I'm either proud of myself or horrified. Hard to say.

"Why do I get to do that?"

"Because it includes an interview that makes me uncomfortable. I'll cut it if you ask me to."

"Who's the interview with?"

"Maya Harper."

My stomach clenches the way it always does when someone mentions Maya. Savvy's little sister.

"Send me the interview."

Listen for the Lie Podcast with Ben Owens

MAYA'S INTERVIEW UNEDITED SEGMENT

Hello, friends. I'm back, earlier than expected, because something happened last night. I met Lucy at a local bar—which you all know already, because you've seen the pictures on Twitter. Yes, we were having a drink, and no, it's not nearly as scandalous as you all seem to think it is.

As we were leaving the bar, Matt pulled into the parking lot and got out of his car. Here's what happened.

[*scuffling noises*]

"Hello, Matt."

"You son of a bitch, I should wring your neck."

[*scuffling, grunting*]

That sound you hear? That's Matt punching me in the face.

"I am going to sue you for every penny you're worth."

"I'll give you my lawyer's number. Can you take your hands off me, please?"

[*banging noise*]

Matt slams me into the car here.

"Matt!"

That's Lucy. She's standing nearby as this happens.

"Beverly is a [inaudible], and that one is a fucking liar!"

"That one" refers to Lucy here, because he points at her.

That's the general consensus, right? Lucy is lying. Lucy is hiding something.

Well, we've already established that Matt is lying too—he wasn't at home the night Savannah died, even though he told police that he was.

And Kyle Porter suggested on this podcast that something might have been going on between Savannah and Matt. Savannah's younger sister, Maya Harper, gave me a piece of her mind about that.

Maya: Savvy never slept with Matt. It's bullshit that Kyle said that, and it's bullshit that you put it on your podcast.

Ben: Okay. Can you tell me more about that?

Maya: About how you're an asshole?

Ben: About why you think it's bullshit that Savvy slept with Matt.

Maya: She hated Matt. The first time she told me about Lucy, she said all this nice stuff about her and then goes, "And she's married to this total dipshit who kept looking at my boobs when I talked."

Ben: And her opinion of Matt didn't change over the next couple years?

Maya: Nope. But even if it had, she never would have slept with her friend's husband. She wasn't like that. Savvy loved Lucy, and she never would have hurt her.

Ben: What makes you think that Savvy never warmed up to Matt? She talked to you about him?

Maya: She said some things. She'd mention him offhand occasionally, like, "She couldn't get rid of Matt, so I had to have dinner with him too." Stuff like that. And she . . . well, this is just my interpretation, but I think Savvy thought that something was going on with Lucy and Matt.

Ben: Going on?

Maya: Like . . . something abusive? I don't know. Maybe I got it wrong. But not long before she died, we were watching this show together, and there was a story line about an abusive husband. And I looked over at one point and she was rolling her eyes, and I was like, "What?" She said that they were portraying the guy to be this total monster, and that wasn't what those guys are usually like.

And I got kind of concerned, and I was like, "How do you know what those guys are like?" And she goes, "Oh, not me, not me. But I know someone. And the guy . . . a lot of people like him."

I didn't ask if it was Lucy. But it had to be. Savvy wasn't close friends with anyone else at that point. And she said *know*, not *knew*. "I *know* someone." I'd always wondered why Savvy had this, like, burning hatred of Matt when everyone else seemed to love him. It made sense suddenly.

CHAPTER TWENTY-NINE

LUCY

I text Ben when I finish listening.

> Can you cut out everything she says after "Savvy loved Lucy, and she never would have hurt her"?

I walk downstairs to toss the rest of my bagel in the trash as I wait nervously for him to reply. It comes as I'm walking back up the stairs.

> Yes. No problem.

I blow out a breath. My hands are shaking a little.

> Out of curiosity, do you want me to cut it because it's not true, or because it is?

I stare at the question for a long time before typing a response.

> The truth doesn't matter.

Maya Harper doesn't live in Plumpton, and I wish I had better things to do than take a five-hour round-trip drive to Austin to see Savvy's sister, but I don't. So I go.

I don't tell her I'm coming, because she hates me and will probably call the cops. Ambushing her so that I have at least fifteen minutes before the cops arrive seems like the best option.

I have no idea where she lives, and even if Ben does, I can't bring myself to ask him. I don't want him to know that I'm going to see her. He already knows too much.

But I do know where Maya works. She's an assistant at an accounting firm, which has their hours listed on their website. They're in a half-empty strip mall between an employment agency and an empty storefront with a *For Rent* sign in the grimy window. I park my car at the back of the small lot by four thirty and wait.

"*He fucking deserved it,*" Savvy sings in my ear.

I close my eyes, my heart pounding. I don't want to think about this, but I'm sitting here waiting for the only other person in the world who knows Savvy's darkest secret.

"*I killed—*"

Savvy appears next to me, both feet up on the dash, blue toenail polish chipped. She flashes me a grin. "Want to know a secret?"

I nod.

"I killed a dude and I'm not sorry. He fucking deserved it."

LUCY

Savvy was still staring at me expectantly, waiting for me to take her up on her offer to murder my husband.

"Even if *we* wanted to kill him," I began slowly, "I think we'd be in way over our heads. Seeing as how neither of us has actually ever murdered someone before."

"Speak for yourself."

I barked out another laugh, but she didn't crack a smile. Her demeanor shifted, something dark and serious flashing across her eyes.

"Wait, you . . ." I trailed off, my breath catching in my throat.

She lowered her gaze from mine and nodded, once.

I stared at her, my heart in my throat. "Seriously?"

"Yes." The word was a whisper, but then she straightened, shaking her head like she wanted to clear it of bad thoughts.

"Yes, seriously," she said, her tone now with a hard edge to it. "I killed a dude and I'm not sorry. He fucking deserved it."

"Savvy." I grabbed her hand. I didn't think I believed her about not being sorry.

Or maybe I was wrong. Apparently I didn't know everything about Savvy.

"It's okay. I don't have trauma about it." She shrugged in a way that was supposed to convey how casual she felt, but it seemed forced to me.

"Who was he? What did he do to you?"

"Troy. An asshole I met in a bar who thought he could put his hands on me. He was wrong." She flashed me a dark grin.

"Jesus, Savvy—"

"I'm fine."

"Did you go to the police? It was self-defense, right?"

"The police." She snorted. "No. I think the self-defense argument would have looked a little thin, given how many times I stabbed him."

"How—how many times did you stab him?" My voice was a whisper.

"Maybe a few more times than was strictly necessary. Plus a couple more for good luck."

I didn't know whether I was horrified or impressed.

"I thought the blood would bother me more, honestly." Savvy shrugged. "It was a mess, which was annoying. This guy saw me coming out of the restroom with blood all over my hands, and I panicked for a minute, and then just went, 'Oh my god, my period is so bad today!' You should have seen the look on his face."

I gaped at her.

"And then I put him in my car, drove him out to the swamp, and dumped him in there. I thought for sure they'd find the body eventually, but I never heard anything. Maybe the gators ate him."

Impressed. I was impressed.

"You put him in your car? A dead body? How did you even get him in there?"

"Hey." She flexed her biceps. "I'm strong."

"Lifting-a-dead-body strong?"

"He wasn't a big guy."

I gave her a skeptical look.

"It took fucking forever," she mumbled. "Thank god I had a

hatchback. I could just sort of drag the body in there and cover him with a blanket."

I barked out a laugh. I quickly clapped my hand over my mouth to cut it off. "I'm sorry. It's not funny."

"It's *hilarious*." She poured a shot of tequila into a glass and nudged it in my direction. She poured one for herself and immediately tossed it back.

I lifted mine as well, but hesitated as I watched her fill her glass again.

"That's why you left college," I said quietly. "Your mom keeps telling everyone that you missed home, but that wasn't it."

She rolled her eyes and threw back the second shot. "Who the fuck *misses* Plumpton? No. I didn't like college. I'm supposed to take out tens of thousands of dollars in student loans just so I can sit in a lecture hall while a bored professor recites everything I just read in the wildly overpriced textbook? No thanks."

I watched as she downed another shot. She lowered the glass to the bar, and I reached for her hand, lacing our fingers together.

"I'm sorry that happened to you."

She shrugged.

"Seriously, Savvy," I said softly. "You don't have to pretend with me that it wasn't a big deal."

She nudged her glass with her finger, glancing up at me briefly. She lifted one shoulder, like *no big deal*, but her eyes told a different story. She squeezed my hand tightly.

"He deserved it," she whispered. "And so does Matt."

CHAPTER THIRTY

LUCY

Maya comes out of the office after five. There are only two other cars left in the lot, and I'm guessing hers is the purple hatchback. I lurk next to it.

She stops short when she sees me. Her car key is sticking out from between two fingers, like they always say to do to ward off would-be rapists.

"Lucy." It comes out as a gasp, like she's scared.

She probably is, come to think of it.

I raise both my hands in surrender. "I just want to talk."

She squints at me. She was a teenager last time I saw her— eighteen, just graduating from high school and getting ready to leave for college.

"*I shouldn't have told her.*" I can still see Savvy sitting on her bed in her tiny apartment with the sloped ceilings. "*Fuck. She's still a teenager, but . . .*"

"*You were a teenager when you killed him?*" I'd guessed, and she'd nodded, clearly relieved I understood.

Maya stares at me. She and Savvy never looked much alike. Maya's hair is lighter, the kind of blond that people usually have to buy from a bottle. Her features are sharper than Savvy's were—the long nose and pointed chin are different from her sister. She's wearing a full coral skirt and a button-up white blouse with a rounded collar. It's a sweet outfit. Savvy didn't do sweet.

But the eyes are the same. Blue, furious. Sweat trickles down my back.

"Can we go somewhere?" I ask. "It's hot out here."

"I don't have anything to say to you." She presses the button to unlock her car.

"Please, Maya . . ." I take a step forward but then trail off, because I don't know how to start a conversation about this.

She glares at me. "Look, I know that everyone has decided you're innocent now, but I still don't want to talk to you."

Everyone's decided I'm innocent? That's news to me.

"It's not that," I say. She opens her car door and throws her purse inside. I say my next words in a rush. "I know about Troy."

She slides into her car seat, gathering her skirt up so it won't get caught in the door. "I don't know who that is."

I grab the door before she can shut it. "The man Savvy killed."

Her head snaps to me, her face draining of color. She stares at me for a minute.

"Get in the car."

Maya starts driving, and then seems to think better of taking me wherever she was originally thinking. She pulls into the parking lot of a long-deserted restaurant and parks beneath some trees.

"That was his name?" she asks. "Troy?"

"Yes. She didn't tell you?" I unbuckle my seat belt so I can face her. I can't stop noticing how her white shirt is still pristine, even though it's the end of the workday. I would have spilled my coffee and lunch on it by now.

She chews on her bottom lip and shakes her head. "And I didn't ask. I don't think I wanted to know."

I'd wanted to know. I wanted to know his name and what he looked like and what blood smells like when there's that much of it.

Maya looks at me quickly. "Do you know his last name? I've

always wondered if maybe someone knew that it was Savvy and they're the ones who—" She stops as I shake my head.

"Troy Henderson. I looked into it years ago. Hired a PI, actually."

I didn't have the money for it back then, but it was my only solid lead, and I refused to tell the police about him. I wouldn't betray Savvy like that.

"Nothing?" She already looks crushed.

"No, I'm sorry. His body still hasn't been found. From what my PI gathered, he'd been known to get wasted and start fights with people. The case is still open, but I don't think anyone is looking for him all that hard. When the PI talked to his sister, she didn't even realize he was missing. She thought he'd moved away and never called."

"Oh."

"I'm sorry. I should have told you earlier, but . . ." But she was young, and starting her freshman year of college just having lost her sister. I didn't want to pop up like, *Hi! Remember how your dead big sister murdered someone?*

"I wouldn't have wanted to hear from you back then anyway."

"Do you want to hear from me *now*?"

She cocks a blond eyebrow, almost amused. "Good point."

"I can send you the stuff my PI found, if you want."

She leans back in her seat, blowing out a long breath. "You really don't remember that night, do you?"

"No."

"My mom never believed you, but it doesn't make much sense to hire a PI to investigate a lead if you killed her yourself." She turns to meet my eyes. "And then not even tell us about it. That was the best defense you had, you know. Her killing Troy."

"I know."

"Would you have told someone, if they'd actually arrested and charged you with her murder?"

I look out the window. "Maybe." I liked to think I wouldn't have, but it's possible that the prospect of a few decades behind bars would have broken my loyalty to Savvy.

I clear my throat and look at her. "As far as I know, Savvy never told anyone except the two of us. Right?"

"She said that only you knew when she told me."

"I'm not telling Ben," I say. "Just so you know. No matter what happens, I'm not telling him."

"You're really talking to that podcaster? Like, giving him an interview?"

"Yes. We've already started."

"Wow." She stares out the front window. "I told him some stuff about Matt, but he said he cut it out."

"I know."

"You know?"

"He asked me about it. I wouldn't confirm it, so he cut it. Legal reasons, I think." I have no idea whether that's true, but it sounds true. "Matt's already threatened to sue him."

"I'm sorry. I shouldn't have said it. I regretted it after we hung up."

I shrug. I wish she hadn't, but I can't bring myself to be mad about it. "I'm glad you said something about Savvy and Matt. You're right that she never would have slept with him."

She shudders, like just the thought of it grosses her out.

"I just wanted to make sure that we were on the same page," I say. "About never telling anyone about Troy. Ever."

"We're on the same page."

She reaches for the shifter and then stops, pulling her hand back and meeting my gaze again. "I wish she'd told me that you knew too."

"Why?"

"Because I thought that you didn't really know her. Most people didn't really know Savvy."

"No, they didn't."

"I should have guessed, though. You were different than her other friends. She stopped hating Plumpton so much after you moved back. She was happier."

I swallow around the lump in my throat. I knew this, but it feels different, coming from Maya. Like it's actually true, and not just a wild hope. I have to close my eyes and take a breath, because for a moment I miss Savvy so much that it physically hurts.

"I was happier too," I say quietly.

I look up at Maya to see her roughly wiping away tears. We share a sad smile.

She clears her throat and throws the car in reverse. "Promise me you'll do everything you can to catch the asshole who did it, okay? Savvy deserves that much."

"I promise."

CHAPTER THIRTY-ONE

LUCY

I text Ben the next morning as I get in my car. I turn the key in the ignition, the warm air blasting in my face as the car starts.

I'm going to Matt's. If I turn up dead, do a podcast about my murder.

He hasn't responded by the time I pull up in front of my old house.

I bound up the front walkway before I can change my mind. This is probably a deeply stupid idea, but Matt won't answer my calls, and if I don't confront him soon, I'm going to explode.

"Let's kill your husband."

Shush, Savvy. We're not murdering anyone today.

The door swings open before I reach it, and I stop short.

A woman steps out, dragging two large suitcases behind her. She's tiny—five feet, maybe—and she struggles with the bags, which probably weigh more than she does. One of them topples over on its side and she curses.

"You want some help?" I ask.

Her head snaps up. Her eyes are blue, and bloodshot. The red curls she has tied up in a bun are coming loose, hanging over one shoulder. She's a mess, but still stunning.

She stares at me.

"Wife number two?" I guess.

"Julia," she says.

"Lucy."

"I know."

She hasn't answered my question about help, but I grab the toppled bag anyway. We drag them to the Lexus in the driveway and I help her load them both in the trunk. She slams it shut and turns to me.

"What are you doing here?" she asks.

"I need to talk to Matt."

"About what?"

That seems intrusive, considering we just met, but I guess she's still technically married to the man.

"Murder."

She bursts into tears.

My phone buzzes, and I don't know what to do about this crying replacement wife, so I open my purse and glance at the screen. There are two texts from Ben.

THAT'S NOT FUNNY.

Are you really at Matt's right now?

Julia sniffles, drawing my attention back to her. She grabs my hands. Hers are very cold, which is weird in this weather.

"Don't go in there," she says. "He's in a bad mood."

I'll bet he is. My phone buzzes again.

"Let me help you," she continues.

I cock my head, confused. "Help me?"

"You know that podcaster, right? I want to talk to him."

Ben and Paige meet us in his hotel room. I want to leave, but Julia keeps tearfully looking at me like we're in this together.

I avoid Ben's gaze as we step into the room and Paige introduces them. Maybe I'm worried that both Paige and Julia will immediately know we're having sex if I look at him.

Maybe I'm just really, really annoyed that the man I'm sleeping with has so much information about my life, and now he's going to have so much information about my marriage. I miss Nathan, and that glazed, far-off look he got when I was speaking.

Ben gets Julia a cup of coffee, and I sit beside her on the couch while she holds it in her freezing hands. Ben's microphone is on the table in front of us, but he hasn't turned it on yet.

"I want to do an interview," she says. "About Matt."

"Okay." Ben smiles in this soft, gentle way that I think is meant to be nonthreatening. He's never smiled at me like that, thank god. "What about Matt?"

"About . . . our marriage. And some things he said about Lucy." She glances at me apologetically.

"Did you know Savannah?" Ben asks, even though I'm fairly certain he knows the answer to that question.

Julia shakes her head. She's fixed her hair and is far more put together now. She's one of those women who can do an effortless messy bun, and I dislike that about her. "No. I never met her. I don't know anything about her or . . ." She looks at me again.

"Should I leave?" I ask hopefully. "This will probably be easier to talk about when I'm gone."

"No." She grabs my hand, wrapping her icy fingers around mine.

"Lucy can step out when you begin the interview," Paige says. I try not to look too relieved. I carefully extract my hand from Julia's grip.

"I want to talk about what Matt is actually like. What our marriage is like. Because all the things that the women in our neighborhood said about him . . ." She reaches for her coffee and takes a slow sip. "I can't let them do that. I thought I could let it go, but if I don't say something, I'm never going to be able to live with myself."

Paige's eyes dart to mine, and I can tell from that quick look that Ben didn't share the end of Maya's interview with her. She's caught off guard.

"Telling the truth isn't going to do shit for you, honey," Savvy whispers.

I stand, because I really can't take much more of this. Julia looks up at me, startled.

"I should go." I move around the coffee table and head to the door. "If people knew I was here when she tells you . . ." I grab the door handle. "You don't want me here for it."

Julia looks like she's going to protest, but Paige nods. "She's right. We'll see you later, Lucy."

I throw open the door and practically run out.

Listen for the Lie Podcast with Ben Owens
BONUS EPISODE 2

Julia Gardner showed up on my doorstep unexpectedly one day. I received word she wanted to talk to me, and I said sure, even though I was confused about what she would have to say about this case. Matt Gardner's wife never met Savannah, and from what I'd heard from neighbors, they were a perfectly happy couple. Matt hit the jackpot with his second wife, as one person told me.

As it turns out, Matt and Julia have been separated for a couple months now.

Ben: You moved out today?

Julia: Yes. Well, I partially moved out two months ago. I went back for more of my stuff today because he said he'd be out of town. He wasn't, but I should have expected that.

Ben: Let's back up a bit. You and Matt have been married for . . . ?

Julia: Three years.

Ben: How'd you meet?

Julia: I was attending a conference in Houston, and he was there visiting some friends. We met at the hotel bar and just hit it off. We dated long-distance for a while, and then I moved out to Plumpton to be with him. We got married not long after.

Ben: Tell me about Matt.

Julia: He was really— No, I was going to say he was charming, but that's not the right word. He's not charming, exactly. He's comfortable. He's one of those people that, when you meet him, it feels like you've been friends for a long time. He has this way of putting people at ease. I'm not very good at talking to strangers, so I noticed that about him right away. It didn't feel like he was hitting on me in that hotel bar, it genuinely felt like he was just being friendly. Not very common with men.

It all felt very nice, at first. He was very open with me about his past, about Lucy, and it made me feel like he was an honest man. I was looking for that in a relationship. But things moved really quickly, and he pushed hard for me to come to Plumpton. I just thought he wasn't scared of commitment.

Once I got out here, and moved into the house, things changed a little. I brushed it off, mostly. He was moodier, more likely to snap at me, but that's what happens, isn't it? You get comfortable in a relationship and you stop being so polite.

Then he was yelling more, and I realized that he was drinking quite a lot. He'd hide the bottles at the bottom of the trash can outside so I wouldn't see them. He'd been avoiding me in the evenings, holing up in his study by himself, and I realized that it was because he was drinking down there.

I tried to bring it up with him—gently—and he got really mad and told me to stop being such a prude. He said he liked to relax with a drink at night, and that I shouldn't be complaining about him taking out the trash. Did I want him to just leave it all for me to do?

I sort of saw through those excuses, but I also didn't want to badger him about his drinking if he wasn't ready to talk about it. You can't make people accept that they have a problem, you know? They have to come to it themselves.

But, unfortunately, I guess he took that as the all-clear to just drink in front of me. And he was *not* nice when he drank. We'd just gotten married when he really started to let loose—that's probably *why* he let loose, come to think of it—and I was a little baffled about how to handle it all. And I felt like I'd been a bit of an idiot. I knew he had a problem when we got married. I'd gone in clear-eyed about it.

But then the violence started.

At first, it was throwing glasses at walls and taking out his anger on stuff around the house. Then it was me. Slapping and pulling my hair and shoving me into walls. He was always yelling at me about how I'd hit him too, how it was my fault too, and I was just like . . . what are you talking about? I haven't touched you.

Ben: To be clear, he was hitting you—*abusing* you—but telling you that *you* were hitting *him*?

Julia: Yes. Constantly. The next morning, I'd say, if you ever slap me like that again I'm leaving you, and he'd go, you slapped me back, you have no room to talk. Which *never* happened.

Ben: What was his response when you told him that?

Julia: Sometimes he'd look genuinely confused. Like he really had thought that we'd been going nine rounds instead of him just . . . it was only him. I wondered if maybe he was so drunk that he didn't remember what happened, so he was just saying that.

Ben: Did you ever feel safe telling anyone about this?

Julia: My mom. I'd edit it a little, try to make it sound not so bad because I didn't want her to worry. But I definitely didn't want to tell anyone in Plumpton. They were all so crazy about Matt. And I worried he'd tell them all that I'd hit him too, even though it wasn't true.

The thing is . . . this is probably really weird, but the person I most wanted to talk to was Lucy Chase.

Ben: Even though you'd never met her?

Julia: Yeah. And that's weird, right? No second wife *wants* to talk to the first wife. Especially a first wife who has been accused of murder. But I wanted to know if their marriage had been the same, because Matt talked about her so . . . kindly.

Ben: I'm sorry, *kindly*?

Julia: Yeah. It was one of the things I liked about him at first, actually. I've never liked men who speak badly of their exes. It usually feels a bit misogynistic to me.

Matt actually seemed sort of sad when he talked about Lucy. He said she was sweet and kind and he felt bad that she had to leave the town she loved. He openly told me he still loved her, but that they just couldn't be together anymore. He said that he hoped she was happy.

Ben: Did you ask why they got divorced, then? If he still loved her?

Julia: I did, and he said that she left him, which is true, I think. He said that it was all just too much for her, being in Plumpton after Savvy's murder. But, of course, later I wondered if it was because he'd been hitting her too.

And I wondered if it was just me. Maybe he'd been so devastated by that divorce that he started drinking, and he changed. That's why I wanted to talk to her. But I didn't reach out, of course. That would have been too weird.

Ben: You've met her just today, though, haven't you?

Julia: Yes. I met her today, by chance. I didn't ask, though. I wanted to, but it's not my place. I could tell that she didn't . . . Well, she has enough problems. She doesn't need mine too.

Ben: How long did the abuse go on with Matt before you left?

Julia: Only about six months. It ramped up really slowly, and so there was only about half a year of me going, am I really doing this? Is this my life? How have I wandered into this abused-wife narrative? It almost felt unreal. I think I might have left earlier, had I not been so confused about how I ended up in that situation.

Ben: Was it okay? Leaving?

Julia: My mom came up and stood in the house while I packed, so he was forced to be on his best behavior. He yelled a lot when I was there today—I was alone—but it was fine. I told him that my mom and my friends knew I'd come up to Plumpton, just in case.

Ben: Just in case something happened to you? Right? I just want to make sure I have this straight—you felt the need to let someone know you were going to see Matt, because you were worried that something might happen to you while you were there?

Julia: Well, it sounds quite dramatic when you put it like that. But . . . yes.

I start to end the interview here, and Julia almost lets me, but she jumps back in, looking flustered.

Julia: No, I just . . . Can I say one more thing? I need to tell you something.

Ben: Of course.

Julia: It's something Matt said about Lucy once. When he was drunk. *Very* drunk, actually. He was going off on this tangent that he did sometimes. I think it was to make me feel bad. Talking about how wonderful Lucy was. It never really made me feel bad, though. Or, not in the way he probably thought it would? I'd get pissed at him, but just even more intrigued about Lucy.

Anyway. He was talking and talking, and he said, "I should have protected her better." And I was like, "You mean after the murder?" Because I knew that he'd sent her to her parents after and felt guilty about it.

And he was like, "No, that night. I should have protected her better."

I was like, "What do you mean? You weren't there, right? Do you mean you should have left the wedding with her?" I was fishing for information, because Matt *never* talked about that night.

And I could see him have this, like, moment of clarity where he realized what he said, and his face just turned bright red. And he muttered something about how, yeah, that was what he meant, but . . . I don't think that was true.

I think he was there, with Lucy, when Savvy died.

CHAPTER THIRTY-TWO

LUCY

Ben gets Julia's episode up bright and early Monday morning. I listen to it while I run on the treadmill, and apparently, I'm not the only one tuning in first thing, because I have a bunch of missed calls and several texts on my phone when I'm done. I read them as I walk across the parking lot to my car, sweat trickling down my back.

> Grandma: Hon, can you call me? Or come by. Any time.

> Dad: Did you leave already? Your mom and I want to talk to you.

> Nathan: Hey, is everything okay down there? Just because we broke up doesn't mean we can't still be friends. If you want to talk about anything.

> Emmett: Do you want to get lunch soon?

Christ, I'm so popular suddenly. People find out that your first husband has been slapping around his second wife and everyone makes assumptions.

I sit in my car for several minutes with the AC blasting in my face, thinking about what to do about those assumptions.

On the one hand, they're right.

On the other hand, they can all go fuck themselves.

I don't appreciate them turning me into the victim of this story.

Savvy's the victim. She was buffed and polished after her death and turned into the perfect victim I could never be. Let's leave it that way.

Another text pops up on my phone.

Hey, it's Julia. Ben gave me your number.

I told him he could do that. Now I wish I hadn't.

I hope you're okay. I'm happy to talk, whenever you're ready.

I wonder whether she really never fought back. Did Matt just confuse us, or did she snap like me, and decide to get out ahead of the story?

God, I hope it's the latter. She's so tiny and cute, no one would ever believe that she hit him. I hope she beat his ass.

I stare at her texts. I'm never going to give her what she needs. I'm not a supportive shoulder.

I quickly type out a reply.

Thanks. Good luck with everything.

"*If you stab him in the neck, it'll be quick,*" Savvy whispers in my ear. "*Do you want it to be quick?*"

Julia is definitely better off without me.

My phone rings—Grandma—but I ignore it. I have to make a choice. If I tell the truth, and admit that Matt hit me, he will *definitely* tell everyone that I fought back. It won't matter that it was months before I snapped. It won't matter that I suffered through countless nights of screaming insults and stinging slaps and being thrown against walls so hard it's a miracle my head isn't dented.

I did, eventually, snap, and it'll just be further proof of my evil, violent heart.

Of course she killed Savvy! Instead of leaving her abusive husband she hit him right back! Who does that?

If I lie, I leave Julia out to dry. I should care about that. Woman solidarity and all that.

But there's no reason people won't believe her. Julia is not me. She's still likable. Still a good victim.

My options are shitty, but I know what I'm going to do.

No one expects the truth from me anyway.

"He did have a temper when he drank, but my experience with Matt was not exactly the same as Julia's." I say the words like I practiced them. I already said them to Ben, in a long interview this afternoon. Both he and Paige looked at me like they thought I was full of shit.

My mom, however, looks relieved. She's standing in the kitchen, leaning on one crutch. Dad is behind her, a spatula in his hand like he's going to threaten someone with it. Grandma sits at the table. They've all been waiting for me to get home. I spent the entire day avoiding them.

"What does that mean, *not exactly the same?*" Grandma squints.

"Like I said. He had a temper. He threw some glasses at the wall, stomped around a lot."

"But he didn't hit you?" Dad asks nervously.

"Of course he didn't hit her!" Mom exclaims. "She lived five miles down the road then. We would have known."

I lift an eyebrow. I'd planned to be a little more straightforward in my denial, but Mom is making this difficult. My sense of self-preservation is really battling it out with my desire to prove my mother wrong.

"I don't think that anyone knows what's going on inside someone else's marriage," I say. "No matter how close they live."

Everyone freezes.

Dad still has the spatula poised in front of him like a weapon. He has a familiar look in his eyes, one I used to see often as a kid. Like he's afraid I'm about to say something that he'll have to deal with, and it's the absolutely last thing in the world that he wants to do right now.

"But I will not be making any tearful podcast confessions, if that's what you're worried about," I quickly add.

Mom lets out a breath, like that was exactly what she was worried about. Dad sets the spatula on the counter, blessedly free from having to do battle for me today.

"We're worried about *you!*" Grandma says.

"Well, I'm happily single now, so it doesn't really matter anyway." I smile. "What's for dinner?"

"Gnocchi!" Mom says, overly chipper, and points to Dad, who is now struggling to open the package.

Grandma throws her hands up in the air. "What the fuck? Are we going to talk about the fact that it was probably *Matt* who killed Savvy?"

Dad spills the gnocchi all over the floor.

CHAPTER THIRTY-THREE

LUCY

Matt: I'm outside. Can you come down?

The text pops up on my phone after ten o'clock. The house is quiet, Mom and Dad already asleep.

I climb out of bed and creep across the room to the window to see Matt's car parked in front of the house. A dark figure leans against it.

I should probably ignore the text, pretend to be asleep. But I still desperately want to confront him, and I didn't get a chance to in the middle of the replacement-wife drama.

I text back, I'll be down in a minute, pull on a pair of shorts, tie my hair up, and head downstairs. I slip on a pair of flip-flops and walk out into the humid air.

He straightens when he sees me coming, sliding his hands out of his pockets. Behind him, the streetlight shines on the pavement, providing enough light to see him clearly. The knuckles on his right hand are bruised, and I wonder whether it's from a face or a wall.

"I met your wife," I say.

"I know, she told me."

"Seems nice." I lift an eyebrow. "Nicer than me."

His jaw works, and he looks past me at nothing. I hope she told him over the phone, and not in person, because I can feel the fury coming off him in waves.

"You ignored my texts," I say.

He pinches the bridge of his nose with two fingers. "Things are so fucked up."

"You just noticed?"

He laughs, shortly at first, and then again, a bigger laugh that makes a smile linger on his face. "God, I miss you."

"*Poison would be less messy, but also less satisfying, in my opinion,*" Savvy whispers.

"Yes, your wife did make it sound that way on the podcast." I lean against the car next to him.

"She was always too nice for me."

What a load of shit.

"I should have known I would mess her up. I just thought that a nice girl like that . . ."

"Could save you?"

"Yes."

"You don't deserve to be saved, Matt."

He frowns, but doesn't argue. "I heard that you didn't say the same. About me. About . . ." He clears his throat. "You said things were different for you."

"You *heard*?"

"Yeah."

I wonder whether he heard directly from Mom, or if she's just told so many people that it got back to him.

"I said my experience was different than Julia's, which is true. I'm not really eager to rehash the past."

He turns to me, genuine gratitude on his face. "Thank you."

"Trust me when I say that it wasn't even a little bit for you."

"*You can't tell people about us, Lucy.*" Matt's face from five years ago appears in front of me. The day he kicked me out of the house and told me to go to my parents'.

"*Savvy is* dead, *Matt*," I'd choked out. "*Our shit doesn't matter right now.*"

"*It will matter to the police. Don't make me tell them about what we did to each other, okay? Don't make me tell them.*"

I'd realized what he was saying—that if the police were looking for evidence that I'd been violent before, Matt could certainly give that to them. I could try to refute it, try to explain that *he* was the abusive one, but it was muddled now.

People don't believe women who fight back. When a man lashes out, people say he's lost control of his temper or made a terrible mistake. When a woman does it, she's a psychopath.

Matt steps forward suddenly, drawing me back to the present. He pushes me up against the car. The length of his body presses against mine, and then his mouth is on mine too.

He tastes like mint, not alcohol, and it reminds me of our early years. Toward the end, he always tasted like booze. Or smelled like it. It was seeping from his pores, eventually.

But this Matt is the one I liked, at first.

"*I think I'm going to miss him,*" I'd said to Savvy. "*That's fucked up, right? That I'm going to miss him?*"

I tense and want to recoil, but I'm kissing him back instead. It's partly habit. Partly instinct. Always just easier to go along with it and not piss him off.

"*He doesn't deserve you.*"

I bite his lip, hard.

He pulls away, amusement in his eyes, like he thinks that was meant to be sexy instead of a failed attempt to draw blood. "Sorry. It's hard not to kiss you sometimes, you know?"

"Try."

"Come home with me."

"No."

I have one tiny shred of common sense, and I'm proud of it.

He sighs, but doesn't argue.

"Is Julia right?" I ask. "Were you there when Savvy died?"

He shakes his head. "No."

"After?"

"No." He turns to me. "I'm sorry I abandoned you after. That's what I meant when I said that to Julia. I should have stuck by you. Not sent you to your fucking parents, who just let Ivy interrogate you."

I don't know whether he's lying. Matt's a great liar.

"Who was the woman you were arguing with in our driveway that night?"

"I really don't think it's fair to drag her into this."

"Why not?"

"Listen." He puts both hands out, like he needs me to calm down. I consider jumping in my car and mowing him down. Then backing up over the body just to make sure he's dead. "She's not involved in Savvy's death, okay? I promise that she never hurt Savvy."

"How nice that you have so much faith in her," I say dryly.

"I deserved that."

Sweat is starting to trickle down my back. I let the silence stretch out for a long time before speaking again. "You know everyone is starting to think it's you."

He nods, eyes downcast.

"Maybe they have a point."

His head snaps up, genuine bafflement on his face. "You think *I* killed Savvy?"

"How's it feel, asshole?"

"That's . . ." He closes his eyes for a moment. "That's fair. But I . . ." He closes his eyes briefly. "Lucy, please just drop it."

"Just *drop it*? You lied and—"

"Please." He grabs my hands. I try to pull them free, but he holds firm, his eyes pleading. "Go back to L.A., Lucy. Stop helping that podcaster. Trust me, okay?"

"Trust you?" I repeat incredulously.

"I know that it doesn't seem like it, but I've always just wanted to protect you. I'm still protecting you." He squeezes my hands. His eyes have gone shiny.

My heart dives to my feet. I yank my hands away and stumble as I step back. The world is swaying.

"Matt, did we see each other after Savvy dropped you off that night?"

"No." He says it again, immediately, like an automatic response he practiced. I don't believe him.

I push down the panic rising in my chest. "Just tell me who it was, okay? Who came over to see you that night? At one in the morning?"

"Lucy, just . . . don't, okay?"

"Just tell me, Matt. You owe it to me."

He sighs, running a hand down his face. "It was Nina. Nina Garcia."

CHAPTER THIRTY-FOUR

LUCY

It was Nina, I text Ben the next day, as I sit down in Mom's office with my laptop. I'm ignoring Matt's advice to stop helping Ben. Fuck Matt. If I did it, then let Ben figure it out. The smug bastard deserves it, after all his hard work.

The person who Matt was fighting with in our driveway after the wedding, I add.

I'm going to need you to tell me that story with the mic on, he replies immediately. Come over? Do an interview? And stay?

I'm tempted to run over there immediately.

Interview and stay? Is that like the podcaster version of Netflix and chill?

Maybe.

I have to write for a few hours. I can come later.

Okay. Does Nina know you know?

Not unless Matt told her.

Do me a favor and don't say anything yet.

I should be more protective of my high school best friend, but I know exactly why Nina was dropping by to see Matt in the middle of the night, even if he wouldn't admit it.

No problem.

Ben greets me at his hotel room door with a smile. He's barefoot, in jeans and a faded T-shirt. It's cute in a way I both hate and love.

"Let's do this," he says, walking to the small table in the corner where the mics are set up. "Then I thought we could order some food?"

I nod. He turns on the microphones.

"You saw Matt recently?" he prompts.

"Yeah, he showed up at my house last night. He wanted to talk about . . ." I trail off, deliberately. "He just wanted to talk. And I wanted to know who he was fighting with that night after getting home, so I went out to talk to him. I'd been trying to get in touch with him for days, but he's been ignoring me."

"Did he tell you?"

"Yeah. He said it was Nina Garcia."

"*I told you she was a bitch,*" Savvy says. I try my best to ignore her.

"Did he say why she was dropping by in the middle of the night? And why he lied about it?"

"He sure didn't. But . . . well, you've heard what people have been saying about our marriage. I doubt she was coming over so they could go play checkers together."

Ben's mouth twists like he's trying not to laugh. He makes me recount the whole conversation, which means I have to carefully navigate around our discussion of Julia and that moment when I let him kiss me.

Not how innocent people act.

"Okay, it's off," Ben says, switching the mic off when we finish. "I guess we know now why Nina doesn't like me."

"Or it's just your personality."

He winks at me.

* * *

I wake up in his bed, alone. The clock on the nightstand says 3:38, and I roll over to see the bathroom door open, the room dark. Light filters in under the door from the living room.

I slide out of bed, find my underwear and tank top on the floor, and pull them on. I push open the door and peek out.

Ben sits on the ground next to the sliding glass door, wearing a T-shirt and boxer briefs. It's cracked open, and he's smoking a joint, blowing the smoke out the door. A half-finished drink is on the floor next to him.

He turns when I step outside the bedroom. "Hey."

"Can't sleep?"

He shakes his head and then holds the joint out, offering it to me.

"No, thanks." I walk across the room and sit down across from him.

"Matt texted you." He points to my phone, which is on the coffee table.

I reach over and grab it. "You're not even going to pretend that you didn't look at my phone?"

"Nope." One side of his mouth lifts. "In my defense, it flashed on the screen like half an hour ago and I just happened to see his name."

I unlock my phone and read the message. Sent at three in the morning. He must be drunk.

I'm sorry. Can we talk?

"He wants to talk." I put the phone back on the table.

"Are you going to?"

"No. He's just drunk."

He takes a hit off the joint and peers at me. "Do you want to talk about it?"

"My drunk ex-husband?"

"Everything . . . involving your drunk ex-husband."

"No."

"Is there a reason you never want to talk about him?"

"I talk about— Wait, off the record?"

"Yes. We're in our underwear."

"Being in just your underwear means you're off the record?"

"I mean, I think it should."

I stretch my legs out, crossing one ankle over the other. Ben puts a hand on my calf. "I talk about him. But I'm not interested in recounting my sad marriage story for your podcast listeners."

"Your sad marriage story is probably relevant."

He has no idea *how* relevant. I shrug.

Ben slowly blows out smoke. "Was he that big of a dick when you married him?"

I give him an amused look. "No. Or, yes. I don't know. He was a more lovable dick. Or I was more tolerant of assholes then. Probably a combination of the two."

"I don't really recognize the version of you that people talk about." Ben finishes the joint and reaches up to drop it in an empty glass on the end table. "The twenty-two-year-old Lucy who married him sounds like a completely different person, the way they talk about you."

"I was, in a way. I was Plumpton Lucy. Same girl I was in high school." I reach for his drink and take a sip. It's straight whiskey, and it burns as it goes down. "I always admired that about Savvy. She was so different than she was in high school. She wasn't afraid to . . ."

"*I thought it would be more upsetting, being covered in blood,*" she whispers in my ear.

Ben looks at me expectantly.

". . . change," I finish.

"It doesn't sound like you were so bad in high school," he says.

"You were the type of girl who went around punching assholes. I think we would have gotten along."

"Or I would have punched you."

He laughs. His eyes are slightly bloodshot, and he's loose, high. "I was a huge nerd in high school."

"I want to see you as a teenage nerd. Show me a picture."

"No," he says, with little to no conviction.

"Come on. You spend your days obsessing over every detail of my past. You've probably seen every picture taken of me in my early twenties."

He squints. "That's a really good point, actually." He sighs as he reaches for his phone. "Fine."

He swipes for a minute before turning the phone so I can see the screen. I take it from him.

It's a prom photo. He stands next to a pretty brunette girl in a green dress. His tie matches. His hair is too short and he has a giant pimple on his forehead. It looks like he hit his growth spurt later, because he's about the same height as his date, who's wearing flats. Or maybe she was just six feet tall.

"You liar." I pass the phone back to him.

He looks startled. "What?"

"You absolutely had girls lining up for you. You were cute and you know it."

"I was a nerd! A bumbling, awkward nerd. I talked about *Iron Man* a lot."

"Oh yes, talking about the billion-dollar Marvel franchise that everyone loves must have made you extremely uncool."

"Hey. It was slightly less cool back then."

"God, you're so smug. You had hot prom dates and won fancy student journalism prizes. You solve crimes on your own and you get murder suspects to have sex with you."

"Paige would be extremely annoyed to hear anyone thinks I solve crimes on my own. And how did you know I won fancy journalism prizes? You researched me?"

"You hired a PI to investigate me, so I don't think you have room to judge my light googling."

"I wasn't judging, I was flattered."

"Don't be."

He laughs, his fingers moving against my calf. I scoot forward a little, and his hand slides up to my thigh.

"What was your most likely thing?" I ask. "You know, in the yearbook? Like how I was 'Most Likely to Kill Her Best Friend.'"

"You were 'Most Likely to be a CEO by Thirty.'"

"Thanks, stalker."

"We didn't do those. I thought they were just a movie thing, actually. A movie thing and a small-town thing, apparently."

"What would you have been? Most likely to win a Pulitzer?"

He laughs. "I doubt it. Most likely to obsess over unsolved murders? I was known for it back then too."

"I know."

"You know?"

"It's in one of the Reddit threads about your podcast. Some people you went to high school with have weighed in there."

"Jesus, you should not be looking at any Reddit threads about me or you."

"Why? Because they call me a crazy murderer but say they'd still fuck me?"

"Yes! That's exactly why."

"This isn't news to me." I move even closer to him, parting my legs so I can wrap them around him and sit in his lap. His arms circle my waist.

I lean down to kiss him. "As one of the men who would definitely still fuck a crazy murderer, I don't think you have the right to look so scandalized."

His lips brush mine as he speaks. "I prefer not to use the word *crazy*. Not in that context, anyway."

"It's so interesting that it's the word *crazy* that bothers you and not *murderer*."

"I didn't say that word didn't bother me too."

I kiss him, looping my arms around his neck and shifting until I can feel that he's currently only bothered in the good way.

"Let's go back to the bedroom."

CHAPTER THIRTY-FIVE

LUCY

I wake a second time to a door opening. It's morning now, light streaming in through the blinds. Ben is on his stomach beside me, still asleep.

"*Ben!*" It's a familiar voice from the living room. Paige. "*Are you in there? You know I worry that someone murdered you when you don't answer my texts.*"

He stirs, groaning as he rubs a hand across his face. The clock says it's after ten. We were up late.

He rolls out of bed and pulls his boxers on. As he walks to the door, he holds his hand out. I think that means he wants me to stay put. He opens the door a crack.

"Hey."

"Hey— Dude, no. I do not want to see you in your underwear."

"Then don't barge into my hotel room at the crack of dawn."

"First of all, it's practically lunch. Second of all, you gave me a key, so I'm not sure what else you expected me to do with it."

"I need to shower. I'll meet you in your room in like an hour."

"It's going to take you an hour to shower?"

"I have stuff to do. Websites to browse. Political news to obsess over. Just give me a little while."

There's a long pause. "Please tell me you did not."

"Just give me—"

"I know that purse, you stupid motherfucker."

Ben stumbles backward as Paige barges into the room. I sit up, holding the sheet against my chest. Paige doesn't look surprised so much as defeated.

"Hey, Paige."

She presses a hand to her forehead. "Ben, I swear to god."

"Does it help if I tell you that this isn't the first time?" I ask.

Ben gives me a deeply exasperated look.

Paige points at him. "You stupid motherfucker," she says again, to really drive the point home.

Ben takes Paige by the shoulders and gently shoves her out of the room. He shuts the door behind them.

"Ben, what in the hell are you doing?" Paige whispers. I slide off the bed and grab my underwear, edging closer to the door so I can better hear them.

"Can we—"

"I don't know whether to be impressed or horrified that you figured out a way to fuck your own podcast."

"That is—"

"I told you that I would only work on this case with you if you kept it together, and this is not keeping it together. This is the exact opposite of keeping it together."

"Since when have you cared who I sleep with?"

"Since it's the woman we are currently reporting on! You know what people would think if this got out, right? You understand that she could unravel your entire season just by telling people you're sleeping together? No one would trust you."

"I understand that, but one, she wouldn't do that. And two, why would she even want to? This podcast is making her look better than she has in years."

I feel like I should be insulted by that, but he's not wrong.

"And when you say something she doesn't like? Why in the world would you trust this woman? She—"

"Can we talk about this later?" Ben interrupts.

They're both quiet for several seconds. I creep away from the door and pull on my clothes.

"We're still not giving you a heads-up about things coming up on the podcast!" Paige calls suddenly.

"Understood!" I yell, and decide not to tell her about Ben asking my permission to post that clip from Maya.

Listen for the Lie Podcast with Ben Owens

EPISODE SIX—"NINA"

After what we just heard Lucy say about Nina and Matt, I went through some of my old interviews where people mentioned her. I found something really interesting. Here again is Colin Dunn, in our very first interview.

Colin: Of all of Savvy's friends?

Ben: Yeah. Which ones did you know well?

Colin: Not really any of them. They're all older than me, so we weren't in school together . . . Oh! Nina. What's her last name? Branson?

Ben: Garcia. She changed it back to her maiden name after she got divorced.

Colin: Oh shit, she was married?

Ben: She was at one time. She's divorced now.

Colin: Oh, okay. Cool.

Ben: But you knew her?

Colin: A little, yeah.

Ben: But not well enough to know she was married with kids?

Colin: Oh shit, she has kids too?

Ben: Two.

Colin: Damn. Okay. Good for her. Oh no, wait. I think she did mention a kid once. Huh.

Ben: How did you know Nina?

Colin: We hung out a couple times. Just, you know. As friends.

I was unable to get in touch with Colin again to confirm a suspicion I had—which is pure speculation on my part, by the way—so I went to Joanna Clarkson for the scoop.

Joanna: Nina and Colin? Like in a romantic way?

Ben: Yeah. You ever hear anything about that?

Joanna: Hmmm . . . that boy sure does get around, doesn't he?

Ben: He does seem to be popular.

Joanna: Listen, hon, I don't think I should be confirming any rumors.

Ben: But there were rumors? About Nina and Colin?

Joanna: There were a lot of rumors about Colin. Who can say which ones are true?

Ben: Colin did tell me that he knew Nina.

Joanna: Hmmm. Well. Do with that what you will.

CHAPTER THIRTY-SIX

LUCY

Are you free for a drink?

Emmett's text comes as I'm finishing up work for the day in Mom's office, and it sends a flash of guilt up my spine. I never responded to his last text, and now Ben has released an episode in which I imply his girlfriend was sleeping with my husband. And then Ben implied that she was also sleeping with Savvy's boyfriend. Years before Emmett, but still. He's probably not having a great day.

I respond that I'd love to, and an hour later I'm sitting across from him at a slightly shady bar off the highway. I've never actually been to this bar, even though it's been here for years. I always assumed it was full of truckers who'd stare at my ass.

I was correct, turns out. Large men in cowboy hats gawk openly at me. An ancient country song plays softly over the speakers. It's peak Texas in here.

Emmett's at a tiny table in back, a full beer in front of him. He takes a sip as I approach, and then makes a face as he sets it back down.

I laugh. I can't help myself. He's just really cute sometimes, in a little-boy way. I'd forgotten that. It had made him seem a little goofy when we were kids—not the kind of guy I wanted to date—but it's endearing now.

He looks up and a smile flickers across his face. "Hey, Lucy."

"Not a good beer, I take it?" I slide into the seat next to him.

"I don't actually drink much. Not a fan of the taste. But it felt like the thing to do today." He takes another sip and grimaces again. I hold back my laugh this time, since he seems miserable.

I raise my eyebrows in question, and signal to the bartender that I'll have the same as him.

"Is this my fault?" I ask.

"No. Well, not exactly."

"The podcast?"

He sighs. "I hate that fucking podcast."

The bartender delivers my beer to the table. I take a drink. Emmett's looking at me expectantly, like I might agree, but I don't actually hate the podcast.

"She's upset?" I ask, treading carefully. I don't actually know what Emmett's upset about. Maybe that Nina was cheating on her husband? Or sleeping with her former best friend's husband? It's all a bit of a clusterfuck, but nothing that actually involves him.

He lets out a short, humorless laugh. "She is definitely upset." He takes a longer sip of his beer. No grimace this time. He's toughening up. "She's still sleeping with Matt."

I stop with my glass halfway to my mouth. "What?"

"Not all the time, but yeah. There had been some signs that she was cheating on me. I didn't want to believe it, but then that episode came out and she sort of broke down and admitted it."

On the bright side, it turns out I never should have been jealous of Nina. Her choices are just as stupid as mine.

"She said they had a connection ..." He rolls his eyes and sits back in his chair. "Their connection is drinking. They're both drunks."

Nina pounding that margarita floats through my memory.

"She'd been doing really good in recovery, and she said it helped that I didn't even like to drink that much. She wasn't tempted, you know? But Matt . . ." He shakes his head and takes another sip of his drink. "I hate Matt. I've fucking hated him since I met him."

My eyebrows shoot up. "Seriously?"

"Yes. I tried to be nice because he was your husband, but he's such a cocky asshole. And now after what he did to Julia and to—" He cuts himself off suddenly, red crawling up his neck.

I don't help him out.

He looks away. "I just really hate him. Actually, I was considering going over there and punching him, but I thought this might be a healthier option." He gestures at me.

I smile. "I'm always happy to get together to talk about how much Matt sucks."

He leans forward, resting his jaw on one hand. I can imagine how his stubble must feel when you touch it, and I almost reach out and touch the other side of his face.

I look down at my beer instead.

"It was stupid, dating Nina." He wraps his fingers around his glass. He has great hands, but I already knew that about him. "She's not the same person she was in high school, and I knew that. I knew she had issues. There just aren't a lot of options here."

"Why did you stay?" I ask.

"I don't know. It was supposed to be temporary, after college. But then you have an apartment and a job and it just seems so daunting, moving to another city. I kept putting it off and putting it off, and now I'm almost thirty and I guess this is where I live now."

"It's not too late. Look at me. I up and left."

His eyes flick up to mine. "I always admired that."

"Yeah? I think most people thought it was stupid."

"No, it was brave. And smart. No one likes you here."

I let out a surprised laugh. "Wow, Emmett, don't hold back."

"You know it's true." He smiles, and a silence settles between us that feels more charged than comfortable.

A lot of moments between the two of us had felt charged, especially as my marriage started to fall apart. One moment in particular comes back, making my heart pound.

"You can talk to me, you know." Emmett had me cornered in the upstairs hallway. Downstairs, I could hear Matt laughing with our friends.

"I know," I said softly.

"About anything." He jerked his finger in the direction of the living room. "Including him."

I took in a tiny breath and tried to keep my expression neutral. I tried to smile reassuringly, but it was hard when Emmett was looking at me like that. He didn't usually look at me like that. Like he wouldn't mind if I pushed him into the bedroom right now.

He put a hand on the wall behind me, so close suddenly that I could smell his soap. I rose up on my toes, and that was all the invitation he needed. His mouth covered my own, his body pressing against mine.

I almost pushed him into that bedroom. We could do it quickly, while Matt was still downstairs. I loved that idea. Maybe I'd even forget to put my underwear back on, so he could wonder later when he found it if something had happened.

I winced and quickly ducked away from Emmett.

"I'm sorry, I can't." I rushed away without looking at him. New low, considering using one of my best friends to piss off my husband. The friend I knew had feelings for me, probably since high school.

I reach for Emmett's hand. I'm actually a little surprised when he doesn't pull away.

"I wish I'd left with you that night," I say quietly.

He cocks his head in question.

"That night we kissed. I should have just left Matt and gone home with you."

"Oh." The word comes out as a laugh. "I would have loved that. And I honestly would have loved to see his face while you did it."

I laugh too. He squeezes my hand.

"You should come to L.A.," I say. "Just pack your stuff and come.

We can . . ." Hang out? Start over? I don't know how to finish the sentence.

He laces his fingers through mine. "Don't say that if you don't mean it."

I almost say, *Unless it turns out I actually did murder Savvy.* I almost make it a joke, and act like an asshole, as usual.

Instead, I smile. "I absolutely mean it."

Emmett's eyes catch something behind me, and his smile fades. He slowly drops my hand.

I turn. Keaton Harper is walking—stumbling, really—across the room toward me.

CHAPTER THIRTY-SEVEN

LUCY

"Calm down, I just want to talk."

Keaton says the words to me before I've had a chance to react to his strolling up to me and Emmett. I bite back the urge to point out that I'm totally calm. I'd rather not get murdered by Savvy's brother today.

Keaton pulls up a chair and plunks his beer down, sloshing some on the table.

He looks like Savvy. He always has, but it takes my breath away for a moment when he lifts his head to meet my gaze. Same blue eyes, same nose, same way of twisting their lips when they're nervous.

His eyes are clear, steady on mine. He's obviously tipsy, but not totally wasted. He takes a gulp of his beer like he's trying to rectify this.

"Why don't you finish that and I'll drive you home?" Emmett offers.

"I'm fine." He jerks his head in the general direction of the bar. "I have a ride."

He goes silent then, and Emmett and I exchange a glance.

"So, how have you been?" I finally ask. Maybe the suspected murderer is supposed to start the conversation in this situation.

He shrugs. "Fine. Got married. Had a kid."

He looks fairly miserable about both these choices, so I'm not sure how to respond.

"I want to talk to you about Savvy." He drains his beer, wipes the dribble from his beard, and signals the bartender for another.

"I sort of guessed."

"You and that podcaster are chummy now, right?"

A scene from last night, Ben's head between my thighs, flashes through my mind. "I don't think that *chummy* is the word."

"He's on your side," Keaton says.

"Ben is always only on Ben's side."

"When I talked to him, he seemed to be real sympathetic to you."

I shrug. The waitress sets a new beer down in front of him.

"Does he think you did it?" he asks.

"I don't know, why don't you ask him?"

He slumps back in his chair with a long sigh. "You are still a giant pain in the ass, you know that?"

"Hey—" Emmett starts.

"Yes," I say. "I am."

"But in a fun way," Emmett says helpfully. I laugh.

Keaton rolls his eyes. "Listen. I've been thinking."

"A dangerous pastime," I say.

"Yeah— Wait, what?" He waves his hand like he's annoyed with me. No one can blame him, considering I'm making *Beauty and the Beast* jokes while we're talking about his sister's murder. "I didn't know. About Matt."

"About Matt and Julia?" I ask, playing dumb. "No one did, from the sound of it."

Keaton pauses. Emmett takes a sip of his beer and grimaces.

"I didn't know he was a jerk."

Emmett snorts.

"What's that supposed to mean?" Keaton asks.

"Nothing." Emmett drinks and grimaces.

Keaton gives him a weird look. "Anyway. I didn't know he was . . . you know. Violent."

"Yes, a *real* shocker," I say earnestly. Both Emmett and Keaton freeze, and then exchange a glance.

"I didn't know," Keaton continues. "And I didn't know that he left after he got home that night. And that Nina was over there. I don't . . ." He takes in a breath and makes a fist. I lean back, away from him, just a tiny bit.

He stares at me in this open, sympathetic way that makes me uncomfortable. I wish he'd go back to looking like he's about to murder me.

"You really don't remember that night, do you?" he asks quietly.

"*I think about the way the knife went into his throat every night,*" she whispers in my ear. "*It's like my own personal lullaby.*"

"No," I say.

"Did you think Lucy was lying?" Emmett asks, with genuine curiosity.

"Of course I did! We all did."

"I didn't." He says it matter-of-factly, and maybe I'm an idiot, but I believe him.

"Well, good for you, Sunshine, but the rest of us were skeptical. But now . . ." He shakes his head and takes a drink of his beer.

I lean forward, folding my arms on the table. It's damp and sticky with beer. "Keaton, are you trying to *apologize* to me?"

"No." He runs a hand over his mouth. "Fuck, I don't know. But you know what I do know? I know both Matt and Nina well, and neither of them said shit to me about being out that night. They didn't say shit to anyone. And that doesn't sit right."

CHAPTER THIRTY-EIGHT

LUCY

Ben wants to meet at Grandma's again, and he's waiting for me on the porch when I pull up in front of the tiny pink house. He strolls over to me as I get out of the car, tossing his dark hair out of his eyes in a way that seems practiced. Like he rehearsed being sexy in a mirror.

"Why are you always here?" I ask.

"I'm not always here."

"You're not fucking me *and* my grandma, are you? That would really bum me out."

"I am not fucking your grandma. Honestly, I don't think Beverly could fit me into the rotation. She has a lot of men coming around." His tone is teasing, and I step away from him when it looks like he's going to lean in. I'd rather my grandma not know about this particular poor life choice.

"Come on." I head toward the house. "It feels like Satan's asshole out here."

He follows me into the house, where he's already set up his podcasting equipment on the table. Grandma is on the couch, scrolling through her phone. She wears an old, faded T-shirt tucked into a full red skirt, and I marvel again at how much cooler my grandma is than I am.

"Is this now our designated interview spot?" I plop down in one of the chairs.

"It's quiet. And Beverly doesn't mind." He smiles at her. I was only half kidding when I asked whether they were fucking.

"He likes that you're more relaxed here," Grandma says without looking up from her phone.

Ben appears startled, like that was something that Grandma inferred on her own.

I take it back. My grandmother is too smart to sleep with Ben Owens. It's too bad common sense isn't genetic.

"I was hoping we could delve deeper into your relationship with Nina today." Ben slides into the seat next to me.

I sigh, looking past his head, out the window to the empty field behind the house. A breeze blows through the tall weeds. Ben looks over his shoulder and then back at me.

I haven't told him about my conversation with Keaton and Emmett. He doesn't know that Matt and Nina are still sleeping together.

I haven't told Ben a lot of things about Nina.

"*She yelled at me while I was holding a knife,*" Savvy whispers in my ear. "*She probably wouldn't have done that if she knew all the fun things I've done with knives.*"

I laughed when she said that to me. I can't even remember exactly why Nina and Savvy didn't like each other. I'm not even sure that anyone besides me knows how much they truly despised each other.

"Lucy?" Ben says.

Nina didn't like Savvy. So what? I don't like lots of people. It never seemed relevant.

It still probably isn't relevant. And if I say it, I'm doing to Nina what they all did to me—making accusations that will haunt her forever. I should lie, or dance delicately about the truth, like the other people Ben has interviewed have done.

Because she couldn't have done it. My brain isn't letting that scenario even take shape in my head. I've imagined killing so many people, and yet I can't put an object in Nina's hand and watch her smash it against Savvy's head.

"Hon?" Grandma touches my arm. She and Ben are hovering, looking at me with concern.

"I don't want to," I say softly.

The wrinkles around Grandma's eyes crinkle as she squints at me. "You don't want to what?"

"I don't want to talk about Nina."

"But she—" Ben starts.

"Can you just give me a day?" I push a hand through my hair. "Surely you have something else we can talk about today." A text message pops up on my phone, and I angle the screen toward me so I can read it. My stomach drops to my feet. "Fuck."

"What?" Grandma asks.

"The internet figured out that I'm Eva Knightley."

Listen for the Lie Podcast with Ben Owens

EPISODE 6—"NINA"

When I first reached out to her, Nina Garcia was hesitant to talk to me.

Nina: Yeah, I don't know. I felt weird about it.

Ben: Weird?

Nina: Yeah, you know . . . this case has already gotten a lot of attention. Everyone knows that Lucy—

Ben: Everyone knows that Lucy . . . ?

Nina: Um. Everyone *thinks* that Lucy did it. But I was talking to Emmett—you know Emmett, right? Me and Lucy and him were all best friends in high school?

Ben: Yeah, we've talked.

Nina: He thought I should. I just feel bad because I like . . . I didn't really even know Savvy.

Ben: You two went to high school together. In a pretty small town.

Nina: Sure, but we didn't like . . . hang out.

Ben: Okay. But you knew Lucy well. This podcast is as much about her as it is about Savannah. And I've heard you know Matt fairly well?

Nina: I mean, a little, I guess. We're friendly.

Ben: Why don't we start at the beginning. What was Lucy like—

Nina: I'm sorry, can we stop for a minute?

Ben: Why?

Nina: I just . . . I need a minute.

Nina was frequently nervous in our interviews, which isn't unusual. Talking about the murder of someone you knew—even just casually—is difficult. I know this.

But when I began going through her interviews, I found some inconsistencies. Here's Stephanie Gantz again.

Ben: I found this yearbook photo. Of Nina and Savannah?

Stephanie: Oh yeah, that's junior year, I think?

Ben: They were on student council together?

Stephanie: Yeah.

Ben: I've heard they didn't really know each other.

Stephanie: I wouldn't say that. They weren't friends. I think they fought over a boy once, like freshman year? Ugh. I hate that, but we were young. The feminism hadn't kicked in yet.

Ben: Sure. So, they didn't like each other, then?

Stephanie: It wasn't anything dramatic by that point, but no, not really.

Ben: By that point?

Stephanie: There was definitely some drama freshman year.

Ben: What kind of drama?

Stephanie: Just . . . like I said, there was a boy. I think Savvy . . . I think she sort of mean-girled Nina a bit. It blew over, and Savvy wasn't like that at all later, but, you know. We were fourteen.

Ben: Did Lucy know there was history with Nina and Savannah?

Stephanie: She must have. Nina was her best friend back then.

Ben: Did you think it was weird, when Lucy became such good friends with Savannah later?

Stephanie: Nah, we were all adults by that point. If you're going to hold grudges about things from when you were a kid, you're gonna spend your whole life angry, you know?

Ben: Do you know how Nina felt about it?

Stephanie: Uh . . . she might have said something catty about it.

Ben: So Nina *was* holding grudges from when she was a kid?

Stephanie: Maybe. Yeah.

CHAPTER THIRTY-NINE

LUCY

It only takes a couple of hours for the reviews of all three of my books to be flooded with people calling me a murderer. Now, when you scroll down to read what people think of my fluffy fake-dating rom-com, the first thing you see is *"THIS IS WRITTEN BY LUCY CHASE, THE WOMAN WHO MURDERED HER BEST FRIEND."*

So, that's unfortunate.

Ben gives me a worried look as I leave my grandma's house after the interview, but I don't have the energy to deal with his feelings right now. Technically, this is all his fault.

Several times I imagine mowing him down with my car. I feel like I deserve credit for not doing it.

I drive straight to Nina's house. I'm showing up unannounced, which is a real dick move, especially since she has kids, but I've lost all my fucks. I have no more to give.

She answers the door with a rightfully annoyed expression. This is what she gets for inviting me over. There are real benefits to not letting me know where you live.

She's in sweats, her hair up in a haphazard ponytail with a giant piece sticking up in the middle. She rests her head against the side of the door, like even standing here is too much effort.

"I've had a really shitty day, Lucy," she says.

"*I know you two were like BFFs in high school, but I swear to god, that woman is such a stuck-up bitch,*" Savvy rudely declares in my head. I'd pushed back a little on that one. Told her that Nina came off as aloof sometimes, but she was actually very nice.

"Well, I've had a shitty five years, so how about you give me ten minutes?" I counter.

She sighs, glancing over her shoulder to where an animated show is playing on the television, the kids on the couch in front of it. She steps out onto the porch, closing the door behind her.

"I'm not doing another interview with Ben," she said. "I texted him no a few hours ago."

"Smart choice."

She eyes me. "What's that supposed to mean?"

"I mean that you're about to take my place as the cheating, lying whore suspected of murder, so nothing good can come of that inter-view."

She pales, and stutters before she's able to get a word out. "You don't think that *I* killed Savvy?"

I don't, but I just shrug.

"The thing with Matt and me—"

"I don't care."

"I didn't do it on purpose. He was just always there and my ex and I were always fighting."

"Seriously, I don't care. I would have cared back then, but I can't really muster the energy at the moment. I would recommend you stop, considering what we just heard from Julia."

She leans against the side of the house, exhaustion on her face. "I didn't know. It was never really more than sex with me and Matt, so we never fought or . . ." She swallows hard. "I'm an idiot."

"I mean, I married him."

Her eyes shift to mine and then quickly away. She wants to say something in response to that, but is clearly holding it back.

I wonder what else she's been holding back.

"Did you hook up with Colin?" I ask.

"Is there a woman in this town who hasn't hooked up with Colin Dunn? Even your mother slept with him."

"But were you with him while he was dating Savvy?"

"No, before, but we both know that Colin and Savvy weren't exclusive." She raises an eyebrow. "Savvy got around more than Colin, if I remember correctly. Funny how the podcast conveniently leaves that out."

Savvy appears on the porch, mouth open in mock anger, like she's insulted. *"Excuse me, are you trying to imply that I was a slut? I told you I never liked this bitch."*

"Why did you go see Matt, the night of the wedding?" I ask, ignoring her.

"I was drunk. It was stupid."

I wait, but she doesn't elaborate.

"I would never sleep with your husband, for the record," Savvy says. *"Because I'm a good friend, but also because you have terrible taste in men."*

"Oh, you're one to talk," I snap.

And I realize, too late, that I've said that out loud.

Nina freezes, slowly looking over her shoulder to where I've just spoken to my imaginary friend.

"Are you . . . okay?" she asks hesitantly.

I flush. "I'm fine. What did your stupid drunk brain want with Matt that night?"

"I . . ." She pushes a hand through her hair with a sigh. "I knew you two were at the wedding that night, and I decided I was going to go over there and make a scene so that you would know I was sleeping with Matt. He'd been talking big about leaving you, and I was going to force the issue. I went over there and waited."

"What happened when he got there?"

"I asked where you were, and he just started screaming at me to go home. Barely even let me get a word out."

"So he was upset? Or angry?"

"Yeah. I figured it was because he could tell what I was doing, waiting outside his house like that. I just started apologizing and left."

"Was he . . . I don't know, disheveled? Dirty?"

She takes a step back, putting her hand on the doorknob in preparation to flee this conversation. "Matt didn't kill Savvy. I know him. He didn't kill her."

I cock an eyebrow. "You know him so well that you didn't realize he was beating the shit out of his wife?"

Her face hardens. She says nothing.

"Why is everyone so eager to jump to Matt's defense, but the entire town immediately decided I was a murderer?"

"First of all, Matt wasn't covered in Savvy's blood. And second of all, I defended you on that podcast."

"I know you did. And I thought it was because we used to be friends, but I think it's more that you felt guilty for sleeping with Matt. Am I close?"

"Go fuck yourself, Lucy." She walks into her house and slams the door.

CHAPTER FORTY

LUCY

Paige discovering us in bed together seems to have had no effect on Ben, because he invites me over again that night, and I've stopped pretending that I'm going to start making good choices.

I glance around for her when I walk into his hotel room. We're alone.

"I took Paige's key back," he says, walking into the kitchen. Two cups with ice sit on the counter, waiting for him to pour liquid in.

"You know that just tells her we're still sleeping together."

"I'm aware. Paige doesn't get an opinion on my dating life."

"Ben, I don't think *dating* is the word for this."

He pauses with the whiskey bottle hovering over a glass, raising an eyebrow at me. "Everything okay with the books? Your books, I mean?"

"There's either going to be a spike in sales, or it's going to ruin my entire career. I'm excited to find out."

He winces, but doesn't apologize.

If I had any self-respect, I'd leave. I would not have sex with the man who is using my life and the murder of my friend for ad dollars on his podcast.

My self-respect is apparently lacking, because I walk over to the living room and sit down on the couch. There are papers and a laptop on the table.

My own name catches my eye, and I lean forward, turning the

paper so I can see. It's an outline for an episode. Mom's name is on it, as is Nina's. Ben's written a few lines of what he plans to say in neat, clear handwriting, and one catches my eye.

Lucy likely didn't mean to kill Savvy, and my theory is that the shock of what she'd done caused a mental breakdown that completely erased the memory.

I look up to see Ben standing over me, holding the glass of whiskey out to me.

"You think I did it." It's not a question.

His eyes skip from me to the paper. I can't tell whether he meant for me to see it. He's usually so good about cleaning up the evidence when I'm around.

"It's just one of a few possible endings," he says.

I take the glass from him. It's heavy. It wouldn't kill him if I smashed it against his head, but it'd hurt like hell.

I slide the paper to the side, so I can see the ones behind it. He was telling the truth—it is just one possible ending. He's written notes for Matt having killed her, and an ending where there's no clear resolution.

But only mine is detailed. The others have two to three lines written out. Mine is an entire page.

"You think I did it," I say again.

I don't know why I'm disappointed. I never thought he was on my side.

Or maybe that's a lie.

He sits down in the chair across the table and leans forward, putting his glass down. "I haven't come to any firm conclusions."

"Ben—"

"I'm still working on it." He pauses. "That was my original ending, before you got here and agreed to talk to me."

I take a long swig of my drink. It burns as it goes down. I put the glass on the table, too hard, and some of it sloshes onto my podcast future, smearing his perfect letters.

"And you've changed your mind now?" I ask.

He hesitates. "My mind wasn't made up before. It's less made up now."

I guess that's really all I can hope for at this point.

"You aren't telling me the truth about everything, though," he says, cocking an eyebrow. "We both know that."

I just stare at him, because he's not wrong. Maybe I don't blame him for doubting me.

"And not just about your marriage to Matt," he says. "There are other things. Your interview airs tomorrow. I don't want to believe you did it, Lucy, but I still have questions you seem either unwilling or unable to answer."

I cock my head, watching as he takes a sip of his drink. The silence stretches between us, proving his point about my unwillingness to answer his questions. A less guilty person would rush to clarify things for him.

"If you think there's a chance I did it, aren't you're worried I'll kill you too?"

Something sparks in his eyes. "Not really, no."

"Not *really*?" I drain my drink, which is a terrible idea. No one needs to be drunk right now. Certainly not me. "This isn't, like, part of the podcast, is it? You're going to end it by telling everyone how we slept together?"

"God, no, that makes me look awful."

"Oh, it makes *you* look awful." I laugh, without humor.

"And I wouldn't do that to you," he adds with sincerity. I'm still not sure I believe him.

There's a knife on the counter, where he was cutting limes. I imagine grabbing it and sticking it in his chest. In and out, in and out.

"*Fucking* Exorcist *style!*" Savvy shouts gleefully.

The lamp in the corner is heavy enough to do some damage against his head. The pen near my fingers could probably go in his throat, if I put some muscle behind it.

Or I could just put a pillow over his head while he's sleeping tonight.

"*Bo-ring*," Savvy sings.

"Lucy." Ben leans forward, peering at me. "What are you thinking about, when you do that?"

I snap.

"I'm thinking about killing you," I say.

Listen for the Lie Podcast with Ben Owens

EPISODE 7—"THE TRUTH ABOUT LUCY"

The first time I met Lucy Chase was at the Plumpton diner. I was waiting for her. She was clearly surprised to see me.

Her grandmother had set this up. I'd offered to go over to her house, let Lucy meet us there, but she said the diner would be better.

Beverly: Let's not ambush her at my house. The diner is public; she'll have the option to just flip you off and get back in her car, if she wants.

She didn't do that. In fact, she came right over and sat down and was . . . well, I wouldn't say she was *friendly,* exactly. But she wasn't hostile, which was what I'd been expecting.

I was nervous the first time we met, and I think she could tell. I didn't think I was going to be, but when she walked into the diner, she just wasn't what I was expecting.

She looked mostly the same as she did in the pictures. Her features are a little sharper now, and she smiles more than all the photos that circulated online would suggest, but I easily recognized her the moment she walked in.

It was her presence that I think I wasn't expecting. She's tall, and she walks into a room like she knows everyone is looking at her. That's how she walked into the diner. Like she knew people were going to stare, and she didn't care.

I have no idea if she actually cares that people always stare at her. I imagine they always have, given how she looks, but it certainly must be different now.

It's hard to know what Lucy is thinking about this—or anything—because she is very, very guarded. She often takes a couple seconds to answer questions, like she's rehearsing the answer in her head first.

She hasn't done a single interview, ever. She didn't speak to the press immediately after Savannah's death, and she certainly didn't speak to them after people in Plumpton started to pin the murder on her. I know for a fact that many journalists have reached out to her over the past five years, hoping to do a piece on her and Savannah, and her response was always no. Or it was simply silence. I reached out to her repeatedly, for months, and got no response.

I don't know why she changed her mind. Beverly says it's simply because she asked her to.

But here it is. Lucy Chase's version of events, for the first time.

Ben: You look extremely suspicious.

Lucy: I think my face is just showing how I always feel about you, Ben.

I want to jump in here to note that Lucy is extremely sarcastic, and comes off as flip at times, even about serious things.

But what she just said is true—she is clearly always suspicious of me. Of everyone, I think, but most definitely of me.

Ben: You've been back in Plumpton now for what? A week?

Lucy: Yeah.

Ben: How is it?

Lucy: Terrible.

Ben: Why is that?

Lucy: It's hot. And everyone here thinks I killed my friend. Actually, I guess everyone *everywhere* thinks I killed Savvy now, but people actually recognize me out on the street here.

Ben: Will you take us through that day? Everything you remember?

Lucy: Yeah. It was a Saturday, and I woke up early because Matt was in a bad mood. He was stomping around, making a bunch of noise.

Ben: Do you remember what he was mad about?

Lucy: No. It was probably something small. Matt was always mad about something.

Ben: Did you fight?

Lucy: Not really, no. Matt and I weren't really ever getting along at that point, so there was just always some low-level hostility. But we weren't yelling at each other or anything that day.

Anyway, I didn't do much that day before the wedding. Just hung out, watched some TV, cleaned the house a little. And then we left for the wedding around five. And that's it. Those are all the memories I have of that night.

Ben:	Colin said that you originally claimed to have a memory of arriving and walking into the wedding, but you later realized it was wrong.
Lucy:	I created a memory around information that other people told me.
Ben:	Has that happened again since?
Lucy:	No. I specifically stopped trying to remember because of that.
Ben:	You stopped?
Lucy:	Yeah. I can't trust my own memory, apparently.
Ben:	What's the next thing that you do remember, after leaving for the wedding with Matt?
Lucy:	Walking down the side of the road. That guy in the truck asking me if I was okay.
Ben:	Where were you going? Do you know?
Lucy:	I think I thought I was going to meet Savvy at her car? I remember looking at the guy and thinking, "What's he talking about, I'm just going to the car with Savvy."
Ben:	Did you realize you had blood on you?
Lucy:	I thought it was dirt. I kept looking down and wondering why I was so dirty.
Ben:	What was your reaction when they told you it was Savannah's blood?
Lucy:	I became hysterical. They had to sedate me.
Ben:	Did you know she was dead at that point?
Lucy:	I think they had told me, but it wasn't sticking. I didn't believe them.
Ben:	Because of the head injury or . . .
Lucy:	It didn't make sense. To me, I'd just been leaving the house with Matt. It felt like five minutes ago, not twelve hours.
Ben:	The police came to question you right away?
Lucy:	It was a few hours. Technically they tried to ask me questions out on the road, but I wasn't making any sense. I just kept saying, "Where's Savvy? Where's Savvy?" Which, I always thought . . .
Ben:	You always thought?
Lucy:	Well, at that point I wasn't fully aware of where I was or

what I was doing, because of the blow to the head. If I'd killed her, why would I be asking where she was? Wouldn't I have said something like "I hurt her," or "I'm sorry"? Since I wasn't fully conscious? Something that indicated what I'd done? I don't know. Maybe that's just something I tell myself to feel better.

Ben: To feel better, like to convince yourself you didn't kill her?

Lucy: Yep.

Ben: Because you don't know for sure?

Lucy: I can't know for sure. I don't remember that night. I know that I loved Savvy and I can't imagine ever hurting her, but everyone is so convinced that I did it. It's hard not to be like, well, what if I did snap? What if I had a psychotic break? Do people know when they have a psychotic break?

Ben: I . . . don't know.

Lucy: It was rhetorical, Ben.
[*laughter*]

Ben: How do you explain the scratches on your arm and your skin under Savannah's fingernails? The bruises on her arm that match the shape of your fingers?

Lucy: I can't. I don't remember.

Ben: Had the two of you ever gotten into a violent altercation before?

Lucy: Of course not.

Ben: But you had been in a violent altercation before. With Ross. Was there anyone else?

Lucy: Nope, just him. I still maintain that he deserved it.

Ben: What about Savannah? Do you know if she had ever been in a fight or any kind of altercation?

Lucy: Not that I know of. Can't really imagine it, honestly. Savvy was a really sweet, levelheaded person. I mean, you've heard it from lots of people on this podcast. Everyone loved her. She never could have hurt anyone.

CHAPTER FORTY-ONE

LUCY

Ben doesn't look particularly concerned about me killing him.

Or surprised, actually.

He cocks his head, his face betraying nothing. "You're thinking about killing me." It's not so much a question as a calm repeat of what I've just said.

"I do it all the time." I don't know why I've decided to tell all my secrets to the absolute worst person to confess them to, but here we are. He did say that he wanted the truth from me. This is one I can actually give him. "With everyone. I think about killing them."

"Like . . ." He shifts, and then pauses, and I see his gaze flick briefly to the bag by the door, which has the microphone. He wants to ask whether he can record this.

He doesn't. He's good enough at this to know when the answer will be *no*.

"Like intrusive thoughts," I say. "I can't stop them. I pick a weapon, and I imagine killing people."

"You pick a weapon." He speaks slowly.

"Whatever's around. I get creative."

His lips twitch. Maybe in amusement, maybe in fear. I don't know which one I'm rooting for.

"Which weapon did you choose in here?"

"The glass first." I point to it. "That wouldn't kill you, though. So, the knife." I touch my own throat. "Then the lamp."

"The *lamp*?"

"I'd bash it against your head."

"I think it's too heavy for you to get enough momentum to do that."

"I'm not always realistic."

"Sure."

"And suffocating you with a pillow. Later. When you're asleep."

His neutral expression cracks with that one. He takes in a slow breath.

"That one's realistic," he says, his voice strained.

"Maybe not. You could wake up and fight me off."

He lifts an eyebrow. "Maybe."

"Depends on how long it takes you to wake up," I say.

"And how strong you are." He's staring at me with a look I can't identify, until he shifts slightly in his chair, and I see it. He's turned on.

I stand and walk to him. I hike up my dress as I lower onto his lap, straddling him.

I put both my hands around his neck.

"Or I could just strangle you right now."

He meets my gaze. His breathing is ragged.

I take one hand off his neck to unzip his pants. I move my underwear to one side. He sucks in a breath as I raise my hips, and then lower them so he slides inside me.

I put both hands around his neck again, squeezing tighter this time.

I lean closer, my lips against his ear. "You took Paige's key back. How long do you think it would be until they discovered your body?"

He makes a strangled noise. I grip harder, grinding my hips against his.

"It would be a good ending, don't you think? Podcaster gets murdered by the woman everyone thought he was going to exonerate?

People would remember you forever. The guy who solved the case, but he got killed while fucking the murderer."

I lean back to look at him. His chin is tilted back, his face red.

"*Tighter, tighter!*" Savvy cheers.

Ben's body jerks, another strangled noise escaping from his throat. He goes still.

I slowly let go of his neck.

He lets out a whoosh of air. His gaze doesn't leave the ceiling for several seconds as he breathes heavily.

He finally meets my gaze, his face still flushed.

I lean forward. When I speak, my lips brush against his.

"Maybe I'll kill you later tonight."

He smiles.

CHAPTER FORTY-TWO

LUCY

Mom is sitting at the kitchen table when I come downstairs the next evening, crutch leaning on the wall beside her. The sun streaks through the back door, but she hasn't turned on a light, so it's dim in the kitchen, her phone screen the only bright spot. Her gaze is downcast, and Ben's voice plays softly from her phone.

She looks up at me and quickly pauses the podcast. I pick up my purse from the hook on the door.

"Where do you go every night?" she asks.

"You don't want to know."

She presses her lips together and considers that for a moment. She nods.

"You really published three books without telling me?" she asks.

"You've never been good at keeping secrets."

She lets out a loud, short laugh. I guess that means she disagrees.

"You wouldn't like them anyway," I say.

"Why not?"

"You're a literary snob. They're not literary."

She sniffs. "Well, I barely read at all anymore, but I do prefer good literature when I make the time. There's nothing wrong with that."

"I didn't say there was." I wanted to say it, though. She squints at me like she knows that.

"You've listened to the episode about Nina?" she asks.

"Yeah."

"You can't do this to that poor woman." Her voice cracks a little.

"*I'm* not doing anything to her. Ben doesn't consult me about what to put in the podcast." A lie, but it's true that he's not consulting me about Nina.

"He's implying she did it."

"He's implied that a lot of people did it. It's irresponsible all around. Nina isn't special."

"Matt deserved it." Her tone is harsh, and I'm actually a little touched. I didn't realize she gave a shit. "Your father and I . . . maybe we deserved it too. And Colin's too dumb to care."

"Agreed."

"But Nina doesn't deserve to have her whole life put on display. So what if she didn't like Savvy? The girl they're talking about on that podcast bears little resemblance to the actual woman. She wasn't actually very nice."

I say nothing to that, because it's true. Savvy was often kind, but she often wasn't. Certainly not in high school.

"Nina's got two kids. A boyfriend, who is a significant upgrade from her ex-husband, who seemed like a real asshole to me. She doesn't deserve this."

"And *I* do?"

Her gaze shifts to mine. She doesn't need to answer that.

"I can't stop Ben from saying stupid shit on his podcast," I say. "But just wait an episode or two. He's probably going to end the whole thing by saying he thinks I did it."

Her eyebrows shoot up. "What?"

"He's got a whole ending written out summarizing his theory about how I killed her. This is just some . . . I don't know. He's exploring every angle. Or just trying to get every dime of advertiser money that he can."

"But he's pointing the finger at Nina anyway?" She looks outraged.

"I like how that's the part that upsets you," I say dryly.

"Oh Lucy, give me a break," she snaps. I blink. "Does he have any hard evidence?"

My chest seizes as I consider the possibility. Would he have told me if he did? I doubt it. "I don't . . . I have no idea. I don't see how he could."

She blows out a breath. "Okay. Good. That's all that matters. They can't charge you unless he uncovers something new."

I open my mouth to ask her why she's always been so convinced I did it. I haven't asked in years, and when I did, I bitterly screamed it, so maybe it doesn't count. I didn't actually expect an answer then.

I close my mouth. I don't want one now either. I don't want to know whether she just has a low opinion of me or she actually knows something. Just the thought makes me want to vomit.

I turn and walk quickly out of the house.

Listen for the Lie Podcast with Ben Owens

EPISODE 7—"THE TRUTH ABOUT LUCY"

Ben: Matt and Mrs. Harper have mentioned that your father was extremely protective of you right after Savannah's death. He wouldn't let people speak to you without being present. Is that correct?

Lucy: Yes. He wouldn't leave the room, even if I asked him to.

Ben: Do you know why?

Lucy: Yeah. He thought I killed Savvy. He was trying to protect me, I guess.

Ben: He said that directly? He thought you killed Savvy?

Lucy: Not *exactly*, but it was obvious he thought I did it. He said . . . Let me try and get it right. He said, "I don't need to know what happened, I just need you to know that I'm on your side." And he said, "If you suddenly remember anything, do not say a word to anyone until you talk to me."

Ben: What was your reaction to that?

Lucy: I was confused and honestly kind of devastated. I didn't understand why he thought I was capable of killing anyone, much less Savvy. On the one hand, it was nice that his first reaction was to protect me, but on the other hand, why wasn't the reaction disbelief? Why didn't he immediately say to me, "I know you could never do this. I know you're not capable of this." Neither of my parents said that to me.

Ben: You're aware that Ivy said your mom acted like she knew what happened a few days after Savannah's death? She said your mom said that she'd make it right.

Lucy: I wasn't aware of that until I listened to her interview.

Ben: So, you don't know why she would have said that?

Lucy: If she knows something, she didn't share it with me.

Ben: How about Matt? How did he act after you got home?

Lucy: He acted like he was scared of me. He asked me to go to my parents' house.

Ben: Can you elaborate? How did he act scared?

Lucy:	He didn't want to come near me. I remember him standing by the door, this pleading look in his eyes. He looked genuinely frightened.
Ben:	So both your husband and your parents immediately thought you killed Savannah?
Lucy:	They never said it directly, but, yes.
Ben:	What did that do to you? Emotionally, I mean.
Lucy:	It certainly didn't help.
Ben:	Can you expand on that?
Lucy:	What do you want me to say, Ben? It felt like shit.
Ben:	Do you think it affected your memory?
Lucy:	How do you mean?
Ben:	Colin said that you shut down when he went to talk to you, after you created the false memory and he corrected it. He said you stopped trying to remember at all after that.
Lucy:	I didn't stop—
Ben:	Have you ever done any sort of memory retrieval therapy?
Lucy:	No. Those methods are controversial, and they can lead to false memories. I was already creating those. I didn't want any more.
Ben:	Have you actively done anything to try and remember what happened since just after the murder?
Lucy:	Like what? I'm in therapy. I've talked about Savvy a lot with my therapist. I think something would come up, if I was going to remember.
Ben:	Do you think it's possible that you can't remember partly because you don't *want* to remember?
Lucy:	No, I think it's the head injury.
Ben:	But all the hours before the head injury. Is it possible that you can't remember because of the trauma of both your parents and your husband immediately deciding you did it?
Lucy:	Fuck, I don't know. Ask a therapist.
Ben:	I did. She said yes, it's possible.
Lucy:	Well, there you have it. Thanks for nothing, Matt. And Mom and Dad.
Ben:	Do you want to know?
Lucy:	If I killed Savvy? Of course I want to know.

Ben:	Are you sure?
Lucy:	Yes!
Ben:	Have you visited any of the places where you saw Savannah that day? Your old house? The wedding venue? You and I went to where her body was found near the Byrd Estate, and that was very traumatic for you.
Lucy:	I haven't, no. I haven't been inside my old house, though I'm sure it looks different now. Same with the wedding venue. They change it for every wedding.
Ben:	Still . . . shouldn't you have gone to jog your memory?
Lucy:	Yes.
Ben:	Yes?
Lucy:	Obviously I should have gone. I don't know why I didn't.
Ben:	Why did you go to the woods where she was found?
Lucy:	My mom made me.
Ben:	But nowhere else?
Lucy:	We talked about going to the wedding venue, but . . . no. I think I said the same thing back then. It would have been set up differently for a new wedding.
Ben:	Would it be fair to say that you've stopped trying to remember? That, in fact, you never really tried to remember what happened that night?
Lucy:	No, *never* isn't accurate. I tried really fucking hard the first couple days.
Ben:	But after that?
Lucy:	I guess I stopped trying, yeah. But not because I didn't want to know! Because I thought it was one of those things where if I didn't think about it, it would finally come to me. That's what you're supposed to do when you can't remember, right?

CHAPTER FORTY-THREE

LUCY

"Get your fucking microphone and meet me outside."

"Oh, hello, Lucy, how nice to hear from you," Ben says on the other line.

I shift the phone to my other ear as I pull my bedroom door shut behind me. "Just get it. I'll be there in ten minutes."

"Okay. Why?"

"We're going to the damn wedding venue."

Ben meets me outside his hotel, and we drive to the Byrd Estate. I take us slowly through the winding dirt road that leads up to the event center. Huge, old trees provide shade, and the historic house looms up ahead, a large white tent set up behind it. I can't imagine what kind of masochists are having an outdoor wedding in August.

A woman in an alarmingly bright white suit scurries out of the house as I park and we get out of the car.

"Well, hi, y'all!" she says. "Are you my five thirty?"

"No," I say.

Her smile falters, but then she spots Ben. "Ben! How nice to see you again!"

"Hi, Trudy." He swings his bag over his shoulder, holding his portable mic in one hand. The light is on; he's recording. "Sorry to just show up unannounced."

"Oh, it's fine. What can I help you with?"

"Do you mind if Lucy and I take a walk around? We want to see if anything jogs her memory."

She recoils at my name. "Oh. Well . . . sure, if you think it will help."

"I fainted last time we did this, but I'll do my best to stay upright this time." I try to sound flippant, but my voice actually trembles a little.

I don't think Trudy notices, because she just frowns at me. "You may tour the Byrd Estate at your own risk."

"Thanks, Trudy," Ben says. She turns and walks back into the building, casting a disapproving glance over her shoulder.

"You want to tell me why you wanted to come here today?" he asks me once she's gone.

"Because maybe you're right. I'm very sad to contribute to your already wildly overinflated ego, but, yeah. You're right that I haven't really tried to remember. So here we are."

"I think my ego is average-sized."

"Ben, focus. And we both know that it is not."

He rolls his eyes. "All right. What should we do—" He stops as a truck rumbles up the road and comes to a stop on the other side of the parking lot. Matt jumps out.

"I invited Matt, by the way." I wave to him.

"What the hell, Lucy?" he calls as he strides over to us. "You didn't tell me the podcaster douche was coming."

"Podcaster douche is recording, by the way," Ben says, holding up the microphone.

"Of course you are." Matt stops beside me, his fingers brushing against my arm. I move away.

"If it makes you feel better, she didn't tell me you were coming either," Ben says.

It doesn't appear to make Matt feel better.

"I need someone who was there to tell me what we did that

night," I say. "Otherwise, we're just going to be wandering aimlessly."

"Lucy, are you sure ..." Matt begins softly, but he trails off, glancing at the mic. He sighs, running a hand through his hair. "Fine, whatever. I'll walk you through it."

"Thank you," I say sincerely.

"Thank you," Ben says, flipping him off with his free hand.

Matt returns the gesture and then turns around, pointing at his truck. "I parked over there. Like Colin said, we got here before him and Savvy, and we talked to a couple in the parking lot, but not him and Savvy. The Nelsons."

"What did you talk about?" Ben asks. "Do you remember?"

"Only because I told the police at the time. It was just small talk—the weather, how hot it was already for May. Just a quick conversation, and then we all went that way." He points. "It was an indoor reception." He walks around the house, and we follow him to the side doors and inside the room.

It's empty, chairs stacked in a corner. There's a bar at the back of the room, and my sandals click against the wood floor as I walk across it.

"Does it look familiar?" Ben asks.

"Only because I'd been to other weddings here, before that night." I turn to Matt. "Do you remember how it was set up?"

"Like a wedding? I don't know." He points across the room, opposite the bar. "DJ was over there. I'm pretty sure the tables were set up along the sides? Round ones? We were sitting ..." He turns in a circle, then points in the direction of the bar. "Oh! We were near the bar. I remember, because Colin said something about it. Something like, 'Cool, easy access.'"

"Nice! Right next to the bar. Best seat in the house."

I freeze. I can see Colin standing in front of me in his rumpled suit, grinning as he points to the bar. Savvy, already holding a glass of wine, stands on her toes and kisses his cheek.

She looks so beautiful in that pink dress. The thin straps show off all her tattoos, and it swishes around her knees as she walks. I'd forgotten what that dress looks like when it isn't covered in blood and dirt.

The crime scene photos flash through my mind. Pink dress twisted around her legs, caked in grime. And then it's not the crime scene, it's right in front of me. I'm staring down at her.

But, no, that can't be right, because it's daylight. I never saw Savvy dead in the daylight.

I don't think.

"Lucy." There's a hand on my back, and I look up to see Matt, his brow furrowed in concern. Ben, standing across from me, looks ready to catch me swooning again.

I blink, stepping away from both of them. "What else? Did we mostly stay in here?"

"I'm sorry, but most of the actual reception is a blur," Matt says apologetically. "And you and I weren't really getting along that day, so we didn't actually stay together most of the evening. Savvy didn't like me, and she didn't pretend otherwise. I can't really blame her, I guess."

I look at him in surprise, but his gaze is across the room.

"You and Savvy stuck together that night, for the most part. Not the whole time, though. At one point I looked around and Savvy was at the table without you, and then I looked again like half an hour later and I still couldn't find you."

"I remember you telling the police that." I glance at Ben. "You never found any guests to confirm where I was?"

"No. No one remembers seeing you anywhere out of the ordinary." He points across the room. "The restrooms are that way, right? Let's take a walk down there."

My heart thumps frantically as I follow him across the room. I take a slow breath. There's no reason to be nervous. I'm walking through an empty wedding venue.

Savvy's in the hallway, wearing her pink dress, holding a bloody knife. She grins and holds it up to Matt's face as he walks by her.

"*You're always just using whatever's around,*" she says. "*Be prepared, like a Boy Scout! Bring your own murder weapon!*"

I shake my head, willing the image away.

We turn a corner. I stop. I look to my left.

There's a door to the outside, sunlight shining through the small square window like it's beckoning us over to it.

"I think I went that way," I say.

"Outside?" Ben asks. "Why? You hate outside."

I almost laugh as I walk to it. "I know. But I think I did."

I push the door open, squinting in the bright sunlight. There isn't much on this side of the building. Just a dumpster, way down at the other end of the building, and what looks like the remains of a broken canopy resting against the brick.

"Are you sure?" Matt stands with Ben in the doorway. "The outdoor area where people were smoking is on the other side."

I take another step. There's a little alcove, currently filled with several nearly empty cans of paint.

I can feel the brick against my back suddenly. I can smell fresh paint as lips press into mine. One of the straps of my dress has slipped down, and there's a hand on my breast. I kiss him again. It's a man. I can still feel the way he smashed his lips into mine.

"Lucy," Ben says.

"*Lucy,*" Savvy said sharply.

I jolt. I remember the air on my breast as he'd moved his hand. I'd pulled my strap back up while she stared at me with an expression—anger? Was she mad?

I try to see the guy. I can't. I can feel his breath against my lips. His hips grinding into mine. But there's just empty white space when I try to see his face.

"*Let's go,*" Savvy barked, and turned on her heel.

And then there's nothing. I don't know whether I said goodbye to whoever the guy was. I don't know whether I followed her right away. Maybe I stayed and had sex with the mystery man. The way he was grinding his hips into mine, we may have been headed that way.

I look at Matt.

"What?" he says. "You remember why you were out here?"

One thing's for sure. The guy wasn't Matt.

And whoever it was, he hasn't bothered telling anyone.

"No," I say. "I don't remember."

Matt cocks an eyebrow.

He knows I'm lying.

CHAPTER FORTY-FOUR

LUCY

I drive Ben back to his hotel and make an excuse for why I can't stay. I've slept over nearly every night for the past week, but he doesn't argue when I claim I'm exhausted and I'm going back to my parents' house. He probably wants to edit everything into an episode anyway. He seemed pretty thrilled by today's turn of events.

I drive across town to my old house. To Matt's house. He opens the door and steps out onto the porch as soon as I pull up to the curb, like he was waiting for me.

Dammit. I hate how predictable I am.

I walk up the path. Matt sweeps his arms out toward the house, as if welcoming me back. The shutters are open today, the light inside warm and inviting.

"Good timing," he says. "I was just about to order us some dinner."

A tiny part of me thought that maybe Matt had turned over a new leaf and stopped drinking this week after Julia's episode aired, but I see the loaded bar cart as soon as I step inside. It's still on the same side of the living room, to the right of the huge teal couch.

The same teal couch that I bought. The same bar cart that I bought.

I stop, looking left and right. There are a few new pieces of artwork—there's some abstract art that's either flowers or just some random blobs of blue and yellow paint that I don't particularly care for—but everything is mostly the same. Beautiful dark hardwood floors, high ceilings, a sleek white kitchen to my right with a huge island in the middle. I always thought that those enormous kitchen islands were the best thing ever, and it turns out I was right.

But it's weird how much everything looks exactly the same. If I hadn't known that Matt remarried, I wouldn't have guessed it walking in. Julia didn't leave much of a mark on the house. Or even on him, maybe.

"I need a drink," I say, even though I know I shouldn't drink with Matt. I should encourage sobriety with Matt. That would be the mature, responsible thing to do for someone you know has a drinking problem.

"A stiff drink," I continue.

He laughs. "Me too."

No one here is mature and responsible.

He doesn't ask what I want; he just grabs the vodka and cranberry, because he knows what I like when I've had a hard day.

I sit on the couch (my couch) as he makes the drinks.

"I'm glad you finally came over," he says as he shakes the tumbler. He's making himself a martini.

"Why is everything the same?"

He strains the liquid into his glass. "What do you mean?"

"Julia didn't want to redecorate?"

"Why would she? You have great taste."

"Ah."

He walks across the living room, two glasses in hand, and passes one to me. "What does *ah* mean?" He sits down next to me.

I take a sip of my drink and then set it on the coffee table. "It means I just realized that you didn't *let* her redecorate."

"I wouldn't put it like that. I mentioned that I liked the way things were, and she didn't seem bothered by it."

That seems unlikely, but I don't know Julia. Maybe she hates decorating. Maybe she really did think I have great taste.

"Are you going to tell me?" he asks.

I raise an eyebrow like I don't know what he's talking about. I do.

"What you remembered when we were outside." He puts his glass on the coffee table. He's already finished half of the rather large martini.

I look at the photo over the fireplace. It's of Julia and Matt's wedding day, her in a sleeveless mermaid-style wedding dress with shoulders that look like they were perfectly sculpted in a Pilates class. Our wedding picture once hung there.

I think it's even the same frame. They just took the old one out and stuck the new one in.

Christ, that's weird.

"I was kissing someone out there," I say.

I turn my attention back to Matt. His jaw twitches, like it always does when he's angry. His mouth is set in a hard line.

"Give me a break," I say.

"I didn't say anything!"

"I know your angry face. And you have no right to an angry face. You were fucking Nina that night."

He blows out a breath. "Not that night, but you're right. I have no room to judge."

I can't hide my surprise.

"I'm trying to be more honest," he says, noticing the look. "With you. About everything. I thought that if I pretended to have a good marriage, I would magically have one. I should have always just been more honest with you. I don't think you ever would have cheated if I hadn't done it first."

I actually have no idea whether that's true. I absolutely slept with Kyle as a "fuck you" to Matt, but I kept doing it because I enjoyed the thrill of it.

I decide not to tell him that.

"Who was it?" Matt asks. "Will it make me mad?"

"What *doesn't* make you mad?" It slips out before I can stop it. I used to love to antagonize him.

But he just smiles, a little sadly. "That's a good point."

Jesus. I reach for my drink and take a long gulp.

"I don't know," I say as I put it back down. "I remember being out there, and kissing him, but I can't see his face. But I remember Savvy interrupting us, and she looked kind of pissed."

Matt's eyebrows shoot up. "Pissed?"

"Yeah. She looked mad, and I think we must have left after that, because she said, *Let's go.*"

"Must have been Colin," Matt says.

"No, there's no way," I protest. "I didn't really even like Colin, and I never would have made out with Savvy's boyfriend."

"He wasn't really her boyfriend. They saw other people."

"Still, I don't think that I would have . . ." I trail off, considering. I make a face and shake my head. "He slept with my *mom* that night. Are you saying he made out with me, and then went back inside and started hitting on my mother?"

"Why not? You guys kind of look alike." He laughs at the expression on my face. "There's a solid chance he didn't even know that Kathleen was your mom. The guy is dumb as a bag of rocks."

"True." I run a hand down my face. "I just can't see it. Even if I was drunk. It had to be someone else."

He reaches out, nudging my skirt up to put a hand on my knee. "It doesn't matter," he says gently.

I slap his hand away. "Of course it matters! It's the first important thing I've remembered in years."

"It's not going to bring her back. Nothing will bring her back." He puts his hand back and squeezes my knee. "I know that this whole podcast thing has been hard on you, but it's almost over. And it doesn't matter what that guy says. Whether Ben points the finger at you or me or Colin or Nina or whoever. He's not the police."

"It doesn't matter what he says, but it matters to me who killed her. I want to know if it was me or you or Colin or Nina or my mom."

"Your *mom*?"

"She was out that night! It could happen! Her alibi is Savvy's boyfriend."

He gives me a look that is both amused and a little pitying. I take another sip of my drink and consider whether I should do something about the fact that his hand has moved from my knee to my thigh.

I glance over at the wedding photo above the mantel. If I squint, it could be our wedding photo. If I squint, this whole house is mine again. This whole life is mine again. My pulse begins to race. A sick feeling rises up in my throat.

Matt leans forward and kisses me, and I kiss him back, despite the frantic beating of my heart. I want to knee him in the balls, but I force myself to sink into this for a moment. I need to be twenty-four again, in this house, feeling everything I felt the night that Savvy died. I don't want to push it away anymore. If I can remember what it's like to be that fucked-up twenty-four-year-old again, maybe I can remember everything.

He slides an arm around my waist, pulling me closer. I remember always feeling conflicted when Matt and I would have sex. Because on the one hand, I wanted to fucking murder him.

On the other hand, we always had really fantastic sex.

He pulls away to press his lips to my neck. "Stay here with me," he murmurs against my skin. "Don't go back to L.A."

I say nothing, and maybe he takes my silence to mean I'm thinking about it, because he pulls back and looks at me seriously. An uncomfortable feeling unfurls in my gut.

"Or we can go somewhere else. Start over. Just the two of us." He pushes my hair back, and then leaves his hand on my cheek. "I've missed you. What happened to us?"

"What happened to you? Lucy, what happened to you?"

The memory slams into me so suddenly that I reel back with a gasp.

Matt stood in front of me. Matt of five years ago, with longer hair and a horrified expression on his face. His eyes were bloodshot. He was drunk.

"Jesus, is that your blood?"

What did I say to him? I can't see myself. I can only see him, and that look in his eyes.

He kept glancing down at something. What is he looking at?

Something in my hand. I can almost feel it. It's wet and rough and—

"Whose blood is that?"

"Lucy, no." Matt's voice is sharp. I blink and he comes into focus. Present Matt. He's got both hands on my cheeks, forcing me to look at him. "Stop."

"No, I remember something, I remember—"

"Oh my god Lucy, what did you do? Oh god. Is she dead?"

"Let's kill . . ." I say the words out loud. I said the words then, to Matt. The forest takes shape around me.

"Let's kill . . ." My brain was short-circuiting. I could hear Savvy in my head, on a loop as I stood in front of my frantic husband. Fat raindrops hit my skin, landing on my eyelashes and blurring Matt's face.

"What?" Matt dropped his hands from my face in shock. "You killed someone?"

"Deserved it," I muttered. "We had a plan."

"Jesus Christ." He took a step back, his horrified expression intensifying. "Savvy tried to . . ."

"To what? Lucy, what did Savvy try to do?"

"I know." Matt shakes me gently, bringing me back to the present. "Lucy, I know that you had to."

I can see it now. I was holding a tree branch. Huge and thick and covered in blood.

I screamed, and I dropped it.

And then I ran.

I'm breathing too fast. My vision is tunneling. Matt still has his hands on my cheeks. I think he's holding me upright.

"I don't know what went on between you two out there in the woods, but I know that you did what you had to do," he says firmly. "I am so sorry that I got there too late and I couldn't protect you."

"Why did you . . ." I can't get words out. Tears stream down my cheeks. "Why didn't you call the police? When you saw me that night? Why did they find me the next morning . . . ?"

"I looked for you. But I grabbed that tree branch first and I took it to the trunk of my car, because I knew it would be harder for them to convict you without a murder weapon. I drove it down to the main road and dropped it in a dumpster behind a bar. When I came back, it had started raining really hard, and the road was flooded and I couldn't get to where you'd been. I thought you'd go home, but when I got there . . . well, you weren't."

I shake my head. I'm fully sobbing now.

"It's okay," he says gently. "I was trying to protect you back then, and I completely botched it. I was drunk and stupid and then I freaked out about everything when you got home. It's my fault."

A shudder goes through me.

He puts a hand to his chest. "Seriously, it's my fault. Things had gotten out of hand between us back then, and I knew it. I should have stopped us. I shouldn't have let it go on so long."

I blink at him, confused.

"The fighting," he says. "The way we used to go at each other, hurt each other. It got to you and changed you, and I know that's partially my fault. I don't think you could stop yourself, that night."

I draw a ragged breath. The way he's describing the violence in our marriage—the violence *he* started, the violence that only ever left *me* with serious injuries—doesn't seem right.

None of this seems right.

"Blame me," he continues. "Scream at me. I deserve it."

I stand and stumble backward, away from him. "No. I didn't kill her. I never would have—no."

He stands as well. "She tried to hurt you. I don't know why, but you told me that she did. I should have just called the police right that second and we could have claimed self-defense, but I was drunk and I panicked. And—" He cuts himself off.

I look at him sharply. "And?"

He hesitates. "Why don't you go lie down? Or take a bath? You love that tub. I'll run it for you."

He reaches for me. His fingers brush my wrist before I yank it away.

I rush to the door like he's going to chase me. He doesn't.

I throw it open and look back at him. "You're lying."

He slides both hands into his pockets with a sigh. "Lucy, please just let it go. You don't want to remember anything else. *Trust me.*"

I don't trust him. I didn't then, and I don't now.

I walk out, slamming the door shut behind me.

LUCY

"Lucy."

I turned to see Matt walking out of the reception, a couple fist-pumping to the music on the dance floor behind him. The music faded as the door shut.

He put an arm around my waist, pulling me close. I let him. It was just the two of us in the dimly lit hallway, the murmurs of voices distant.

"I'm sorry about earlier," he whispered.

"You're always sorry."

He kissed me. I should have pushed him away. I might have slapped him if we were at home.

Instead, I looped my arms around his neck. I kissed him back. He tasted like whiskey.

"I'm going to do better," he said as he pulled back to look at me.

I wondered whether by "do better" he meant that he was going to stop smacking me around, or whether he was going to stop sleeping with other women.

He wasn't going to stop doing either, no matter how many times he claimed he was trying to be better.

He slid both hands over my ass, pressing his lips to my neck. "Remember how we had sex in the bathroom at the last wedding we went to here?"

Vividly. My body remembered too, because it was angling toward him, ready to get bent over a counter again.

Someone coughed, and I quickly stepped back from him to see Savvy standing outside the bathroom door.

"Am I interrupting?" she asked, her tone dripping with judgment. I couldn't blame her.

My face heated. I didn't know why I kept falling back into Matt's arms, after everything. There was something wrong with me. Something broken that kept drawing me toward him, like a painful bruise I couldn't stop poking at. It's just that when it was good with Matt, it was *good*.

I was so deeply fucked-up.

A group of women trailed out of the bathroom behind her, laughing as they paused in the hallway. Nina was among them, and she nodded at me once.

Savvy walked past me, and I reached for her arm.

She yanked it away, my fingers only barely brushing her skin, and I heard the laughter from the women abruptly stop.

"The fucker doesn't deserve you," she said through clenched teeth. "You know exactly what he actually deserves."

She stomped away, and I swallowed as I watched her go. For all my big talk, I didn't think I could actually ever go through with killing Matt. I didn't think I could kill anyone, but especially not him. He'd already turned me into a rage-filled monster I didn't recognize. I wasn't going to let him turn me into a murderer too.

Savvy, however, seemed ready to actually go through with it. I was almost reluctant to tell her the plan was off.

I turned to see the women headed back into the ballroom, stealing glances at me as they went.

Matt was still grinning at me, oblivious to Savvy's words. "Looks like the bathroom is clear."

The look on Savvy's face had strengthened my resolve. "I'm not fucking you hours after you tried to drown me in the bathtub."

He rolled his eyes. "Don't be so dramatic. I didn't try to *drown* you."

I could still feel his hand around my neck, holding me under the water as I struggled and splashed. He'd laughed when I came up sputtering after he finally let me go. He shrugged it off so easily that I was, once again, wondering whether maybe his version of events was the true one.

I had this wild urge to start pounding my hands against my head. Like if I smacked my skull hard enough, I'd be able to think straight. I just needed to get my brain into the correct position, and then I could trust my own memories more than Matt's.

I resisted the urge and brushed past Matt. He caught my arm.

"You know I could just find someone else." He curled his lip. He always had the ugliest expression when he reminded me of how much other women loved him. "There are ten women in there who would immediately take me up on the offer."

I yanked my arm away. "Then go grab one and do it. I don't care."

His eyes glinted. "Don't test me."

"Go crazy, Matt. You're already fucking half the town anyway."

He blinked, clearly startled that I was aware of his (incredibly indiscreet) cheating.

"And there are way more than ten guys in there who would love to fuck *me*." I laughed as I gestured at the doors to the reception. "Maybe I'll give it a go too."

His face twisted in rage. I would have been in real trouble if we were at home.

But the door opened, bringing music and laughter with it, and he was forced to hide his anger. He ducked his head and walked past me, roughly bumping my shoulder as he went.

"Hey, Lucy, you okay?"

I turned at the sound of the familiar voice.

CHAPTER FORTY-FIVE

LUCY

Matt's lying.

I go back to my parents' house after leaving Matt's, and barely sleep. Savvy is screaming in my head, and I have no idea whether it's a memory or a figment of my imagination.

"She tried to—"

What? Kill me? She bashed me over the head and so I returned the favor and accidentally killed her?

I wake with only that thought swirling around in my head. I grab the trash can from under the desk and puke in it.

Ben texts asking whether I want to visit the woods near the Byrd Estate again.

I book a flight home to L.A.

Savvy stands in the corner of my room in her bloody pink dress, arms crossed over her chest, judging me.

I deserve it. I'm giving up. I don't want to know anymore. Even though I told Ben that I didn't think Matt did it, I have to admit that a tiny part of me was holding on to the tiniest hope that he did. Now that I can so clearly see in my memory the shock on his face, the absolute horror as he looked at me, I can't hold on to that hope. Matt didn't kill her.

I was the one holding a bloody tree branch, mumbling about murder. I was probably talking about Matt, about *him* deserving it, but that doesn't change anything. Maybe I snapped. Maybe I told Savvy that I didn't want to kill Matt and she went after him anyway. Maybe I stopped her.

The thought makes me feel sick. I can't imagine a world where I decided to kill Savvy instead of letting her kill Matt, but it could have been an accident.

And I don't want to know. I'd rather live with the uncertainty forever than the knowledge that I murdered her.

I decide I can't completely ignore Ben, because he's already decided I'm guilty, and shutting him out will just make things worse.

I drag myself out of bed by noon, throw away my puke-filled trash can, and shower.

"I enjoyed killing that guy. Why weren't you scared of me? Why is it so hard to believe I'd snap? It happened before."

I close my eyes as the water drips down my face. Savvy's voice is too loud. It's not her. It's me, projecting my fears onto her.

Panic swells in my chest, and I turn the water off.

"I will kill you!" Savvy screams.

This is why I stopped trying to remember. I couldn't tell what was real.

I close my eyes and desperately try to shut out everything.

"Leaving?" Ben repeats. I'm standing near the door of his hotel room, hoping to make a quick escape. He takes a step back, into the kitchen, like he hopes I'll follow him. I don't.

"Day after tomorrow." I try to keep my expression neutral. I've forgotten how to have a face.

"Why?" He's wearing his gray T-shirt, the one with the tiny hole at the collar. I've pulled that collar to the side so I could kiss his neck. I look past him.

"I've been here two weeks. It's hot. I have to get back to L.A. and move my stuff out of my boyfriend's apartment."

He blinks. "You have a boyfriend?"

"Ex-boyfriend. He doesn't want to date a murderer."

"Oh. Sorry." He doesn't look sorry. "Can I call you for some follow-up interviews in L.A.?"

"Ben, I have spent hours talking to you. Just tell the world I'm guilty and let's move on."

He leans against the kitchen counter, staring at me. "What happened?"

"Nothing happened."

"What did you remember?"

"I remembered that I hate true crime podcasts."

"Lucy."

I reach for the doorknob. "Say whatever you want about me. I don't care." I pull open the door and walk out.

CHAPTER FORTY-SIX

LUCY

"**D**ad."

He jumps a mile high, dropping the knife he was using to cut an onion. It clatters across the kitchen floor and stops near my feet. It's a big knife, a chef's knife, and I stare at it.

I can't actually bring myself to imagine killing him.

At the moment, I can only kill Savvy. Over and over, on a loop in my head. A tree branch straight to her skull.

"Lucy." Dad puts a hand on his chest. "You scared me."

"I know." I pick up the knife and put it on the counter.

"Are you all packed?" He doesn't hide his cheerfulness at my leaving.

"I don't leave until day after tomorrow. And I'm having dinner with Grandma tonight."

"Oh good, she'll appreciate that." He reaches for the knife, turning on the water to rinse it off.

"Did Matt tell you I killed her?"

He turns off the water. When he looks up at me, it's not in surprise. Matt clearly already told him this conversation was coming.

"Yes."

"When?"

He wipes off the knife with a towel, for longer than necessary. An excuse not to look at me. "He came over that night."

I take in a breath as it clicks into place. "That's where he went. After he came home." I frown. "Does Nina know as well? Why was she at my house that night?"

"No. Apparently she was drunk and had planned to cause a scene so you'd know they were together. Just bad timing. He sent her away."

"And then he came over to the house and told you both I killed Savvy."

"Just me. I told your mom a couple days later. She . . ." He trails off, putting the knife aside and then bracing both hands against the counter. "She wanted to come clean right away. Said that even if it wasn't self-defense, you'd get a light sentence. But Matt and I disagreed. You genuinely didn't seem to remember anything, and we both thought we should just wait. I figured your memory would come back in a few days, and then you could tell us exactly what happened and we'd go from there."

"And when it didn't come back?"

He looks away, uncomfortable. "I figured you either just wanted to move on or you really had blocked it out. The trauma of that . . ." He sighs. "I can't blame you, I guess."

"You guess."

"I would have preferred to face it head-on. I regret not going to the police. Matt said that your memory started to come back when Ben pushed you to remember. I chastised your mother for pushing you. I thought you needed space to do the right thing. She was right, of course."

"You believed him, then? Matt."

Dad looks up, startled. "Should I not have? I didn't know then that . . . Well, I didn't have the full story. But I didn't have any reason not to believe him."

"He was drunk. He didn't actually see me do it. There could have been someone else there, it could have been—" My voice has gone too high, hysterical, and I stop abruptly. I know how it sounds.

"He didn't mention anyone else being there," Dad says gently. "He said . . . Well, he explained what he saw, and what you said to him."

"*He* could have killed her."

"Do you think he did?" He's humoring me.

I see Matt's hysterical face in front of me. I've already tried to convince myself a hundred times that he could have been panicking because he just killed Savvy, but it seems unlikely. I know him too well. I know what he's like when he's just gone too far, caused more pain than he intended. He goes calm. Fix the problem. Be nice. Convince her that it's partially her fault.

He wouldn't have been hysterical about killing Savvy, even drunk. He wouldn't have had that look on his face.

"No," I say. "But you weren't there. You just had Matt, telling you that I killed someone. You thought I was capable of that?"

"I didn't want to. But sometimes you have to do the best with the information you have. That's the information I had. And Matt wanted to protect you. I saw that right away." He gives me a sad look. "We both did."

"And Mom wanted to hand me over to the cops."

"She was also just trying to do what was best."

"It wasn't a criticism."

He looks startled. I might have done the same thing, if I were in Mom's place. Just get the truth out there and let the chips fall where they may.

Or maybe I wouldn't have done the same thing. I didn't immediately run to Ben or the cops when the memory of Matt resurfaced.

I booked a flight home to Los Angeles.

I eat a quiet, awkward dinner with Grandma. I can't tell her the truth, the only family member who believed in me. She believed in me so strongly she turned over all our secrets to a smug podcaster.

"Ben says something happened," she says, once she's deep into her second gin and tonic. The television is on, muted, but I keep getting distracted by a woman on the screen with very long red fingernails. She taps them against her chin, over and over. She could take someone's eye out with those fingernails.

I gather up the remains of my burger and walk to the trash can. "Nothing happened. I told him that."

"I don't think he believes you."

I laugh hollowly.

"*Did* something happen?" she asks.

"Well, I had sex with him," I say, because I want to change the subject.

"Oh, hon." She smiles, a bit sympathetically. "I know. It was obvious that night you two came over for dinner after going to the crime scene."

"We hadn't actually had sex yet at that point."

"Obvious that there was tension, I mean. I don't blame you. I would have done the same thing. He does look like an Avenger, after all."

I laugh despite the crushing weight on my chest. "Thanks, Grandma."

My phone dings, and I glance down at it as I slump into the couch next to her.

It's an email from my agent, informing me that I shouldn't worry about my books being sold out everywhere, because the publisher is already in the process of printing an additional fifty thousand copies of each of them. "*So exciting!!*"

I guess it is, but I can't really feel anything but numb right now.

"Turns out people actually did want to buy romance novels from a suspected murderer," I say as I lower my phone.

"Of course they do," Grandma says. "Like I told you, better to be interesting than likable."

She flips the TV off. "Ben told me you're convinced that he thinks you did it."

I frown. "That's basically what he said. He wrote out a whole ending about how I did it."

"He says that was just one rough draft, and you weren't supposed to see it. Just him working through some thoughts. He sounded really frustrated, if you want to know the truth. I don't think he has an ending."

"He'll decide I did it, just like everyone else did." I swallow around the lump in my throat.

"Not *everyone*," Grandma says softly, putting a hand on my shoulder.

I close my eyes and tilt my head back in an effort not to burst into tears, but I fail. They leak down my cheeks and suddenly I'm crying on my grandmother's couch like I'm ten years old again. She scoots closer to me and wraps an arm around my shoulders.

"I think I did it," I whisper, eyes still closed. "I think I killed her."

"No, you didn't."

"You don't know."

"Neither do you! You just said you *think* you killed her. You still don't remember, do you?"

I open my eyes and roughly wipe my hand across them. "No."

"You didn't do it." Her mouth is set in a hard line, the wrinkles around her eyes more prominent as she frowns harder.

"Stop having so much faith in me."

"No."

"I don't deserve it."

"Horseshit."

"I haven't told you everything." My hands are shaking, and she reaches over and clasps them both.

"I don't need you to tell me everything." She holds my gaze, her dark eyes serious. "I don't need you to lay out every single secret and detail of your existence for me to judge. I *know* you."

I dissolve into tears again, and she wraps her arms around me and pats my back.

"Don't give up, sweetheart. Don't give up."

CHAPTER FORTY-SEVEN

LUCY

I drive home slowly. It's dark, and the streets of Plumpton are empty. I almost roll down the windows like I would on a quiet night in L.A., but the humidity is as thick as ever.

When I stop at a light downtown, I look out to see Emmett decorating the window of the art shop.

A guilty voice in the back of my head reminds me that I never answered his last two texts. I also haven't told him I'm going back to California.

The light turns green. He's noticed me staring at him. He lifts his hand in a hesitant wave.

Shit. I press lightly on the gas and park the car on the side of the road. I step out.

"Hey." I point to the big yellow sunflower he's painting on the window. "That's pretty."

"Oh. Thanks. Some kids wrote 'vagina' over the last one, so the owner asked me to do one that's less erotic."

I bark out a laugh. "Was your last flower *erotic?*"

A grin spreads across his face. "Well, I didn't think so, but apparently some kids saw something I didn't."

I lean against the brick wall next to the art shop. "They could have at least been more creative. *Vagina* isn't very clever graffiti."

"I agree. Put some effort in, kids." He turns back to the window, brush poised.

"I'm sorry I didn't answer your texts. It's been ..."

"Busy?" he guesses without looking at me. He sweeps yellow across the window, forming a petal.

"No. I'm never busy."

He shoots me an amused look.

"Horrible," I finish, trying for honesty. "It's been horrible being back, reliving everything with Savvy and my marriage ..." I take a deep breath, and I'm mortified to realize I'm about to start crying again. I thought I had gotten it all out at Grandma's. I try to blink quickly enough to hide it, but tears slide down my cheeks.

Emmett lowers his brush. Men usually look terrified when women start crying, but he looks more intrigued than anything.

"Sorry." I wipe my cheeks.

He steps forward and kisses me, which is the last thing I expect. Maybe he's trying for comfort. I don't love it.

I'm still against the wall, and he presses his body against mine. His lips are too rough, his tongue too eager. His saliva is all around my mouth far too quickly. No one asked for this.

I consider pushing him away, but it seems easier to just ride this out, smile politely, and then bolt while discreetly wiping my face off.

I don't remember him being a bad kisser the time we made out in my house. My memory of that night is fuzzy; I must have been drunker than I realized.

He puts a hand on my breast over my shirt. Seriously, no one asked for this.

I put a hand on his chest, ready to push him away. His other hand is on my cheek. I smell paint on his fingers.

"Lucy."

His hand is the one on my breast five years ago, I realize. The sounds of laughter and music drifting over from the wedding. He'd slipped one of my straps down, and his thumb was tracing circles over my nipple. He had green paint underneath his fingernails.

"*I've wanted to do this for so long*," he'd said to me, his lips against my neck. He reached for his zipper, and I realized he intended to fuck me right there, with the smells of rotting food drifting over from the nearby dumpster.

What the hell, I'd thought. I'd been drunk. Not too drunk, but enough to think that fucking Emmett was a great way to get back at Matt, who probably had a woman bent over the bathroom counter right at that moment.

"*Lucy*." Savvy's voice was sharp, almost angry. I'd turned to see her standing a few feet away, hands on her hips. "*Let's go.*"

Her voice, her look of disapproval, had snapped me back to reality. I'd quickly put my boob back in my dress and hurried after her.

"*No, Lucy, wait*." Emmett had caught my hand, not gently. I'd yelped as he pulled me back to him.

"*I'm sorry*." I'd apologized to the man who had just hurt me, in a baffling choice. "*I shouldn't have done that*."

I'd run after Savvy then, and that's where the memory fades.

In the present, I'm still kissing Emmett.

Actually, it would be more accurate to say that *he's* kissing *me*. I'm mostly a statue at this point.

Someone loudly clears their throat, and we both turn.

Nina.

She's standing near the curb, wearing light blue scrubs. She shoots me an icy glare as Emmett steps away from me.

"Can I talk to you?" she asks Emmett.

He sighs heavily but nods, and then shoots me an apologetic look. Nina walks inside the art store, and he follows. The bell chimes as the door closes behind them.

I walk quickly to my car, and then sit in the driver's seat, breathing heavily.

Why did Savvy look *mad* about my making out with Emmett at the wedding? Did she have feelings for—

I freeze as the memory comes into focus.

LUCY

Savvy stomped to her car and threw open the door.

"Wait, are you mad?" I asked as I scurried behind her.

"Just get in," she snapped. She climbed into the car and slammed the door.

I slid into the passenger's seat, kicking an old fast-food bag aside. "Are you seriously angry that I was kissing Emmett? What's this expression?"

"I'm not mad." She closed her eyes for a moment, like she was gathering the strength to deal with me. "I'm just concerned."

"Give me a break," I said with a laugh.

Her expression was still serious. "First I find you kissing your asshole husband, when you should be plotting his fucking demise."

I swallowed hard.

"And then I find you with your boobs out, getting ready to—"

"*One* boob! One boob was out!"

"Getting ready to have sex against a wall next to a dumpster. You are acting like me, and that is extremely concerning."

"I am not. You would have had both boobs out."

"Harsh, but true." Her expression softened as she turned on the car. "Okay, but what the hell are you doing letting Matt grope you like that? He *hurts* you, Lucy."

Shame burned in my throat, and she took her hand off the gear shifter and turned to me when she caught the look on my face.

"I'm sorry," she said quietly. "I didn't mean to be all judgmental."

"No, you're right. I don't know why I . . ." I trailed off, because that was a lie. I did sort of know why I stayed with Matt, why I kept falling into the same patterns over and over. "Sometimes it feels like we deserve each other, you know?"

"No," she said firmly.

"You don't understand. The things I say to him, the way I've screamed at him . . ." I shook my head. "A better woman wouldn't talk like that. She wouldn't hit back. I think we were drawn to each other because we're both garbage."

"Lucy, *no*." She grabbed my hand. "Absolutely not. He did this to you. He drove you to the brink of your sanity and then blamed you for doing what you had to do to survive. All of this is his fault."

I looked down at our hands and nodded, even though I wasn't sure I believed her. "And now I'm being a total asshole by hooking up with Emmett."

"How does that make you an asshole?"

"He doesn't deserve to be used like that. He's a sweetheart."

She gave me a truly baffled look. "He is absolutely *not* a sweetheart. He's only nice to you because he's been in love with you since you guys were kids."

"He's not in love with me. He had a crush, maybe, but—"

"You're right. He's not in love with you. He's got you up on a pedestal. He thinks you're the perfect girl."

I didn't argue with that, because I knew she was right. It was one of the things I'd always secretly liked about Emmett. He had stars in his eyes every time he looked at me.

"Listen, I wasn't going to tell you this, but . . ." Savvy trailed off, making a face. "I slept with him a few months ago."

"Oh." My voice was too high, betraying my jealousy. I'd thought she knew I had a soft spot for Emmett. He was off-limits.

But that was dumb. I tried to reason with myself. I was married to someone else, and I'd never mentioned having feelings for him.

"I'm sorry, I know he's your friend," she continued, biting her lip. "And I knew that he had a thing for you, but he stayed late at the bar one night, and I got drunk, and we just . . . Well, he's pretty aggressive. Sometimes when a guy takes charge like that you just go along with it, you know?"

I thought of him unzipping his pants after exposing my boob to the world. "Yeah."

"That's not to say I didn't want to," she said in a rush. "I did. I was game. But it was just . . . not good."

I wince. "No?"

"No. I mean, the kissing was . . ."

"Sloppy," I finish for her.

"God, yes. And then the actual sex was pretty rough, which I don't always mind, but it was also just . . . bad. Zero concern for me. Just jackhammer and run, you know?"

I made a face.

"And he was rude, after. He asked me not to tell you—"

"He did?"

"Yeah. I felt sort of bad about it anyway, so I figured I could just not mention it." Her expression was sheepish. "But then he was also pretty mean to me? Like, he came by the next week and got really handsy and rough and when I told him I didn't want to, he got all mad and said, 'I thought you were always down to fuck.'"

I reeled back. "Wow. Rude."

"So, he's an asshole, and I really suggest you find someone else because you can do so much better. How about that new bartender? You should probably have some good sex before we murder Matt. It'll look tacky if you're flashing your boobs all over town too soon after."

Headlights flashed across my face, and I looked over to see Emmett turning his truck onto the road. Our eyes met. I quickly looked away.

"I have really bad taste in men, don't I?" I said.

"I wasn't going to say anything, because I really have no room to judge."

I laughed, and then sat back with a long sigh. "I have to leave him. Matt."

"Yes."

"And Plumpton. I can't stay here after."

She put the car in drive. "You don't want to kill him on the way out?"

"I'm not sure I ever really wanted to do that, Savvy." My desire for revenge was fading, and slowly being replaced by a desire for a new life. My life so far had been a series of supposedly "good" choices—I met a guy in college, married him, moved back to my hometown and into a dream house. And it all turned to shit.

I didn't want revenge so much as I wanted to find out what would happen if I made different choices. I needed to start over. I didn't want to be the girl trapped in a marriage because I was too scared to leave, too scared of what other people would think of me if I didn't have a shiny, enviable life.

And I didn't want my fresh start to involve a possible prison sentence.

"Did *you* actually want to kill Matt?" I asked Savvy.

"Absolutely." She flashed me a grin that made it impossible to tell whether she was serious.

"No," I said softly, looking out the dark window. "I can't."

She turned onto the dirt road. "Where would we go? If we left town?"

"I don't know. Anywhere. I've been thinking I should pack my bags one night while Matt is sleeping and disappear. But I don't think I'm brave enough to go by myself."

She smiled at me. "You know where I've always wanted to go?"

"Where?"

"California. Los Angeles."

"It's so expensive," I said wistfully.

"It's expensive because it's great." She pounded the steering wheel with one hand. "Let's do it."

"Seriously?"

"Yep. Like, as soon as possible. Fuck the Texas summers; I don't want to do one more. Let's go tomorrow night."

My heart thumped. I'd just been dreaming, but she was going to take me up on it.

"Yes," I said before I could change my mind.

She let out a little squeal of delight. "Okay, but if Matt comes to find you, we're fucking murdering him."

"Deal."

Her smile faded as she squinted at something in the darkness. "What the hell?"

CHAPTER FORTY-EIGHT

LUCY

I squeeze my eyes shut, trying to make the rest of the memory come into focus.

But it's fading. Savvy's laugh, her smile, start to drift away, and all I have left is an ache in my chest.

We were going to leave Plumpton, together. I can see Savvy in L.A. She would have loved the beach and hated the traffic. We probably would have shared an apartment.

I can't breathe, thinking about what could have been.

What the hell? What the hell? What the hell? Savvy's words go round and round in my head. She's in front of me, smiling as blood drips down her face. I'm trying too hard.

Through the storefront window, I can see Nina standing in front of Emmett, arms crossed over her chest. His face is red, angry. He's yelling at her.

He left the wedding. I blink as I remember—I clearly saw his face as he turned his truck onto the road to leave.

I grab my phone from my purse. Ben picks up on the first ring.

"Hey, Lucy."

"Didn't Emmett say he stayed at the wedding until it ended?"

"What? Uh ... yeah. Wait, wait, can I record this?"

"Fine, whatever. Just—"

"Hold on. Okay. Ask that again."

"Emmett said he stayed until the wedding ended?"

"Yeah. Wedding went until three a.m. People saw him there. He helped organize rides for people to get home."

"No one remembers him leaving and coming back?"

"No. He said he was there the whole time."

"I remember him leaving. Right before Savvy and I left."

There's a long pause. "Are you sure?"

"Yes. I got in the car with Savvy, and I clearly saw him driving past us, down that dirt road that leads to the highway. He saw me too. Our eyes met."

"Lucy, do you remember what happened?"

"It ... it's coming back in bits and pieces. I remember parts of the wedding, and I remember getting in the car with her. We were talking about leaving. Going to Los Angeles together."

"Were you fighting or ... ?"

"No. We weren't. We were happy." My breath catches in my throat.

"Let's go back there. Now. It's dark out; maybe that will help. Where are you?"

"I'm outside the art shop." My words come out breathless.

Through the store window, Emmett gestures angrily.

I see Nina flinch. She draws her arms into her body, turns her face away, and squeezes her eyes shut.

I've done that.

I know that pose.

It's what you do when you're bracing to be hit.

"Lucy?" Ben says.

Emmett doesn't hit her. He grabs both her wrists.

"Why are you at the art shop?"

"Because Emmett ..." I trail off. I can tell that Emmett is holding Nina's wrists too tightly. Tears are streaming down her face, and she's trying to pull free of his grasp.

"He's hurting her," I say quietly. I should move. I should help.

"Emmett? Who's he hurting?"

Nina breaks free. She bolts from the shop and practically dives into her car. I watch in the rearview mirror as it disappears around the corner.

A knock on the window makes me jump.

It's Emmett.

And now I remember.

LUCY

"What the hell?" Savvy asked, squinting in the darkness.

I leaned forward. A truck was parked in the middle of the road. A tall figure stood in front of it. Savvy's headlights caught his face. Emmett.

She slowed to a stop, rolling down her window. She put a hand out like, *What the hell?*

Emmett walked over to my side of the car. I rolled down my window.

"Can I talk to you?" The words were breathless, a plea. I was having a hard time reconciling the Emmett I'd known since I was a kid with the version Savvy told me about. This Emmett had his fists clenched at his sides, his eyes wild and desperate as he looked down at me.

"Dude, now?" Savvy said, exasperated. "Can't it wait until tomorrow?"

Emmett ignored her. "Please?"

I sighed, reaching for the door handle. "Sure. Savvy, it's fine, Emmett can drive me home." I looked at him for confirmation, and his face brightened. He nodded.

"No, it's cool," she said. "I can wait."

She said it like there wasn't room for argument, and I caught

Emmett's annoyed eye roll. I climbed out of the car and shut the door behind me. It smelled like rain, and it was actually a little cool for May.

Emmett walked away from the car, a few steps into the thick trees around the road. I glanced back. I could still see Savvy sitting in the driver's seat, peering at us.

"I'm sorry, I know this is weird, but I had to talk to you." He squinted, putting a hand up over his eyes. "She's really not going to turn those off?" He stepped further into the trees, away from Savvy's headlights.

"I probably shouldn't have run away like that," I said, following him into the trees. The moon was full, and Savvy's headlights were still providing some light. I could see his face clearly. His eyes were wide, a little desperate.

"No, I shouldn't have . . ." He trailed off, shaking his head. "I shouldn't have kissed you. I got carried away. You just have to understand, Lucy, I'm crazy about you."

I swallowed. Even if Savvy hadn't just told me what she did, I didn't think I would have reacted to this revelation with excitement. It was too hard to imagine anything after Matt.

I was a mess, and I didn't need Emmett's feelings on top of everything.

"I've been crazy about you, for years," Emmett continued, oblivious. "I know that Matt is an asshole to you, and he's cheating on you. You know that, right? That he's cheating on you?"

"I know," I said.

He took a step closer to me. "Leave him. Be with me. I love you. I've loved you since we were kids."

He grabbed me around the waist and kissed me. It was sloppy, like he was trying to devour my face. I pushed him away.

"I can't, I'm sorry." I took a step back.

He immediately grabbed me again. "Yes, you can. I know you

think that you have the perfect life in that house, but I know how unhappy you are. I know that you don't actually love him. That you never have. I know you feel like you have to stay and project this image of the perfect wife, but you don't. Let me help you."

It was strange how he seemed to have taken a sliver of truth and crafted a whole narrative for me. A narrative where he could rescue me. I certainly was unhappy, but I *had* loved Matt. It was why I hated him so much. Because I'd been madly in love with him at one point, and he hadn't beaten it all out of me yet.

And I didn't think I'd ever been trying to project the image of a perfect wife. I was doing a piss-poor job of it, honestly.

"I can't," I said again. "I'm sorry. You're right that Matt and I aren't happy, but I can't jump into something else right now."

"I'll wait for you," he said in a rush. "If you need time. Please, Lucy, just—" He didn't finish. He cut himself off by kissing me again. I wasn't sure what he meant by "I'll wait" if he was going to immediately kiss me again.

"Emmett, stop." I pushed him away again. "This isn't going to happen, okay? I'm sorry."

All the hope drained from his face. "What?"

"I'm not, I don't . . . I don't feel that way about you. We've been friends forever, we shouldn't—"

"You don't feel that way about me? Why do you keep kissing me then?"

"I'm sorry, I—"

"You wouldn't keep kissing me if you didn't feel something!" His voice had an angry edge to it now.

"Okay, time to go!" Savvy yelled. I heard her car door slam, and she appeared through the trees a moment later.

I felt a rush of gratitude that she'd ignored me when I said Emmett could drive me home.

"For fuck's sake, Savvy, would you stop sticking your nose in our business?" Emmett snapped. "We're having a conversation here."

"It sounded more like you were yelling at her."

"I wasn't yelling at her, I'm just trying—"

"It's fine," I interrupted. "Can we just continue this tomorrow, Emmett? It's late, and I've had a lot to drink."

"You don't need to continue anything," Savvy said. "She said no, dude. Accept it."

Emmett's nostrils flared. "No one was talking to you. Just let Lucy and me—"

"Get it through your thick skull, asshole. No. Complete sentence." She looped her arm through mine, tugging gently.

"No. We're not done." Emmett grabbed my other hand, roughly pulling me away from Savvy. He had a vise grip on my arm, and I winced.

"You did not just do that!" Savvy planted her hands on Emmett's chest and shoved, hard. He stumbled back but didn't let go of me.

"Don't touch me," he growled.

"Let her go."

"No."

"Emmett, please let me go," I said, trying desperately to stay calm. My brain was flashing *Danger, danger* at me.

My fists curled, almost against my will. I was ready to fight. I'd been here so many times with Matt.

"My god, you are such a dick," Savvy yelled. "Just let her go!"

"Just fucking mind your own business for once, you stupid little—"

I punched him. My fist connected with his jaw. I'd had some practice with Matt, but it still wasn't the best punch. I lost my balance, and it didn't land as hard as I'd intended.

Still, he stumbled back, sputtering, and released my arm. Wasn't used to taking a hit like Matt was.

"I said no!" I was screaming. I hadn't meant to, but it felt like my brain had short-circuited. I wasn't fully in control. "I don't want your fucking help! I don't care about your stupid childhood crush!"

Emmett gaped at me. I was shaking as I turned away. Savvy gave me a thoroughly impressed look.

"Time to go," she said, and then laughed.

I glanced back at Emmett in time to see him lunge at me.

CHAPTER FORTY-NINE

LUCY

"Hey," Emmett says, his voice muffled through the car window, bringing me back to the present. He opens the door. I wish I'd locked it. He kneels down so we're at eye level. "Don't leave. Come inside for a minute."

"*Lucy?*" Ben's voice is small, coming from the phone I have lowered onto my thigh. Emmett glances down at it.

"Who is that?" Emmett asks.

"Ben," I say faintly. I'm frozen. All I can see is Emmett's angry face as he lunges for me.

"Hi, Ben!" Emmett says loudly, cheerfully. He smiles at me.

I don't know whether my face shows how baffled I am. I'm too numb to feel anything.

"Are you going to hang up with him or . . . ?" Emmett laughs a little.

And then he swallows, and I see it. He's nervous.

My mouth is dry. I grip the phone too tightly, until my hand hurts.

Emmett reaches over and takes it from me. He presses it to his ear. "Hey, Ben. I think Lucy needs a minute. She'll call you back, okay?"

I don't know whether Ben protests. Emmett ends the call and slides the phone—*my* phone—into his pocket. He puts a gentle hand on my arm.

"Why don't you come inside? You want a glass of water or something?"

I shake my head.

"Well, I can't let you drive like this. You're white as a sheet." He reaches over and takes my keys from where I'd dropped them on the passenger's seat. I realize suddenly that I'm sweating. I've been sitting in this hot car for several minutes.

"*Run, Lucy,*" Savvy screams in my head. "*Run!*"

"Come inside," Emmett says again. He puts a hand on my cheek. "Let me take care of you."

Emmett unbuckles my seat belt. I didn't know I had it on.

"Come on." Emmett puts both hands on my arms. "Let's just get out of this car, okay, Lucy?"

His voice is gentle.

It's confusing, because in my head he's screaming.

LUCY

Emmett lunged, knocking me into Savvy. We both tumbled to the ground.

"Oh god." Savvy was on her feet first, reaching for me. I gripped her arm.

Emmett punched her. My fingernails scraped her skin as she stumbled away from me.

"You fucking bitch! I've spent my whole life waiting for you, being the nice guy, being the friend, and this is how you repay me?" He grabbed me by the shirt, hauling me to my feet.

Savvy flew at Emmett, locking her arms around his neck. He twisted and squirmed, letting go of my shirt.

He yanked one of Savvy's hands free, and she tumbled off his back.

Emmett whirled around, desperately grabbing for me. I darted around him, reaching for Savvy's hand. She grabbed my hand again and took off, pulling me with her.

We ran, ducking through the trees. I dared a glance over my shoulder. I didn't see Emmett.

"Oh shit," Savvy gasped suddenly. "I went the wrong way."

I stopped, looking over my shoulder. It was dark, and quiet. We'd run away from the road, and Emmett was nowhere to be seen.

My breath was coming in short gasps. I tried to reach for my purse. My phone. It was in the car.

"Do you have your phone?" I asked.

"Yes!" She slid her hands into the pockets of her dress and took it out. Her face fell as she looked at the screen. "Shit. It's dead."

Tears streamed down my face, and I wiped them away with a shaky hand. "I'm sorry. I shouldn't have gotten out of the car. I didn't know that he . . ." I sniffled.

She shook her head. "It's not your fault. But later, after we call the cops, I want you to remember that I probably saved you from being raped and murdered. I expect eternal gratitude."

I laughed through my tears. "Eternal gratitude. Got it."

Savvy took my hand. "Let's go back to the venue," she said, pointing to the dark trees. "Emmett's probably waiting for us by the car."

"It's like a mile, isn't it?"

"Yeah, but I think it's the safest option. She reached down to pull her heels off. I did the same.

"Are you even sure that's the right way?" I looked up at the sky, like I might magically gain the ability to tell direction by the stars. I could barely tell north from south when the sun was up.

"Uh." She looked left, and then right. "That's a good point."

"We came from that way, right?" I pointed.

"Yes? I can't see my headlights anymore." She pressed both hands to her forehead. "Oh my god. How did people live before phones?"

"Wait, we weren't that far from the main road," I said. "Let's listen and see if we can hear the cars. We can go that way instead."

A fat drop of rain landed right in my eye, and I blinked, startled.

"Great," Savvy said, holding her hand out to catch a drop. "Rain is just what we need right now."

The sound of leaves crunching made me turn.

Emmett ran out from the darkness, something poised over his head. It looked sort of like a hammer, though not the kind used for construction. It was just a metal block at the end of a stick.

"Run," Savvy whispered.

We took off together, bashing through the trees. We were faster without our heels on. I threw mine behind me, hoping to hit Emmett.

I missed. And he was gaining on us.

Savvy let go of my hand. She was gasping for air. "Go, Lucy. Run."

I tried to grab for it again. "Don't stop. I can hear cars."

"No. You're faster than me. Just go. Get help. I can take him."

"No, you can't—"

I screamed as a hand yanked on my hair. I stumbled backward, and a fist connected with my face. Stars danced in my eyes. Even Matt had never hit me that hard.

I was on the ground. I didn't remember how I got there. Savvy ducked as Emmett swung the hammer at her.

She lunged at him, trying to wrestle the hammer from his grasp. It hit the ground with a thud.

She dove for it, scrambling across the dirt. He yanked on her ankle, and she yelled as he dragged her back through the dirt.

I dove forward, dove for her. My brain was still misfiring, spots in my vision. I wrapped my fingers around her arm and desperately tried to pull her toward me. I was holding on to her so hard my hand was starting to ache.

Emmett let go of her suddenly and grabbed something off the ground.

He swung a tree branch, heavy and thick.

It connected with her skull.

She grunted as she hit the ground. I scrambled to her. She slowly sat up, blood pouring from a cut on her head.

Emmett stood over us, breathing heavily. He'd tossed the tree branch aside in favor of the hammer again.

I wrapped my arms around her, protecting her. "Please stop," I begged. "We won't tell anyone if you just stop, okay? We were planning on leaving anyway. We'll just go and you'll never hear from us again. I promise. Please, Emmett."

He stared down at me, his eyes black in the darkness.

"Lucy?" Matt's voice rang out in the quiet. "Savvy? Emmett? Are y'all out there?"

I froze. We'd run back to the car, not to the main road. The car I'd heard was Matt's.

"Ma—"

Emmett cut off my scream with a hammer to the skull. It barely grazed the left side of my head but still knocked me back. Savvy caught me before I hit the ground.

"Matt! Help!" she screamed.

Emmett lifted the hammer again. I swayed. I was dizzy. I opened my mouth to scream, but nothing came out.

I looked up. Emmett had his arm drawn back, eyes locked on mine.

"You made me do this," he growled.

The hammer was coming straight at my head.

Savvy shoved me out of the way. He smacked the hammer into her head so hard that the crack reverberated through the trees. She collapsed across my lap. Blood pooled on my dress.

My hands were covered in blood.

There was a buzzing in my brain.

"Savvy?" Matt's voice was still distant.

Emmett looked over his shoulder, cursed, and then swung the hammer again.

Everything went black.

CHAPTER FIFTY

LUCY

"You've been trying too hard to remember things," Emmett says.

I'm out of the car. I don't remember getting out, but now I'm standing next to it, and Emmett is looking at me worriedly. His fingers are wrapped around my wrists.

"It's not good for you," he continues. "Remember what happened last time you tried too hard? You started creating things in your head."

The crack of the hammer against Savvy's skull is replaying on a loop in my brain.

Too real to be something I created.

"Matt told you I was there that night, didn't he?" Emmett asks.

I blink. "What?"

Emmett's expression goes dark. "He told you I was there. He promised he wouldn't, but I should have known that asshole wouldn't be able to keep a secret." He puts both hands on my cheeks. "*I* would never hurt you, you know that."

"Matt told me you were there," I repeat, even though it's a lie. Matt didn't tell me shit.

Emmett was *there*? And Matt *knew*?

"I left the wedding for like twenty minutes because I had to go home to let my dog out," Emmett says. "I saw you . . . Well, you don't want to know."

"Yes, I do," I whisper.

"We fooled around, at the wedding," Emmett says. "We were . . . Well, we kept doing that. You remember, the times before that. You and I are always making our way to each other."

That was one way to describe my getting drunk and kissing him twice, I guess.

"Savvy saw us, and she got really mad. I don't know if she ever told you, but she and I had a brief fling. It was nothing, just a couple of times, but she acted really cold to me after. I think maybe she thought it was more than it was?"

That was one way to describe Savvy avoiding him after bad sex.

"You two left together. I decided to run home to let my dog out, and I came across Savvy's car on the side of the road on the way out. I thought it was weird, because most of the guests took the main road out. It was supposed to rain that night, and the people at the venue had told us not to take that road, that it flooded easily. I guess she forgot. *I* forgot, until later that night."

"You came across her car, already parked," I repeat.

"Right. I got out, and you two were off in the trees, yelling at each other."

"About what?"

"I don't know. It was too hard to follow. But you seemed really upset. She slapped you, and you scratched her. I started to intervene then, but you grabbed the tree branch and just . . . I don't think you meant to hit her that hard. You panicked, and started screaming, and you ran."

"You forgot about my head injury," I say to Emmett.

He drops his hands from my cheeks. "What?"

"My head injury. You forgot that *I* got bashed in the head too."

"Oh." Something like panic flits across his expression and then disappears. "I don't know how that happened, but you were running like a bat out of hell. You must have hit your head on something. I actually tried to chase you, but you took off."

"And you just left Savvy there to die?" I ask.

"She was already gone," he says quietly. "There was nothing any-one could do."

"And you didn't go to the police because . . . ?"

"Because I love you." His gaze is steady on mine. "I don't care if you made a mistake once. Technically, she hit you first. And you didn't mean to do it. I know that."

"What did you say to him?" I ask. The buzzing in my brain is back. It's hard to think. "To Matt."

"I told him the truth. That I saw you kill Savvy."

"Why did I . . ." I squeezed my eyes shut. "Why did I run?"

"I think you were scared to face what you'd done."

"And Matt didn't call the police either?"

"We wanted to take care of it ourselves. We were going to find you, but the road washed out and we couldn't get back to find you. And then that guy found you before we could, and it just . . . it seemed better to say nothing. You didn't remember anyway."

I look up and meet his eyes. "That must have been a real relief for you."

His eyebrows draw together. "For *me*? I was relieved for you. I never want you to remember that trauma. I was disappointed that you didn't remember our moment at the wedding, because we were finally—"

"About to fuck next to a dumpster?" I finish for him.

"We were finally acknowledging our feelings for each other."

"I guess we were. Like when I said I didn't care about your child-hood crush, and I just wanted you to fucking leave me alone."

He freezes. "You never said that."

"Why did Matt believe you when you said that you saw me do it? I hit you. You didn't have any evidence of it on your face?"

"You never hit me," he says.

"I think Savvy hit you too, but she wasn't very good at it. She was so short, and small. She was better with knives."

Emmett looks startled by this.

"*I* should have punched you harder. I've had practice." A knife to the gut would have been better. Savvy was right.

"Lucy." He speaks like he's talking to a child. "Let's take a step back. You're getting hysterical."

I punch him in the face.

CHAPTER FIFTY-ONE

LUCY

Emmett stumbles into the road, sputtering. He gives me a thoroughly baffled look.

Which quickly turns to rage.

I should run. I wait for Savvy's voice to pop into my head, telling me to run.

Instead, I see her next to Emmett in her pink dress, blood dripping down her face.

"*I have an idea,*" she says with a grin. "*Let's kill Emmett!*"

I smile. That's a great idea.

I stride into the road, hands balled into fists. My right hand already hurts from hitting him once.

I don't care.

He grabs me by the collar, drawing back to hit me. I duck and slam my fist into his gut.

He gasps and doubles over. "Lucy, stop," he wheezes.

I aim my fist at his face, but he twists away from me. I catch a flash of the rage in his eyes before he punches me in the face.

The world goes white for a moment. I'm on the ground, gravel digging into my palms. Something wet drips down my face and into my mouth. I taste blood.

He grabs me underneath my arms and begins pulling me off the road. I'm dizzy, and he has me halfway to the art store before I begin kicking and squirming.

"God dammit, Lucy!" he yells. I break free and spring to my feet. I lunge at him.

We topple to the ground together, rolling twice before I manage to pin him down. I put my hands around his throat and squeeze as hard as I can.

He kicks his feet. His face turns red.

Let's kill let's kill let's kill

He bucks, throwing me off him. He scrambles to his feet and runs into the store.

I follow as he crashes through the store, knocking over a display and sending paintbrushes onto the floor. I leap over them.

He grabs a hammer from the shelf—the same sort that he used to kill Savvy, and I realize suddenly that he must have had it in his truck that night. He went back to his truck to grab something to kill me with.

This asshole.

I grab him by the back of his shirt, but it rips as he frees himself. He darts out the back door.

I sprint through after him, back into the thick, humid air.

He's waiting for me on the other side, hammer poised. He swings it at my head, and I lean back just in time. The edge of it barely grazes my forehead.

I stumble back. He swings again, misses again, and I reach up to grab his hand, trying to yank the hammer free.

He shoves me and swings again. The hammer catches me on the chin this time, and the pain sends me scrambling back.

A moment of clarity flashes through my rage. I should run. I glance behind me, to where my car is just visible around the corner of the store.

He took my keys, I suddenly remember. My keys and my phone. I can run, but it would be with nothing.

A viciously satisfied expression crosses Emmett's face as I stand there, blinking from the hit. It's a familiar feeling—the panic of being trapped, the frustration of his having all the power.

I scream. It's guttural, a sound I've never heard myself make before.

I charge at him, and the shocked expression on his face as I do it might be the most satisfying thing I've ever seen. We crash hard into the ground, a mess of limbs and grunts.

I claw at his arms, trying to grab the hammer. My knee connects with his chest, and his grip on the handle loosens as he gasps. I snatch it from him and spring to my feet.

He scrambles up as well, lip curled, his chest rising and falling too quickly.

I swing the hammer into his stomach.

He buckles over with a gasp and heaves. He holds out a hand, like he wants me to stop. I pause with the hammer poised to strike again.

He bolts upright suddenly and takes off running.

"Emmett!" I scream. I consider, briefly, sprinting in the opposite direction. But my feet have other ideas. I'm chasing him before I realize I made up my mind to do it, my anger driving me forward.

Distantly, I hear my own name. I don't know whether it's real, or whether it's Savvy.

There's a small patch of trees behind the store. Emmett runs into them, and I push my legs as fast as they'll go. Emmett casts a terrified glance over his shoulder. Something about it is satisfying. Maybe this is what Savvy felt like when she killed that man. *He deserved it.*

"Better run faster, asshole!" I scream.

"*Lucy!*" the voice yells again. Not Savvy. Closer.

I'm close enough to almost reach Emmett. I stretch my hand out, my fingers grazing the fabric. I snatch it, yank it back into my fist. He yells as he tumbles to the ground, and immediately tries to get to his feet.

I lift the hammer over my head and bring it down hard on his leg. It makes a very pleasing *crunch* sound as he screams.

"Lucy!"

Emmett uses one leg for leverage as he dives forward on his knees, yanking the hammer from my grasp. It goes flying.

And comes to a stop at Ben's feet.

He's breathing heavily, eyes wide and horrified as he looks from me to Emmett.

"Oh my god, Ben," Emmett pants. He uses his good leg to scoot away from me. "She's lost it. She's fucking lost it. She's trying to kill me."

Ben holds my gaze. I wipe the back of my hand across my mouth. Blood smears across my skin.

I look down at the hammer. Back up at him.

He slowly reaches down and picks it up.

"He killed her." My voice is low. It doesn't sound quite right. "He killed Savvy, and he tried to kill me."

Surprise flickers across Ben's features. I can see the wheels turning, the interviews starting to loop in his head. I have no idea whether his research will back up my claim.

"Matt saw him that night," I continue. "You can ask him. Emmett was there, and he fucking killed her."

Ben stares at me. His expression is unreadable.

"No," Emmett says. He shakes his head desperately. "No. I never would have hurt Savvy. Or you, Lucy. You have to believe me."

Ben cocks his head.

"You saw her!" Emmett points at me. "She was about to kill me! She would have, if you hadn't come along!"

Ben looks down at the hammer in his hand.

"Let's find out," he says.

He tosses me the hammer.

CHAPTER FIFTY-TWO

LUCY

I sit in a hospital bed, staring at a police officer.

He's standing just outside the curtain surrounding my bed, talking to Ben. I can see them both through the crack where the fabric isn't closed all the way.

"You heard him say that?" the officer asks.

"Yeah," Ben says. "Emmett yelled something about how he'd tried to kill Lucy once."

I blink. My head is swimming and aching, but I'm pretty certain Emmett said nothing like that.

"And Matt Gardner saw Emmett that night," Ben continues. "You should ask him about that."

The officer nods, writing something down. He pushes the curtain aside and fixes me with a hard stare. "We'll have more questions for you in a minute."

I nod numbly.

He walks away, and Ben steps inside the curtain with me. His eyebrows are drawn together, the nerves and stress obvious in the way he keeps crossing and uncrossing his arms.

"*She's lying! Why aren't any of you listening to me?*" Emmett's scream is distant from down the hall somewhere.

"I could have killed you both," I say to Ben.

He looks startled. "Sorry?"

"When you tossed me the hammer. I could have killed him, and then you. Your sense of self-preservation is lacking."

He lets out a breath of air that's like a laugh. "Like you said before, that would have been a better ending. You kill the real killer and the host of the podcast trying to solve the crime. I think a lot of people would have liked that ending better."

I side-eye him. "There's something wrong with you."

"I know." He smiles. "I never thought you were going to kill me, Lucy."

I don't know whether I believe him.

I'd like to, though.

"Emmett didn't say that," I say after a brief silence.

"What?"

"You know what. He didn't yell anything about killing me. He told you he was innocent."

He shrugs.

I imitate his shrug. "That's it?"

"Whatever. It's close enough to the truth. People are going to believe whatever I say. Your word isn't enough."

"The truth doesn't matter."

Savvy's words sound gentle this time. Less angry.

I shift my attention back to Ben. "The truth is whatever you say it is."

CHAPTER FIFTY-THREE

LUCY

Matt is waiting for me outside the hospital.

I look like absolute shit—a black eye, three stitches in my eyebrow, a bruise starting to form on my chin. Luckily my nose isn't broken, but my entire face is vibrating in pain.

"Oh my god." Matt rushes over to me. I see my parents, not far behind him. Ben left a while ago, because I was tired of his hovering. I told him I didn't need him to call anyone for me, but I can see that my request was ignored.

"I'm going to kill Emmett," Matt says.

My parents stop not far behind him. Dad's chest is rising and falling too quickly. Mom's eyes are red, and she won't look at me.

"You saw him that night," I say. Matt has the decency to look embarrassed.

"After you," he says. "You ran away, and then Emmett appeared a second later, crying and saying he'd seen you kill her."

"And you just believed him."

"You said—you said . . ." He clenches both fists in frustration, and I instinctively take a step back. "You were covered in blood, mumbling something about killing! And you said she deserved it, and 'Savvy tried to.' What was I supposed to think?"

"She tried to save me," I say. "That was the end of that sentence. Savvy tried to *save me*, and he killed her."

"Oh, Lucy," Mom says, and moves like she's going to hug me. I step back, shaking my head.

"The cops want to talk to you," I say.

Dad gapes at me. I thought that I was too exhausted to feel even more annoyed, but apparently I'm not. I don't know where he finds the nerve to look surprised.

"You lied to them. Hid evidence. Good luck with that."

Mom's mouth drops open.

"We were protecting you," Matt says. "You have to understand. Me, your parents—we thought we were protecting you."

"No, you didn't," I snap. "You protected *yourself*, Matt. You knew what would happen if I started telling people the truth. You knew what would come out."

Matt's face reddens. Both my parents are statues, tears streaming down Mom's face.

I step away from them. "The only person who ever protected me was Savvy."

Listen for the Lie Podcast with Ben Owens

FINAL EPISODE

Police have charged Emmett Chapman with Savannah Harper's murder. Matt, Kathleen, and Don have been charged with withholding evidence.

I spoke with some of the people of Plumpton a few days after the news broke. First, let's hear from Beverly, Lucy's grandma.

Beverly: Well, it's a lot to deal with, if you want to know the truth. I always knew she didn't do it. I knew it when Lucy didn't know it. I just wish that other people would have had more faith in her.

Ben: Kathleen and Don never shared with you what Matt told them? That he saw Lucy the night Savannah died?

Beverly: They sure didn't. If they had, I would have screamed it to the whole town. How do you believe that man over your child? How did Matt believe Emmett over his own wife?

Ben: It does seem strange.

Beverly: Well, not strange, exactly. Typical. Men always believe each other.

I also talked to Ivy, Savannah's mother.

Ivy: We're still processing it all. There are still questions to be answered.

Ben: What kind of questions?

Ivy: Just . . . we don't want to rush to judgment.

Ben: Because that's what happened with Lucy?

Ivy: We're done talking about this.

And I talked to Joanna.

Joanna: Emmett's saying he didn't do it. He says that Lucy created a new memory. He says it's not even her fault. He's being really nice about it.

Ben: You don't believe Lucy, then?

Joanna: Hon, I'm just confused. She's created memories before, right? She admitted it. And now suddenly, five years later, she remembers everything and can very conveniently pin it on someone? It's suspicious.

Ben:	What do you make of Matt and the Chases withholding important information about the case?
Joanna:	Obviously they shouldn't have done that. But they were covering for Lucy. You can't blame the Chases for protecting their daughter.
Ben:	Did you know I was there when Emmett tried to kill Lucy again? I heard him yelling about killing Savvy.
Joanna:	Wait, you did?
Ben:	Sure did.
Joanna:	I . . . I didn't know that. Well . . .

Lucy was generous enough to talk to me one last time to answer a few lingering questions.

Ben:	Do you regret not going back to Plumpton sooner?
Lucy:	Yes. I regret a lot of things. I wish I hadn't let my parents and Matt get into my head. I think that if they hadn't immediately acted like I did it, I would have been better equipped to deal with everything. I could have pieced it all together sooner.
Ben:	Speaking of piecing it all together, I do have a few lingering questions. First of all, did you ever get your memory back of the time after Savannah's death? The hours you were wandering?
Lucy:	No. The head injury erased most of that for good, I think.
Ben:	You don't know why you left her body? Or why you had that bloody tree branch when Matt saw you?
Lucy:	No. My guess is, some part of my brain was thinking I needed it for self-defense.
Ben:	Emmett is claiming he's innocent, and a lot of people still don't believe you. They say you're still hiding something.
Lucy:	I could explain all day and these people will never believe me. Most of us don't change our minds once we've settled on a version of events. Everyone has made their mind up about me, and it's not changing, no matter what.
Ben:	Does that bother you?
Lucy:	Sort of. I don't think it's too much to ask, that everyone not think the absolute worst of me all the time. But I'm not all that concerned about it anymore. I am not responsible for the fake version of me you created in your head.

Ben: One of the biggest questions I've been getting is this—Why would your husband believe Emmett over you? Matt very quickly put the blame on you. Why was that?

Lucy: Well, Matt saw me that night, and it admittedly didn't look great. I think the only way I can explain it is to say that Matt never gave me the benefit of the doubt about anything. Just like most of the people listening to this podcast, he thought the worst of me. And to be fair, he *saw* the worst of me. We had a very bad marriage—which I'm not going to go into here—and when you already hate your spouse as much as he hated me at the time, thinking I murdered my best friend isn't a huge leap.

Ben: Still, it's weird, isn't it? Shouldn't Matt have questioned Emmett's version more, given how injured you were?

Lucy: Sure, he should have. But Emmett actually had a whole plausible story and I had nothing. Matt, like most men I've known, is always more inclined to believe the guy's version of events.

Ben: And your parents? They were convinced you murdered Savannah, because of what Matt told them. Why do you think *they* were willing to make that leap?

Lucy: Matt didn't tell them about Emmett being there. I'd like to think that they would have been more skeptical if he had.

Ben: That's a generous way of looking at things. You don't feel angry that they also didn't give you the benefit of the doubt?

Lucy: Sure, I do. I'm not all that surprised, though.

Ben: What do you think Savannah would say, if she were here?

Lucy: I think she'd be happy I was okay. She died trying to protect me. She saved me. We were a team, me and Savvy, right up until the end.

CHAPTER FIFTY-FOUR

LUCY

Grandma is leaning against her doorframe as I pull up to the tiny house, still looking smug as hell.

"You headed to the airport?" she asks as I climb out of the car and walk to her.

"Yes. Finally." I can't believe I just spent over three weeks in my hometown. I deserve a medal. "You're coming to visit me next time. This town doesn't get the pleasure of my company ever again."

She snorts. "That's fair." She steps back, letting me step into the air-conditioning. I flop down on her couch.

Grandma goes into the kitchen to make a drink and then slides into a chair at the table with her drink.

"It isn't everything," I say quietly.

"What isn't?"

"The story Ben told on the podcast. It isn't the whole truth." I meet her gaze. "I know you know that."

"I do," she says softly.

"I'd tell you, but it's the only thing left I can do for her." I lean forward, resting my elbows on my thighs. "Keeping the secrets. It's all I can do."

"Oh, hon, I understand." She reaches forward, taking one of my hands in hers. "You don't owe anyone your whole story. Or Savvy's."

I nod, swallowing hard.

"Let Ben think he found the truth. He did what we needed him to do. You're right that some people will never believe you, no matter how hard you explain yourself. Trust me, there's no pleasing people. If they're determined to think the worst of you, they will."

"They think the best of Savvy, so I guess that's really all I can ask for."

"Absolutely. Who she actually was, and the secrets you two shared, that's just for you."

I scoot forward, wrapping my arms around her. "Thank you for badgering me into coming back and doing this."

"You're very welcome. I am happy to badger you into doing the right thing anytime."

My phone dings, followed up immediately by a second ding. I suppress a sigh as I sit back and glance at the screen. I've been getting a strange mix of messages these days—some from people I know, saying they knew I was innocent all along (*I never really doubted you*, Nathan sent this morning, a text too absurd to warrant a response), and *many* comments on my Eva Knightley social media accounts, ripping into me for all sorts of things. A substantial portion of the internet hates me more than ever. Some of them acknowledge that I didn't kill Savvy but *still* hate me.

It's an email from a journalist, asking for comment on an article he's writing about me. Linked is a video that is apparently making the rounds on social media. It's titled, *Lucy Chase: How a Manipulative Psychopath Framed Emmett Chapman.*

I shake my head in amusement and delete the email. As usual, Grandma is right.

There really is no pleasing people.

"Did you see Ben before he left yesterday?" she asks.

I nod.

I have a text from Ben on my phone, sitting there unanswered since last night. I still can't decide if he's the best or worst idea I ever had.

Can I take you out when you get back to LA? I promise to ask fewer intrusive questions this time.

"Are you two going to see each other when you get back to Los Angeles?"

Savvy appears behind Grandma, casually leaning against the door. The dress from the wedding gone, replaced by jeans and the white tank top I used to see her in so often. A red bra strap peeks out at the shoulder. She grins at me.

"*Fuck yeah you are*," she says. I can't help but laugh, grin back at her, even as Grandma gives me a puzzled look.

I pull out my phone and type a reply to Ben.

ACKNOWLEDGMENTS

Listen for the Lie was a leap of faith for me. It took two years of writing and rewriting and pinning color-coded index cards to giant boards to shape Lucy's story into a book. I am eternally grateful to everyone who took this leap with me and helped bring the book into the world.

A huge thank you to my agent, Faye Bender, the first champion of this book, who believed in it with such passion and enthusiasm.

Thank you to James Melia for all your insights and positivity and for making me rewrite those last few chapters so many times. And thank you to Amy Einhorn for taking over and bringing the book over the finish line (and for making me rewrite the ending one more time—now it's truly perfect). Thanks also to Lori Kusatzky for all your work making sure every stage of the process went smoothly. A big thank-you to Ryan Doherty for stepping in to take care of this book as it made its way into the world.

Thank you to everyone at Macmillan who put in their time and effort to make the book shine—I don't always get to meet all of you, but I deeply appreciate your behind-the-scenes work.

Thank you to Shannon Messenger, who read a few chapters in the very early stages and told me that it did indeed make sense and told me to keep going. A shout-out to Kaitlyn Sage Patterson, who, when I shyly confessed I was thinking of writing an adult thriller, immediately said that the genre was a great choice for me. I thought of that often when writing this.

I am so grateful to the authors who took the time to read and blurb *Listen for the Lie*—Stephen King, Courtney Summers, Liane Moriarty, Alex Michaelides, Alice Feeney, and Chandler Baker. You are all amazing and I'm honored to have your words on my book.

Thank you to my mom and my sister, the only people I let read a completed draft before querying agents. I appreciate you reading and giving me hope that it was safe to send out into the world.

Thank you to all the authors who answered my questions and were so generous with their time when I was panicking about finding an agent who would like this book. Thanks especially to Maurene Goo for helping me find such a great fit.

And thank you to Laura (again), Emma, and Daniel, with my apologies. This is what happens when you let a writer live with you for six months.

ABOUT THE AUTHOR

Amy Tintera is the *New York Times* bestselling author of several series for young adults. She earned degrees in journalism and film and worked in Hollywood before becoming an author. Raised in Austin, Texas, she frequently sets her novels in the Lone Star State, but she now lives in Los Angeles, where there's far less humidity but not nearly enough Tex-Mex. *Listen for the Lie* is her adult debut.